EDGE

The peaceful Welsh valley where
Catherine had come back to live was
threatened with destruction when lead
was discovered there—and it was largely
up to the squire, Rafe Glyndower,
whether or not the scheme would go
ahead. It was also up to Rafe to decide
what was going to happen about his relationship with Catherine—and about his
relationship with his wife . . .

Books you will enjoy
by ANNE MATHER

SMOKESCREEN

On the face of it, after her tycoon husband's death Olivia had the world as her oyster: a rich and powerful widow, she could do anything she wanted. Anything—except have the love of the only man in the world she could ever love.

DUELLING FIRE

Left alone in the world after her father's death, Sara was glad to accept her 'aunt' Harriet's invitation to become her companion—at any rate for the time being. But there were problems, chief among them the mysterious Jude. What exactly was his relationship with Harriet?

INNOCENT OBSESSION

Because Sylvie's selfish sister refused to go to Greece to live with her husband Leon and her small son who needed her, Sylvie found herself persuaded to go instead. And all she got by way of thanks was the hostility and suspicion of Andreas Petronides, Leon's unbending brother, who refused to think anything but the worst of her!

CASTLES OF SAND

Little Hussein was Ashley's son—but she had not seen him since his birth seven years ago. Now his formidable uncle Alain had offered her a job as Hussein's governess in his home in the Middle East. But Ashley must never let the child know who she was—and she must put up with all the suspicion and hostility of his relatives, who had taken the child from her all those years ago . . .

EDGE OF TEMPTATION

BY

ANNE MATHER

MILLS & BOON LIMITED
15–16 BROOK'S MEWS
LONDON W1A 1DR

First published 1982
Australian copyright 1982
Philippine copyright 1982
This edition 1982

© Ann Mather 1982

ISBN 0 263 73844 2

Set in Monophoto Baskerville 10pt
01–0682 – 62585

Made and printed in Great Britain by
Richard Clay (The Chaucer Press) Ltd,
Bungay, Suffolk

CHAPTER ONE

IT was surprising how small the valley looked from the helicopter. Perhaps it was the fact that it was a valley that accounted for that feeling of compression, of compaction, of hills giving on to hills with little between but the restless waters of the Llanbara. The sweeping slopes where he had ridden all his life, the high pastures where Powys herded his sheep and Meredith had his forestry plantation, were telescopically condensed into narrow bands of green and brown, the trees so close the sun could not penetrate. It was an illusion, of course. As the blades of the propellers swept them lower, the rocky outcrop of Morfa Crag could clearly be seen, the sun-dappled hillside a patchwork of shifting shades and shadows, with the roofs of farm buildings clustering together in settlements dotted about the valley floor. *Penwyth*. His home, and his heritage. And what was it worth?

'Lead has always been in demand, of course,' Sir George Marland was saying now, 'but really, it's only during the last few years that we've turned back on our own resources. I think the oil crisis in 1974 alerted the government to its dependence on other countries for its essential needs, and awakened a kind of national determination to avoid any exploitation of that kind in the future.'

Rafe nodded. In all honesty, he was not paying a great deal of attention to what Marland was saying. Marland was a government official, and like all government officials, in Rafe's opinion, he said what he had to say in as many words as possible, instead of as few.

'Man is a hungry individual, Glyndower—some might say greedy. He's a consumer, and in this day and age, he consumes more than he has ever done before. World mineral deposits are running low. Even the oil we're presently pulling out of the North Sea may not see us to the turn of the century. We must constantly be on the alert for new sources, new deposits, and lead is a very valuable commodity.'

Rafe glanced at John Norman, his eyes expressive. What did Marland think he was? A moron? He knew the state of the world's economy—who better, when it was brought home to him constantly in the day-to-day demands of the estate. He knew that cash was in short supply, and that any substantial deposit of ore on his land would benefit him and the country both. Ever since they lifted off, Marland had been expounding in this vein, and quite frankly, Rafe was sick of the sound of his cultivated tones. He didn't need some pompous bureaucrat implying where his duties lay, explaining the situation to him as if he was some ignorant schoolboy, not conversant with the simple mathematics of economics.

'I think Mr Glyndower understands your position, Sir George,' Norman interposed now. 'However, Penwyth has belonged to his family for many generations, and the far-mers—the tenant farmers, that is——'

'Farmers!' Marland's tones mirrored the contempt he felt for such an interruption. 'My dear John, the wealth accrued from such land is negligible. What is it? Sheep country at best! There's your equation. In my view, there is no problem. And let us not forget that it's Lord Penwyth's decision, not Glyndower's.'

'My father has put the affair into my hands,' retorted Rafe tersely, pulling a case of the narrow cheroots he smoked out of the pocket of his tweed hacking jacket. When both men declined his offer of the case, he put one of the slim cigars between his teeth, and added: 'Conversely, I'm of the opinion that there are conflicting interests here. Interests of humanity, and ecology. This country of ours—and I mean Wales, not England, or Great Britain, as it sometimes suits the government to call us—has been torn apart by mining of one sort or another. Pits, spewing slag and slurry all over our hillsides, belching black dust into air that was once clean and pure. Is that an equation, Sir George? Is that what you mean by mineral wealth?'

Marland's plump shoulders stiffened. He was not used to such plain speaking. His heavy jowls above the starched white collar of his shirt visibly stiffened. Brushing an imaginary speck of dust from the ironed crease in his

pin-striped trouser leg, he adopted an air of frosty for-
bearance.

'I trust you're not about to enter that as a serious point
of opposition, Glyndower,' he observed sourly. 'With your
apparent concern for humanity, you should be the first to
realise that without the coalmines, the people you so
staunchly defend would have starved.'

Rafe put away the lighter he had used to light his che-
root and drew deeply on the tobacco, exhaling a cloud of
aromatically-flavoured smoke into the enclosed cabin of
the helicopter. He supposed it was impolite of him to
smoke in such a confined atmosphere, when neither of his
colleagues was doing so, but right now he needed the sus-
tenance it gave him. Lucy would not approve, he knew
that, but then there were a lot of things he did of which
Lucy did not approve, and at the moment her approval
was not in question.

Of course, he knew he had been a fool, bringing up the
subject of coalmining. Marland could cut any argument
he might make to ribbons, and the humane aspects of
rheumatic diseases and silicosis were more than compensated by the rewards offered. Or so it seemed. There
were still plenty of men willing to risk life and limb to
bring up the energy-bearing carbon, and his own ancestors
had not been unwilling to take their fair share of the pat-
rimony offered. It was as well Marland knew nothing of
his own history, and besides, what bearing did it really
have on what was happening here?

'I'm simply saying that—enough is enough,' he replied
now, weariness descending like a shroud. 'I don't know
that in this case, the end justifies the means.'

'Rafe!' It was John Norman who spoke, his good-
natured features drawn into an uncharacteristic frown.
'You know perfectly well, Penwyth needs the capital.'

Rafe moved his shoulders impatiently. 'I don't deny
that. But is that sufficient reason to deny a man his livelihood?'

Marland cleared his throat. 'I understand that without
a—shall we say—substantial investment of capital, the
estate may have to be sold any way.'

Rafe stiffened now. 'Where did you hear that?' He

glanced at John Norman again. 'Was that your opinion, too?'

The president of the Norcroft Mining Company shifted uncomfortably. 'One doesn't have to be a fortune-teller to see for oneself, Rafe,' he demurred. 'You've said yourself . . .'

'We're going through a rough patch, yes.' Rafe inclined his head. 'But it's been rough before. We've survived.'

'An estate like Penwyth is an anachronism,' declared Marland heavily. 'Too small to be efficient, too hilly to farm economically. Who would want this land anyway? Fields and fields of rough turf, climbing among acres of second-rate timber. Pretty, maybe—valuable, it's not.'

Rafe stilled the ready retort that sprang to his lips. Now was not the time to sentimentalise or offer emotive reasons why he wanted Penwyth to stay the same as it had always been. In all honesty, Sir George was probably right: Penwyth was not a viable proposition. It never had been. The house was a rambling mausoleum, badly in need of roofing and repair, and the acres of garden that surrounded it were gradually running to seed. Old Laurence did what he could, but there was a limit to one man's abilities in that field, and the man was old—too old to handle a garden like the Manor's, yet not old enough to pension off. And if they did pension him off, who would take it on? The young people left the valley in search of work in Cardiff or Swansea, and he hadn't the time to handle it himself. Not along with everything else.

How much easier it had been years ago, he reflected bitterly. The rents from the farms had never contributed much towards the upkeep of the Manor, but in those days, the subsequent lords of Penwyth had had independent means. They had had the money to maintain the valley as an oasis of peace and tranquillity in a world being torn by economic collapse and starvation, money derived from sources it was not always polite to question. They had not been crippled by a series of taxes and death duties, supplemented by rising costs and soaring prices, that left Penwyth almost bankrupt and struggling to survive. Now the rents from the farms were a much-needed necessity, though they went only a small way towards the upkeep of the estate, and his father's lengthy illness had even eaten into Lucy's allowance.

'What would you suggest I tell my tenants?' he asked Marland now. 'Like me, they were born and brought up in this valley. They don't know any other life. It takes some swallowing, doesn't it? Destroying a whole community!'

'How many farms are involved? Six? Seven?' Marland sniffed. 'You can't seriously consider the needs of half a dozen families more important than the wealth of the nation as a whole.'

'How dramatic!' Rafe's lips twisted. 'No, Sir George, I'm not that arrogant—or altruistic. I know what granting exploratory rights means, and I'm aware how important such a find might be.' He shook his head. 'It just seems ironic that it was Mervyn Powys who brought that axe to me. He had no idea what it would lead to.'

Marland shrugged. 'The luck of the game, Glyndower. Now, can we discuss primary claims?'

It was after five before they had completed the aerial survey. The helicopter belonging to the Norcroft Mining Company came down on the field below the manor, and levering himself out beneath the lethal blades of its propellers, Rafe felt it was incumbent upon him to offer his guests some refreshment before they returned to their hotel in Llandrindod Wells. Lucy would expect it, he knew, and besides, he would be interested to have her opinion of Sir George Marland. Lucy was quite a shrewd judge of character, and just because he didn't like the man, it did not mean he was unlikeable. He was not surprised when his offer was accepted. No definite decision had yet been made, and he knew both Marland and Norman would welcome this opportunity to further their mutual ends.

While the pilot stilled the noisy propellers, Rafe walked towards the Land Rover he had left parked earlier in the afternoon. His dog, a golden-haired Labrador named Rufus, awaited him, sitting patiently in the front of the vehicle, only exploding excitedly when he opened the door.

'Easy, boy, easy,' he murmured, fondling the golden

head affectionately, as the dog displayed its welcome, and then fastening his fingers around its collar as Sir George and his satellite came importantly across the turf to join them.

'You sit up front, Sir George,' urged John Norman, politely climbing into the back, and Rafe's mouth drew down in a wry curve as he allowed Rufus to bound into the back beside the mining company president.

Sir George used his handkerchief to dust the dog hairs from the seat before joining his host in front, and Rafe turned on the ignition with an inward grimace. He wished he could be done with the whole damn business, without the decision which he knew he was going to have to make.

Penwyth dreamed in the late afternoon sunlight. It was a beautiful house, built on the site of an ancient Cistercian monastery, destroyed in the sixteenth century. Stones from the original building had been used to build the manor house, and from time to time, rumours were spread of a shadowy monk being seen in the grounds, or a certain coldness being felt in various parts of the building. Rafe himself had never seen any ghost, or experienced any sense of chilling as he worked in his study, sometimes late into the night, but the Welsh were a superstitious people, and he respected their beliefs.

The house itself was built of mellowed stone, liberally covered with ivy. It was a constant battle trying to keep the creeping tendrils off the windows, but tinged with the russets and reds of autumn, as it was now, the vine gave the building a warm, welcoming appearance. It was approached beneath a Norman arch, set in a high stone wall, that gave on to a cobblestoned courtyard, where Rafe's mother had cultivated plants that clung as tenaciously as the ivy to the uneven bricks. Here was honeysuckle and clematis, but late in the year, only the lingering scents of their blossoms remained, like a memory of summer.

Rafe brought the Land Rover to a halt to one side of the ivy-hung porch, and warning Rufus to remain where he was, invited his guests into the house. Sir George was mellowing, too, beneath the undoubted influence of historic architecture, his admiring gaze moving along the mullioned panes that flanked the porch at either side, and John Norman, who had seen it all before, exchanged an encouraging glance with their host.

William Morgan appeared as Rafe entered the hall, his elderly features expressing polite interest in the two men who were following his employer. The old man had been butler at the Manor for more than forty years, since the days when the Glyndowers had employed a housekeeper, too, and not relied on the mistress of the house to perform such menial duties. He was a luxury they could ill afford, Rafe had acknowledged many times, but like Percy Laurence, Morgan was too old to cast adrift.

'Will you be wanting tea, sir?' he enquired now, relieving Rafe of his jacket. 'I believe Mrs Glyndower is in the library. Master Thomas is with her.'

For a moment Rafe forgot the presence of his guests, forgot the unpleasantness of the decision he was going to have to make, and felt only a sense of crushing disappointment.

'Tom?' he echoed. 'Thomas is here?'

'Yes, sir.'

'*Damn!*'

Rafe felt his jaw clenching angrily, and then was reminded of his position once more as Sir George remarked: 'Capital house you've got here, Glyndower. This panelling—magnificent! Seventeenth century, isn't it? Beautiful.'

'It's early eighteenth, actually,' replied Rafe absently, his mind still buzzing with the implications of his son's arrival. Then, forcing a politeness he was far from feeling, he added: 'Part of the foundations date back to the sixteenth century, and there are stone racks in the cellars, which we think were used for storing wine by the monks who used to live in the monastery that originally stood on this site.'

'Is that so? Fascinating, fascinating . . .'

Sir George was clearly disarmed by his surroundings, and while he and John Norman shed their sheepskin jackets, Rafe had a swift exchange of words with the butler.

'When did he arrive?' he demanded in an undertone, and Morgan wasted no time in pretending he did not know who his employer was talking about.

'Just after you left, sir,' he exclaimed, rather reluctantly Rafe felt. Morgan had a soft spot for the youngest member of the household. 'I—er—I understand he came up from Cardiff by train.'

'Hitched a ride, you mean,' muttered Rafe dourly. 'God Almighty, this is all I need! I don't suppose his mother was pleased.'

Morgan's mouth turned down at the corners. 'No, sir.'

'I thought not,' Rafe thrust impatient fingers through the thickness of his hair. Dark, like his Celtic ancestors, it was now streaked with grey, no small contribution coming from the problems Thomas always created.

The opening of the library door brought his silent speculations to a halt. Lucy stood on the threshold, smiling warmly at John Norman, whom she knew, before awaiting her husband's introduction to Sir George. Not very tall, and slender, with the smallest hands and feet he had ever seen on a woman, Lucy epitomised anyone's ideal of a well-bred and attractive wife. But, after twelve years of marriage, Rafe now understood why size should never be equated with weakness. Lucy was strong, and determined, and at times she could display the ruthlessness of purpose her father had exhibited in the boardrooms of the Redvers grocery chain. As when dealing with their son, for example . . .

With the introduction over, Rafe suggested they continued their conversation in the library, and ignoring Lucy's silent signals to adjourn to his study, he entered the room to find Thomas curled up mutinously on the window seat. His eyes widened hopefully when he saw his father, and then dropped again when he saw he was not alone, and Rafe had no opportunity to speak to him before John Norman saw him, too.

'Hello, Tom,' he greeted the boy smilingly, and Thomas was forced to vacate his window seat and come and shake hands with his father's guests.

'Hello, sir,' he acknowledged politely, casting an appealing glance towards his father, and then shook hands with Sir George as he followed the others into the room.

'This is your son, Glyndower?' Marland exclaimed,

taking a seat on the worn velvet sofa beside the fire, and holding out his hands to the blaze. 'A fine boy. Isn't he at school?'

'He was.' Lucy spoke, coming into the room after ordering tea, and urging Sir George to remain seated as he attempted to rise. 'Unfortunately, Thomas doesn't like work, and this afternoon he arrived home—unannounced.'

'What my wife means is—this is the third time Tom has run away from his school,' Rafe put in flatly. 'Isn't that right, Tom? You have made yourself absent without leave, haven't you?'

Tom drew himself up to his full height of some four feet eight inches. At ten years of age, he was quite a tall boy, but so thin Rafe felt he could have snapped him in two.

'Yes, Father,' he answered now, making no excuses for his behaviour, and Sir George let out his breath in a puffing sound of disapproval.

'Won't do, young man, won't do,' he declared, as Lucy came to join him on the couch. 'We all need to learn, as much as we possibly can these days. And accept discipline. That's what keeps the wheels of industry turning.'

Tom made no reply, looking to his father for some sign that he at least understood why he had come home, but his mother was still in command.

'Go along and see your grandfather, Thomas,' she directed, as Morgan came in with a tray of tea. 'Talk to him for half an hour. I shall speak to you later.'

Tom's hesitation was minute, and although Rafe was tempted to countermand the order, he didn't. But talking to old Lord Penwyth could be a trying business. His father had lapses of memory, a symptom of the disease that had stricken him down five years before, and he was poor company for a small boy.

Still, Tom went obediently out of the room, and Rafe moved to the drinks cabinet. He guessed his guests would prefer something stronger than tea to ward off the chills of the late September afternoon, and he ignored Lucy's tightening lips when both Marland and Norman accepted Scotch.

With their glasses full, Rafe seated himself opposite his

wife, long legs splayed carelessly, considering the mud on his boots with a critical eye. Lucy, as usual, presented an impeccable appearance, and he supposed he ought to be grateful she had her own allowance. Without it, Tom could not have attended his public school—however reluctantly he remained there—or Lucy herself been able to maintain her wardrobe in the manner to which she had become accustomed. This afternoon, her plain mushroom-coloured dress, of fine woollen jersey, proclaimed its exclusiveness in the simple elegance of its lines, and the chestnut darkness of her hair curved softly into her nape, styled by an expert hand. He knew she would not approve of his own informal attire of moleskin breeches and roll-necked sweater, but she would not say so, not in so many words. Like everything else, it would be implied, alluded to, and only aired if his own patience gave out and he brought the subject up.

Realising a conversation was going on around him, Rafe made an effort to pay attention to what was being said. But his thoughts were with his son upstairs, and he longed to go after him and find out why he persisted in disobeying orders like this. So far, all they had been able to get out of him was that he didn't like the school or being away from home, but Rafe was convinced there was more to it than that. He had not liked boarding school either, but the comradeship and the facilities for sports had gradually compensated for the loneliness he had initially experienced. Of course, he had been older than Tom—twelve, before he left home for the first time—but Lucy found the boy so trying, he had eventually been obliged to consider boarding school as a solution.

'Rafe! Rafe, did you hear what Sir George said?'

He lifted his head rather blankly to discover Lucy staring at him with scarcely-concealed disapproval. He hadn't the faintest idea what Marland had said, and she knew it, and with some compunction he made his apologies.

'I'm sorry,' he said, the blue eyes which could change so swiftly from sapphire to steely-grey warming in conciliation. 'I was miles away. What were you saying, Sir George?'

Marland's sniff was expressive, but Glyndower's Scotch

was good, and he was feeling considerably more mellow. 'I was just telling your wife, and Norman here, how much I admire this house. Ever thought of selling? I'd guess it would make a tidy sum on the open market.'

'I think not.' Rafe had no intention of being rude, but selling Penwyth was never on the cards. 'Besides, you're too generous, Sir George. No one in his right mind would want to buy this white elephant. Woodworm, dry rot, a leaking roof—you name it, we've got it. Penwyth needs a small fortune spending on it, and even then, of what use is a house as large as this to anyone?'

Marland's eyes flickered. 'It's a show-piece, and you know it, Glyndower. Dry rot and all. With a few thousands invested, it could rival the stateliest homes in the country.'

'You're not suggesting I should put it into the hands of the National Trust, are you, Sir George?' Rafe enquired shortly, and Lucy cast him an impatient look before hurrying into speech.

'I'm afraid you've touched on rather a sore point with us, Sir George,' she declared. 'Penwyth is my husband's one weakness; nothing and no one will induce him to leave this house voluntarily.' She made an expressive gesture. 'I can't imagine why.'

'Can't you?'

The challenge was unexpected, and she gave her husband another disapproving stare before offering their guests another drink.

John Norman chose to intervene at this point, turning the conversation into less explosive channels, and for a while there was no contention between them. But Sir George was not a patient man, and soon he returned to the subject which had brought him to the valley.

'You will let us have your decision soon, Glyndower,' he remarked, making it more a statement than a question, and Rafe inclined his head. 'You do realise there's the possibility of a public enquiry if the scheme is mounted, and that could delay us even further?'

Rafe frowned. 'A public inquiry?'

'Of course.' Marland sighed. 'Norman, didn't you explain all this?'

'Until Mr Glyndower agrees to a test bore, I see no

reason to anticipate the worst, Sir George.'

'In my experience, it pays to anticipate the worst. Then one is never disappointed, Norman.' Marland shook his head. 'You do appreciate my position, Glyndower? I need a decision to take back to the Minister.'

'And you shall have it. Tomorrow,' Rafe assured him briefly, rising to his feet, decisively ending the meeting.

John Norman hastily finished his drink and rose, too, but Sir George was less enthusiastic. However, he had little choice in the matter, and Rafe saw Lucy's pained expression as Marland offered her his thanks for their hospitality.

'We hope to see you again, Sir George,' she demurred, accompanying them to the door, but Rafe cast an impatient look upstairs as he put on his jacket once more. He had still to drive the two men back to the helicopter, and again, Tom would have to wait.

It was getting dark when he got back to the house. This time Rufus accompanied him indoors, bounding off towards the kitchen for his supper at his master's command. Removing his jacket again, Rafe hesitated in the hall, torn between the desire to speak to Tom and the awareness of Lucy's disapproval emanating from behind the closed door of the library.

Stifling a curse, he turned towards the library, throwing open the door and entering the room with little regard for its occupant. As expected, Lucy was still sitting beside the tray of tea, gazing throughtfully into the glowing embers of the fire. With her shoulders hunched, and her head turned away from him, she had a delicate air of helplessness, and his conscience stirring within him, he closed the door with more consideration. She did not stir, and on impulse he crossed the room towards her, and bent to bestow a light kiss on the curving nape of her neck.

'Don't touch me!'

Her harsh words froze the spark of emotion that had prompted his action. With a jack-knifing movement she put the length of the couch between them, to sit regarding him with angry, resentful eyes.

Rafe needed no reminder of the uselessness of appealing to Lucy in this mood. She could suppress her emotions without effort, so successfully, in fact, that at times he suspected they were as counterfeit as the fragile appearance she presented to the world. It was not in her nature to compromise, and right now, she was in danger of losing everything she had worked for.

Pulling the case of cheroots out of his pocket, Rafe ignored the sound of distaste she made, and bent to light his cigar with a taper from the fire. Then, straightening, he said: 'I might as well go and speak to Tom, if you've got nothing to say.'

It was the match to the dynamite and as he had expected, Lucy exploded: 'Is that all you can think about? Your precious son! When there are matters of supreme importance to discuss, all you can think about is that disobedient little horror upstairs!'

Rafe inhaled deeply. 'He's your son, too,' he pointed out mildly, refusing to be aroused by Lucy's vituperation. It was a deliberate attempt, he knew, to incite his anger, and in so doing, weaken his arguments against Norcroft. In the heat of the moment, he was apt to say things he would later regret, and Lucy never let him forget anything.

'You don't care about anyone but yourself!'

This was another favourite accusation of hers. It wasn't true. He did care. He cared deeply for the people in the valley, the people he had known since he was a boy himself. He cared about Penwyth, and he knew that if ever his father had to move from the house, it would kill him. He cared about Tom—and Lucy, although his feelings for her had changed from the boyish infatuation she had first inspired to a kind of patient toleration. She was his wife, the mother of his son. He could admire her. He freely admitted that she was a better business person than he was. But there were times, as now, when her determination and self-interest, her ambition, appalled him, and he refused to be browbeaten into accepting a situation just to sustain her good humour.

'If that's what you think, I shall go and speak to Tom,' he said now, moving towards the door, and she sprang to her feet, fists clenched in frustration.

'Rafe!' She was obviously fighting the desire to rant at

him. 'Rafe, listen to me. This is our chance, our opportunity; the only opportunity we're ever likely to have. All right, so I know I've got no love for this place, but that doesn't mean I wouldn't like to see it restored to what it was. Just think what we could do! That dampness in your study—the roof——'

'Do you think I don't know that?' Rafe's lips tightened. 'We need the money—I'm not denying it. But . . . I don't know . . .'

'Rafe, Rafe . . .' She sensed his weakening, and came to stand near him. 'I know how you feel. But really, you mustn't confuse compassion with sentiment. Do you think any of these people—these people that you consider of such account—would hesitate, given your opportunities? If they owned their own land? Do you think they wouldn't grant mining rights? Oh, Rafe, you know they would!'

'I don't know,' he persisted grimly. 'Lucy, this isn't your valley. These are not your people. I know that. But they've been good tenants——'

'You're a good owner!' she countered sharply. 'My God, I think they must think you're soft. Those rents haven't been raised for——'

'I know, I know.'

Rafe raked back his hair with a weary hand, wishing his father was still master of the estate, in anything more than name. This shouldn't be his decision, and God alone knew, he was no Solomon.

'So . . .' Lucy's small fingers dug into his forearm. 'Oh, Rafe, don't let's quarrel any more tonight. Let's just talk about it, hmm? We could go out for dinner. Yes, that's a good idea. I've got a dress I bought the last time I was in London. I'd be glad of the opportunity to wear it.'

'Haven't you forgotten Tom?' enquired Rafe dryly, and was not surprised when Lucy's hand was withdrawn, and her features resumed their earlier expression of irritation.

'Thomas!' she almost spat the word. 'I should have known that little horror would come first on your list!'

Rafe sighed. 'As you said a few moments ago, don't let's quarrel any more tonight, Lucy. In any case. I'm too tired to go out this evening. I need a bath, and a change of clothes . . .'

'You don't have to tell me that!' Lucy wrinkled her small nose distastefully. 'You stink of oil and tobacco, and you're covered in dog hairs! I was ashamed, when Sir George was here——'

'It wouldn't be the first time, would it?' remarked Rafe flatly. 'If you'll excuse me now, I'll go and speak to our son.'

'He's going back tomorrow!' said Lucy shrilly.

'I haven't denied it, have I?'

'Well, don't come looking for me after you've let him walk all over you. I shall eat dinner in my room, and I don't want to see you again until the morning.'

'Point taken.'

Rafe reached for the door handle, but Lucy wasn't quite finished.

'By the way,' she muttered reluctantly, 'someone's coming to see you in the morning—some female. I don't know who she is. Says her name is Tempest, or something.'

'Tempest?' Rafe's dark brows descended. 'Who is she? Some friend of yours?'

'Mine?' Lucy sounded amused. 'You must be joking! Her uncle lives in the valley, apparently. She said you would know who she was.'

Rafe stared at his wife broodingly for a moment. Then, recognition dawned. '*Catherine* Tempest?'

'I think that was what she called herself. Why? Do you know her? Who is she?'

'Only Mervyn Powys's niece!' Rafe's jaw tightened. 'I wonder what she wants. Didn't she say anything?'

'Only that she wanted an appointment to see you.' Lucy's lips twisted mockingly. 'Some admirer of yours, is she? One of these "people" you keep talking about?'

'No!' Rafe expelled his breath impatiently. 'As a matter of fact, she was born and brought up near London. Her mother was Powys's sister, but she left the valley twenty-five—maybe thirty years ago.'

'Then how do you know this girl?' demanded Lucy shortly. 'How does she know you?'

Rafe's expression softened slightly. 'She used to spend

her summer holidays at the farm. When I was a boy I used to spend time down there, too.'

'Oh, I see.' Lucy was scathing. 'A boy-and-girl relationship.'

'No, nothing like that.' Rafe was tight-lipped. 'My God, she was only a kid! Nine, ten at most.'

'And you were?'

'Fifteen, sixteen—I don't know.'

Lucy looked amused. 'Hero-worship, then.' She shook her head. 'No wonder Thomas is such an undisciplined little devil! I don't suppose your father approved of you being so familiar with the tenants.'

'My father always cared for their welfare.'

'How feudal!'

'It was why you married me, remember?' retorted Rafe, stung into uncharacteristic bitterness. He had never referred to the reasons why Lucy, the daughter of a self-made millionaire, should have succumbed so eagerly to his amateurish attempts at seduction. Twenty-one, and fresh out of university, his experiences with girls had been limited to minor successes with waitresses, and office workers. Lucy Redvers, a year his senior, and already socially sophisticated, had seemed much too experienced to find him attractive. It was months before he understood, months before he realised the fact that as heir to his father, Lord Penwyth, he was infinitely more desirable in Lucy's eyes than any wealthy businessman might have been. But by then, of course, it had been too late. They were married, and any doubts he might have had he stifled.

Now Lucy's lips quivered, and had he not known better, he might have been disarmed by the break in her voice. 'I married you because I loved you, Rafe,' she declared tearfully, pulling out a handkerchief. 'I don't know why you say such cruel things to me. Just because I'm trying to help us both, to help all of us. You're so bigoted. You won't accept Daddy's help——'

'His charity, you mean? No.' Rafe was adamant, but there was a note of frustration in his tones. 'Oh, Lucy, why do you do this? Do you never try to put yourself in my position? Why do you persistently ignore the human problem here?'

'I have problems, too, and I'm human,' she retorted indignantly. 'You—you're impossible! You know you'll have to give in, sooner or later.'

Bitterness turned to bile in the back of Rafe's throat. The trouble was, he knew she was speaking the truth. In spite of himself, he was going to have to grant that permission; that, or have it taken out of his hands. How much longer could Penwyth survive without an influx of capital? One year? Two, at most. And then what? Bankruptcy? Penury? An unpalatable prospect for himself, an impossible one for Lucy, and for Tom. And his father . . .

'Yes,' he said now, the word torn from him. 'Yes, I expect you're right. But that doesn't——'

The sentence was never finished. Lucy was grasping his arm, gazing up at him with eyes avid with excitement. 'You mean—you mean——'

'I mean—I'm going to speak to my son,' said Rafe flatly, pulling his arm from her grasp, leaving the room and mounting the stairs on leaden feet.

CHAPTER TWO

CATHERINE Tempest swung her small Renault on to the private road that led to Penwyth manor house with some misgivings. The road was a gravel track, loosely made up and moist after the rain, and the tyres protested as they slid across its surface, but Catherine scarcely noticed. She was intent on the interview ahead of her, and in no way convinced that she was doing the right thing. It was strange really. If she had not taken it into her head to open a boutique in Pendower, she might never have become involved in her uncle's affairs, and this business about drilling for lead in the valley would not have concerned her.

But she had always loved the valley. She remembered those holidays as a child, spent on the slopes above Penwyn. She even remembered the horse she used to ride, a disreputable old gelding, with a temper to match its uncertain colouring. Perhaps it was her maternal ancestry which had instilled such a sense of belonging inside her. Certainly she had never felt a stranger here, and although she had lived in London for more than twenty-five years, she had seldom experienced the happiness there that she had enjoyed in the valley.

Of course, in latter years her visits to Penwyn had necessarily decreased, both in frequency and dimension. Since leaving school eight years ago, she had had neither the time nor the funds to spend eight weeks every year running free across these hills, and since opening the boutique in Hammersmith, she had been too absorbed with business affairs to pay more than an occasional week-end's visit to Penwyn.

The fact that the Hammersmith boutique had been so successful had enabled her to look farther afield, however, and despite her mother's opposition, she had decided to open a second branch in Pendower, the small country

22

town only ten miles from her uncle's farm.

Mrs Tempest, widowed these ten years, had recently remarried, so Catherine felt no sense of belonging with her. Her stepfather was all right, but there was obviously friction between them, belonging as he did to one of those freakish political organisations with fanatical doctrines long out of date. Catherine had already moved into a flat of her own in London, in spite of all the empty rooms in the house her father had bought for them, and it was only a small upheaval to transplant herself temporarily into a small cottage in Pendower.

It was a whim really, a foolish ideal of recapturing the dreams of her childhood, and she had told herself she could afford one mistake. The fact that the shop had prospered seemed more good luck than anything, and it was ironic when her affairs were going so well that her uncle's should be going so badly.

Lately, she had spent more and more time at the farm, and the reasons were here, at Penwyth. Her uncle was making himself ill with worry, and her cousin, Owen, was not much better. Owen had recently married, and his wife was expecting a baby. None of them had ever considered having to leave the valley, and the tenancy of the farm had been passed down from father to son for generations.

A gust of wind sent a shower of raindrops from the overhanging trees on to the windscreen of the car, and Catherine automatically set the wipers in motion. She was almost there. She could see the ivy-hung walls of the manor house on the rise above her and she changed into a lower gear to negotiate the slope. Her knees felt distinctly wobbly as she thrust the lever forward, and she had to concentrate on what she was doing to rid herself of the feeling of impending disaster.

What was she doing here? she asked herself uneasily. Why had she allowed herself to be persuaded to speak to Mr Glyndower on her uncle's behalf? What could she possibly say to deter him? And why should she imagine he would listen to her? She wasn't involved, not directly anyway, and just because she had a little more experience in negotiation than either her uncle or her cousin, it did not mean she could conduct this interview with success.

What had bargaining for materials to do with farming, or outfitting boutiques to do with mining for lead?

Her fingers were slippery against the wheel, despite the chilly autumn day outside. She was nervous—*oh, how nervous she was!*—and how she longed to turn the car and drive back to Pendower and put all thoughts of her uncle's problems behind her.

She expelled her breath on a sigh. He would probably not even remember her. It was years since she had seen him, and then only from a distance. They had never been friends, not in the real sense of the word. They had known one another, shared a common interest in horses and riding, even played together, although he had been so much older, almost grown-up in Catherine's eyes, but never really talked together. They had danced together once . . .

Her mind recoiled from that particular recollection. He would not remember that, but she did. After all, it was only—what? Eight years ago? The last year she had come to Penwyn for the summer. Her last year at school. That last holiday before she started work in one of the big stores in Oxford Street, and learned about clothes and the aptitude she had for designing them. There had been a country ball, she remembered, a village affair, with the squire's son and his lady graciously attending the proceedings. A barn dance had been announced, she recalled, and the Glyndowers had been persuaded to join in. Her own partner, a boy of her cousin Owen's age, had swung her into the line, and halfway through the dance she had halted before Rafe Glyndower.

Her lips quivered in remembrance. He had been totally unaware of her identity, and she had not attempted to enlighten him. They had danced a few bars of a waltz together, and then the music had changed again, and they had both moved on to other partners. It had been a perfectly innocent incident, he had been polite, but nothing more, yet Catherine remembered the feel of his hand at her waist, and the strength of his body, long after the ball was over.

She drew an uneven breath. She wondered if he remembered her name, if nothing else. It was unlikely, she supposed. After all, a lot could happen in sixteen years, and it must be that long since he had played with her at the farm. He was virtually the squire now. His father was senile, or so it was rumoured, feeble-minded after the stroke which had put him into the county hospital. Rafe had been married for quite a number of years; his wife was beautiful, and, by all accounts, could wrap him round her little finger; and they had a son called Thomas.

It was smattering with rain as she drove beneath the arch that gave on to the courtyard before the heavy oaken door. So this was Penwyth, she mused, trying to keep a sense of perspective. It was certainly imposing, yet apart from viewing the rooftops from a position higher up the valley, she had never been this close before. The tenants never came here, or very seldom anyway. They paid their rents to the estate's agent, and had no reason to approach the Glyndowers themselves.

Parking the Renault, she quickly pulled down the sun visor above the passenger seat and gave her reflection a critical appraisal in the mirror that was attached. Her nose was not shining and her lipstick was not smudged, but her pupils were slightly dilated. Blinking, to remedy this revealing feature, she tucked the strands of honey-brown hair behind her ears, and wondered if she ought to have worn a skirt instead of slacks. It was too late now to alter this, however, and gathering up her handbag, she opened her door and climbed out.

Drawing the collar of her suede jacket about her ears, she hurried towards the porch, sheltering under the overhang as she rang the bell. It was quite a modern bell, of the press-button variety, but hanging beside it was the iron bell-rope which had once been pulled to gain admittance. Shades of Dickens, she thought ruefully, and then stiffened as the heavy door was opened.

The elderly man who faced her was vaguely familiar. She recognised him from occasions she had seen him about the village. She thought her aunt had told her his name was Morgan, but she couldn't be sure.

'Yes miss?' he enquired now, sparse brows descending. 'Can I help you?'

'Oh—yes.' Catherine glanced round at the downpour

which had opened behind her. 'I—er—I have an appointment with Mr Glyndower. My name is Tempest, Miss Tempest.'

'Mr Rafe is expecting you, miss?'

'I believe so.'

Catherine glanced round again, hoping he was not about to keep her waiting on the doorstep. It was cold, as well as wet, and she felt at enough of a disadvantage as it was.

'You'd better come in, then,' the butler invited grudgingly, and, relieved, Catherine stepped into the warm mustiness of a hall that was panelled in a dark wood that gleamed with the patina of age. The floor reflected a similar lustre, but the wooden blocks were worn and strewn with rugs. As the door was closed behind her, Catherine heard the distinct chink of glass, and glancing upward, she caught her breath in admiration for the magnificent chandelier suspended overhead. She could imagine it illuminated on a cold winter's evening, its warming glow reflected in the panelling, and casting shadows on the shallow treads of the staircase that curved along one wall.

'If you'll wait here, I'll see if the master is in his study,' declared the butler formally, and Catherine hid a smile at the use of the title. *The master,* she thought, shaking her head. One could get delusions of grandeur for less.

'Miss Tempest?'

He had come upon her unawares, and she was annoyed. She had intended to control this interview from start to finish. Now, swinging to face him, she was immediately at a disadvantage, shaken by his sudden appearance, and by the immediate attraction she felt towards him. *That* hadn't changed, even though she had convinced herself that it must, and she chided herself for allowing a girlish infatuation to effect her so strongly.

'It is—Catherine Tempest, isn't it?' he was saying now, holding out his hand towards her, and despite her misgivings she was forced to take it, hoping he would not associate the dampness of hers with anything more than the weather.

He hadn't changed. He was still the most disturbing man she had ever met, and as soon as it was possible she snatched her hand away, twisting her fingers together, forcing herself to appear composed. She had known she should not have agreed to conduct this interview, had known her reasons were not wholly altruistic. She had wanted to see him again, to speak to him as an equal, and now she was here, and she felt tongue-tied.

As if aware of her embarrassment, Rafe turned aside then, gesturing towards the open doorway she now saw behind him, inviting her into his study. On unsteady legs, she preceded him into the room, and schooled her features as he closed the leather-covered door behind them.

As he moved behind the square desk that dominated the room, she allowed herself a surreptitious appraisal of the boy who had grown into such an attractive man. Those summer days at Penwyn had never seemed so distant, or her own relationship with him so remote and unreal. He was truly his father's successor, while she—she was still just the niece of one of his tenants, and no amount of success in her own field would alter that. He was older, of course. There were strands of grey in his dark hair, and the lines beside his mouth were deeply engrained. But his hair was still as thick as it had ever been, and longer than he used to wear it, and his mouth as deeply sensual as his lower lip denoted. He wore casual clothes—moleskin pants that clung to the powerful muscles of his thighs, a black shirt that accentuated the darkness of his skin, evidence of the time he spent outdoors, and a dark green corded jacket, with leather patches at the elbows.

'Now, Miss Tempest,' he said, indicating that she should take the leather chair opposite him. 'Why did you want to see me?'

Catherine made a movement towards the chair, and then stilled. It might be easier standing up, although she sensed his mild impatience when he was obliged to remain standing, too. Clearing her throat, she endeavoured to meet his gaze, and was surprised to find a certain guardedness about his eyes.

'My uncle asked me to speak to you,' she said, and then wished she had not put it quite like that. 'That is—he would have spoken to you himself, but—well, I offered to come.'

'Did you?' His dark eyebrows ascended.

'Yes.' He wasn't making it any easier for her. 'You—you must know why I'm here.'

'I have a strong suspicion,' he agreed evenly. Then: 'Won't you sit down? I'm sure you'd find it much more comfortable.'

Catherine hesitated only a moment longer before moving forward, albeit reluctantly, to seat herself in the chair he offered. With a sigh of satisfaction, Rafe Glyndower took his own leather armchair, and with long fingers beating a tattoo on its arm, he said: 'Your uncle wants to know whether any decision has yet been made about the mine.'

Catherine pressed her lips together. 'Yes.'

He nodded. 'I guessed as much.' His fingers stilled.

'Naturally, he's worried,' Catherine justified herself. 'It is his livelihood—the livelihood of his family. Naturally, he wants to know what's going on.'

'Naturally,' agreed Rafe Glyndower dryly, and she wondered for a moment whether he was mocking her. But his expression was perfectly serious, and in any case, his next words drove all thought of mockery out of her mind. 'You can tell him that no decision has been made—yet. When I do know anything definite, he'll be the first to hear.'

'Thank you.' There was not much else she could say, even though she had still to voice her own opinion in the matter. 'I'll tell him what you've said. I know he'll be relieved.'

'Good.' Was there a trace of anger in his voice now? 'I'm glad to have been of service.'

Was that all? Catherine sought for words to express herself. 'Do you—that is—do you know when you'll have something definite to relate?'

'I'm afraid not.' He was definitely withdrawing now, pushing back his chair, getting to his feet. 'It's been very nice seeing you again, Miss Tempest. Give my regards to your aunt and uncle, won't you?'

Wait a minute!

The words were never spoken, but they drummed in Catherine's head. Any minute now, she was going to be dismissed, and she still hadn't voiced any of the objections she had come here to espouse.

'Mr Glyndower . . .'

He was moving round the desk towards her as she spoke, but her words arrested him. 'Yes?' He was cautious, and pushing back her chair, she rose to face him.

'You—you do appreciate my uncle's position, don't you, Mr Glyndower?' she ventured nervously, and although his lids lowered ominously, she hastened on: 'I mean—there's more to this than just losing the land.'

'I do know the arguments for and against,' he reminded her, his tone colder than before, but now she had his attention, she was not about to relinquish it.

'It would—destroy the whole community,' she continued. 'I don't know what's involved, but I do know that new roads would be needed for the vehicles transporting the ore to the smelting plant—would that be in the valley, too, by the way?—and the cottages in the village simply aren't built to withstand that kind of vibration.'

'Your concern does you credit,' Rafe retorted shortly, but when he would have moved towards the door, she went on:

'That's without the destruction of the beauty of the valley. The river—would it become polluted, too? And what would they do with the rock they dig out? Would there be piles of debris everywhere?'

'Miss Tempest—*Catherine!*' He spoke through his teeth. 'I know very little more about what's involved here than you do. I'm as appalled as anyone else by the possible effects such a scheme might have on the ecology of this area, but there are other considerations. So far, all that's been determined is that there are grounds for believing that a seam of ore may exist in the land above Penwyn. Your uncle knows there have been geologists working in the area. As yet, no actual drilling has been done, so all their work is purely speculative. It could be a cold trail. No one knows. Without further exploration, they never will.'

'And—and that's your decision. Whether or not to grant drilling rights?'

'Yes.'

Catherine gazed at him, trying to read his mind, trying

to penetrate the mask-like schooling of his features. For the first time she noticed the muscle jerking at his jawline, and the lines of weariness around his eyes. They were revealing aspects, and she realised, with a stirring of compassion, that he was not without a conscience. This was not easy for him, and after all, he need not have agreed to see her. For a moment the gulf between them narrowed, but as she parted her lips to utter some conventional words of gratitude for granting her this interview, the door opened behind him, and a slim, dark-haired young woman stood on the threshold.

Catherine recognised Lucy Glyndower at once. Apart from that occasion when she had accompanied her husband to the ball, she was regularly seen about the town. She drove a Volvo estate car, and Catherine had encountered her in the supermarket on more than one occasion. Not that Lucy acknowledged her. She seldom acknowledged anyone other than the manager of the store, and Catherine had heard the girls at the check-out grumbling about her haughty ways. Until this moment she had thought they exaggerated, but the look Mrs Glyndower cast in her direction was completely devoid of interest, and she turned immediately to her husband, almost as if Catherine wasn't there.

'I've just been speaking to Thomas!' she declared, and there was a note of anger in her voice. 'Are you aware——'

Her husband's intervention halted her tirade. 'We have a guest, Lucy,' he reminded her evenly. 'Miss Tempest was just leaving. We can discuss Thomas later.'

His eyes held hers, and Catherine sensed the antipathy between them at that moment. Then, as if unwillingly accepting her husband's injunction, Lucy Glyndower turned to face her.

'Oh, yes,' she said. 'You're Powys's niece, aren't you?' The way she said it made Catherine's resentment bristle, but she managed to disguise it. 'My husband remembered your name. But you don't live here in the valley, do you, Miss Tempest? So the loss of your uncle's farm will mean little to you.'

Catherine squared her shoulders, glad that in height at least she had the advantage, although Lucy's daintiness was obviously more feminine. 'I live in Pendower, Mrs Glyndower,' she retorted smoothly. 'But I've always considered the valley my second home. Anything that affects Uncle Mervyn affects me, too.'

'Oh, dear!' Lucy didn't sound at all sympathetic, though. 'Still, I'm sure he'll be well compensated.'

Catherine blinked. 'Well—compensated?'

'Yes,' Lucy nodded. 'When he has to move.'

Catherine's eyes went straight to Rafe Glyndower's face, and what she saw there in no way reassured her. 'You mean—you mean the decision has been made, then?'

'Oh, yes.' It was Lucy who answered. 'Didn't my husband tell you?'

'*Lucy!*'

Rafe Glyndower's warning came a little too late, however, and Catherine was already gazing at him in angry disbelief.

'You said—you said——'

'My husband was probably trying to avoid any unpleasantness,' Lucy remarked, shaking her sleek head. 'Surely you realise, Miss Tempest, that we cannot allow sentiment to stand in the way of business?'

'Lucy, for God's sake——'

'Oh, please. Let her go on!' Catherine's fingers clenched painfully. 'I'd rather hear the truth than a pack of lies!'

'Miss Tempest!' It was Lucy's protest that rang out then. 'I must repeat, whatever loyalty you may feel towards your uncle, this is not your affair, and coming here in an abortive attempt to appeal to my husband's good nature—presuming on a relationship you may once have thought you had——'

Catherine gulped. 'What do you mean?'

'I mean this—childish aberration you nurtured for my husband . . .'

'Shut up, Lucy!'

'He told me about it,' Lucy continued, ignoring Rafe's furious command, and his fingers digging into her shoulder. 'I suppose you thought it gave you an advantage. Your uncle thought so, obviously. But being insolent is not going to solve anything!'

'I warn you, Lucy——'

But Catherine had heard enough. She could feel the hot colour surging into her cheeks, and knew that if she didn't get out of here soon she would be tempted to slap Lucy's taunting little face. So he had remembered, she thought bitterly, but it gave her no satisfaction. What had he said? What could he have intimated for his wife to get such an impression? It was galling and humiliating, doubly so, because she had never dreamed he suspected her infantile infatuation.

Brushing a hand across her eyes, she hurried blindly towards the door. She had to get out of here. It had been a waste of time coming. The decision was already made, and Rafe Glyndower had only been humouring her. She hated him for that. Hated him, for making a fool of her, for humiliating her in front of his wife. She would never forgive him. Never!

She had the impression that there was somebody in the hall as she stumbled awkwardly across it, someone standing on the stairs who watched her uneven progress with wide, curious eyes. But she didn't stop to look. She wrenched open the heavy door without waiting for anyone's assistance, and ran down the steps to the Renault, uncaring of the rain.

Fortunately, she had not locked it, but her cold fingers fumbled with the handle, and she had just managed to jerk it open when other fingers closed around her arm. Hard fingers, they were, but long and sensitive, powerful in their determination not to let her go.

'Catherine, *wait!*'

The voice was familiar, much too familiar, and she struggled urgently to free herself, her long honey-coloured hair falling forward in a curtain, hiding the heated contours of her face.

'Let go of my arm, Mr Glyndower,' she said, with what she hoped was convincing coolness, but she knew from his angry oath that he had no intention of complying.

'I want to talk to you,' he told her harshly, and she lifted trembling fingers to loop back her hair.

'There's nothing more to be said, Mr Glyndower,' she exclaimed unevenly. 'And—and I'm getting wet.'

'So am I,' he retorted, and then, with an impatient

glance back towards the house, he bundled her into the car and got in beside her, forcing her to scramble over into the passenger seat.

The Renault was a small car, hardly big enough to accommodate a man of his size, and with the rain drumming on the roof outside and running in a concealing shroud down the windows, Catherine felt a suffocating sense of constriction. Their combined breathing clouded the windows, concealing them behind its enveloping mist, and she shifted as far away from him as the narrow confines of the car would allow.

'Now . . .' Rafe rested his elbow upon the steering wheel and pushed back his hair with a weary hand. 'Let's get one thing straight, shall we? No decision has been made, whatever my wife may have said——'

'I don't believe you!'

'Why not?'

Catherine bent her head. 'Why should your wife lie, Mr Glyndower?'

Rafe sighed. 'She wasn't lying——'

'There you are, then!' Catherine was indignant.

'—she was—anticipating.'

'In other words, she knows what your decision is going to be!' declared Catherine, sniffing as drops of rain trickled down her nose from the dampness of her hair. 'You're splitting hairs, Mr Glyndower.'

'I'm speaking the truth,' he retorted, turning his head to gaze impatiently at the clouded windows. 'For God's sake, I don't know why I'm telling you this. Like Lucy says, this has nothing to do with you, Catherine.'

'I think it does, Mr Glyndower.'

'And for God's sake, stop calling me *Mr* Glyndower.'

Her breath caught in her throat. 'What would you have me call you, Mr Glyndower? Rafe? I don't think your wife would like that.'

He turned to look at her then, and she flinched beneath the cold contempt in his eyes. He had the longest lashes of any man she had ever known, but they did little to conceal his antagonism at that moment, and she shrank back in her seat, half afraid he was about to strike her.

'My wife is not my keeper,' he enunciated harshly.

'Whatever you may have heard to the contrary.'

Catherine flushed then. 'I—I didn't say she was.'

'No.' He conceded her protest. 'But I'm not a fool. I know what people think, but they're wrong. Do you understand?'

Catherine shrugged. 'It's nothing to do with me.'

'No, it's not. But it may help to remember that when the decision is finally taken.'

Catherine licked her dry lips. 'You—you are going to allow mining in the valley, aren't you?'

'Oh, God!' He rested both elbows on the steering wheel then, cradling his head in his hands and hunching his shoulders. 'I don't see what else I can do,' he muttered heavily. 'The estate's almost bankrupt as it is.'

Catherine caught her lower lip between her teeth. 'Can't you—can't you borrow money? From—from a bank or somewhere?'

He looked at her pityingly. 'On what collateral? A crumbling manor house and a few uneconomic acres of land?'

Catherine hesitated. 'But I thought—that is—isn't Mrs Glyndower's father—I mean——'

Rafe's mouth thinned. 'You mean isn't Hammond Redvers a wealthy man?' Catherine inclined her head a trifle awkwardly, and he nodded. 'Yes, Redvers has capital. And he'd invest it in Penwyth if he had the chance.'

'He would?' Catherine was confused and showed it.

'Oh, yes.' Rafe shifted his long legs uncomfortably. 'Would you like to know what he has in mind?' He raised dark eyebrows, and gaining her silent assent, explained: 'He would like to sell the valley to one of those leisure consortiums. You know what I mean? Some kind of holiday complex, with swimming pools and sporting facilities, pony trekking, a marina—you name it, he's thought of it.'

Catherine was horrified. 'A—holiday camp?'

'Well, I understand that designation doesn't appeal these days. Complex, is the word they use. But generally speaking, they mean the same.'

'With cabins, and things?'

'Accommodation would be provided,' Rafe agreed dryly, watching her growing concern.

'That—won't happen,' she exclaimed. 'Will it?'

'Not as long as I have any say in the matter,' Rafe declared shortly. 'So now do you understand my position?'

Catherine made a negative gesture. 'Surely—surely, as this valley means so much to you . . .'

'No.' Rafe shook his head. 'Hammond Redvers didn't get where he is today by philanthropising.'

'But he's your father-in-law!'

'Yes. Well, he thinks I'm not realistic, and I think he's a financial leech. We don't exactly see eye-to-eye in these matters.' He shook his head. 'Although why I should admit that to you, I can't imagine.'

Catherine met his gaze reluctantly. 'Thank you, anyway,' she murmured, half afraid of the penetration of those clear blue eyes, so unusual in someone so dark. 'I—I do see your dilemma. I just wish there was some way . . .'

'So do I,' he retorted, with a return of abrasiveness, and thrusting open the door behind him, he levered himself out of the car. 'Thank you for listening to me. Goodbye, Catherine.'

'Goodbye—Rafe,' she answered, although her tentative use of his name was drowned in the brisk slamming of the door.

CHAPTER THREE

THE bar of the Bay Horse was half empty at this hour of a
Friday evening, and Catherine led the way to a table in
the corner, near the crackling log fire. Seating herself on
the banquette, she accepted Robert's offer of a Scotch and
soda, and warmed her hands at the blaze as he went to get
their drinks. It was an attractive room, and her eyes
strayed over the hunting trophies and horse brasses that
decorated the walls. There had been a hostelry on these
premises almost as long as there had been a manor at
Penwyth, and she couldn't help thinking that Josh Evans
would not complain at the increase in trade a development
in the valley might bring.

Robert came back, carrying two glasses, and she trans-
ferred her attention to him. A little over medium height
and stocky, with a fair complexion and drooping moustache, he was an amusing companion, and she forced a
smile to her lips as he seated himself on the banquette
beside her.

'Cheers,' he said, swallowing a mouthful of his lager,
and she took a mouthful of her own drink as he added:
'Nice place.' He waved his glass expansively. 'Can we get
a meal here?'

'We can. A bar meal, at least,' she conceded. 'But we
won't. Aunt Margaret would never forgive me if I didn't
bring you over for supper.'

Robert laughed goodnaturedly. It was an amiable
sound, and Catherine thought how good it was to hear it.
Robert was unfailingly cheerful, and right now he was
exactly what she needed.

'Aunt Margaret,' he said, swallowing more of his lager.
'And Uncle Mervyn, is that right? You see——' He held
up a knowing finger. 'I don't forget these things.'

Catherine's smile was less tense. 'It's good to see you,
Robert. But you should have warned me you were coming.

I promised to have supper at the farm last week, and I didn't make it. I daren't let them down again.'

'That's okay,' Robert shrugged. 'I like meeting your family. It makes me feel that I'm getting somewhere——'

'Now, Robert . . .'

'Oh, don't worry.' He pulled a wry face. 'I'm not going to bring that up again. I just—well, I like being with you, and I don't mind where it is.'

Catherine looked down into her glass. 'You should find yourself a woman who wants to settle down,' she said quietly. 'Not a career woman like me. You know you want a home and family. You're not getting any younger—neither of us are. You should be looking around.'

Robert ignored her and looked round the bar. 'This looks a pretty old place,' he commented. 'Stone floors no less. No wonder the beer's cold!'

'You're right. The cellars are ancient. As a matter of fact, I was just thinking those very thoughts.'

'Really?' Robert grinned. 'You see! We even think alike.'

'Oh, Robert!'

Catherine applied herself to her drink again, and Robert looked about him. 'Tell me who everyone is,' he ordered. 'Come on. The bartender, for example. Is he the publican?'

'No, that's Morris Evans, the publican's son. Josh has the licence.'

'You mean he owns the place?'

'No, again.' Catherine's lips tightened. 'All the property in the valley is part of the Penwyth Estate.'

'Is that right?' Robert's fair brows ascended. 'That would be the estate which has granted drilling rights on your uncle's land?'

'Yes.' Catherine's fingers tightened round her glass. She preferred not to think about that.

Sensing this, Robert went on: 'So, who else is here? That fat old boy in the corner, for instance, with the pipe. Who's he?'

Patiently, Catherine catalogued the various occupations of the people in the bar, realising that Robert was doing his best to cheer her up. He was a nice person, and she had been delighted when he walked into the boutique, right on closing time. She hadn't seen him for over two months, not since the last time she was in London, and it was surprising how much she had missed his humorous face.

A sudden influx of customers caused him to glance round again, and in an undertone, he said: 'Farmers! These days they don't look any different from accountants.'

'They may be accountants, for all I know,' declared Catherine tersely, after giving the men a cursory look. 'They're Norcroft's men—geologists or geophysicists or something. They're the ones conducting the explorations at Penwyn. I believe they're staying here at the inn. They're engineers of some kind, but I don't know them.'

'I see.' Robert considered the newcomers thoughtfully. 'And—is there any news?'

'Not yet.'

'How long has it been?'

'Since they arrived?' Catherine shrugged her slim shoulders. 'I don't know. A month, six weeks—something like that.'

It was exactly six weeks, two days, and eight hours since she had had that interview with Rafe Glyndower, but she wasn't going to tell Robert that.

'Interesting.' Robert nodded now, and then, in an attempt to justify this statement, he added: 'I mean, if it was anywhere else than on your uncle's land, it would be interesting, wouldn't it? If they do find lead, it will be tremendously important. After all, everyone thought lead mining was virtually defunct in Britain.'

Catherine knew he was right. Such a find was potentially exciting, but not if one was personally involved. She could only see the effect it was having on her family, and that negated its importance so far as she was concerned. Not that the men's appearance had interfered too much with the running of Penwyn, yet at any rate. Their present explorations were confined to the top field, and apart from the inconvenience, and an occasional tremor from their boring equipment, they could almost forget they were there. Indeed, it was always possible that their search

would prove fruitless, in which case Rafe Glyndower had
given an undertaking that her uncle should have first
option should the land have to be sold.

It was the only light at the end of the tunnel, but she
knew her uncle had little faith in it. From the moment the
first drillings were heard, he had withdrawn into a shell of
his own making, and no amount of sympathy or cajole-
ment could bring him out of it. He was not eating, he had
lost weight; and her aunt said he was sleeping badly. And
all because his shepherd had found the head of a Roman
axe among some rocks in the top pasture, and he had
been honest enough to hand it over to the Glyndowers.

Yet for all that, she could not entirely blame Rafe
Glyndower for what had happened, even though her attitude had enraged her cousin Owen. Rafe was as helpless
as they were, at the mercy of his own needs and necessities,
and there was no easy solution to any of their problems.

Supper at Penwyn was not a comfortable occasion, even
though her aunt attempted to make it so. Uncle Mervyn
was out attending to a cow that was calving, and apart
from appearing for a brief moment halfway through the
meal, he left his wife to entertain their guests.

'Do you have a dairy herd, too, Mrs Powys?' asked
Robert politely, helping himself to another slice of savoury
flan, and Catherine saw the way Owen glowered at him.

'Oh, no.' Aunt Margaret shook her head. 'Just a few
cows for our own use, that's all.'

'This is a sheep farm,' Owen told him shortly. 'Or at
least, it was.'

'Owen!'

His mother gave him a warning look, but it was too
good an opportunity to miss, and turning on Catherine,
he added: 'We're all indebted to my dear cousin here for
removing the uncertainty.'

'It's not Catherine's fault.' It was Gillian, his wife, who
defended her. 'She only told you what Mr Glyndower had
told her.'

Owen snorted. 'That bastard! I wouldn't believe a word
he said. If he's so desperate for cash, how come that son of
his goes to public school? And what about the servants
they employ——'

'Would you have him dismiss old Percy Laurence?' demanded Catherine, stung by his indifference to anyone's well being but his own. 'And what about the butler? Morgan, isn't it?' She appealed to her aunt for confirmation. 'Neither of them would get any other employment, you know that.'

'They still have to be paid,' insisted Owen moodily, pushing his pie round his plate. 'And I know Linda Jones works there, too.'

'Penwyth is a big place,' retorted Catherine. 'Someone has to work there.'

'Then why doesn't that wife of his get herself off her backside and do something?'

'Really, Owen! At the supper table!' His mother looked apologetically at Robert. 'I'm sorry, Mr Brooke. My son isn't usually so objectionable.'

'Oh, really . . .' Robert was seldom embarrassed, and his smile was reassuring. 'Don't apologise, Mrs Powys. I come from a large family, so I'm used to family squabbles. Besides, I'm enjoying myself. You're an excellent cook, if I may say so. This flan is delicious!'

Aunt Margaret flushed with pleasure, and Catherine felt a surge of warmth towards him. Robert could always be relied upon to smooth over any difficulties, and Owen was forced to apply himself to his supper, aware that any further comment on his part could only be construed as boorishness.

When supper was over, Catherine offered to wash up, and she and Gillian shared the dishes while her aunt showed Robert the family photograph album.

'Don't take any notice of Owen,' his wife urged her awkwardly. 'You know what he's like. He always expected to take over here.'

'I know that.' Catherine cast a sympathetic glance in the younger girl's direction.

'It's different for you,' went on Gillian. 'You don't live here. I know you like coming here, but you have your own life outside the valley.' She paused. 'Are you going to marry Robert?'

'Heavens, no!' Catherine was vehement, and Gillian looked at her strangely.

'No?'

'No.'

'Why not? I saw the way he was looking at you during supper. Hasn't he asked you?'

Catherine was amused, and her gurgling laughter rang around the stone-flagged kitchen. 'Oh, Gillian,' she exclaimed, 'I don't want to marry anyone. Not yet, at least,' she added, sobering as an image of Rafe Glyndower's dark features swam unexpectedly before her eyes.

Gillian was affronted. 'I expect you do things differently in London,' she mumbled, clattering two plates together, and Catherine sighed.

'I expect we do,' she conceded. Then, encouragingly: 'You're looking well. Being pregnant evidently agrees with you.'

Gillian nodded, obviously still brooding over what Catherine had said, and presently she pursued: 'Do you sleep with him?'

Catherine didn't pretend not to understand. 'With Robert?' She shook her head. 'No.'

Gillian frowned. 'But he's staying with you tonight, isn't he? I heard Owen's mother asking where he was staying, and he said at your cottage.'

'There are two bedrooms,' Catherine pointed out patiently. 'Gillian, I know this may not be easy for you to understand, but a man and a woman—they can be *just* friends.'

Gillian looked sceptical. 'Can they? All the men I've known want just one thing—Owen included.' She flushed. 'And you're not getting any younger.'

'Thank you.' Catherine's tone was dry.

'Well, it's true. You're not. I'm twenty-two, and you were always three years older than me.'

'Well, that's one thing that doesn't change,' remarked Catherine wryly, reaching for the towel to dry her hands. 'It's nice of you to be so concerned, Gillian, but there's really no need. I guess I'm just a career woman at heart.'

'Mmm.'

Gillian didn't sound convinced, but Catherine had had enough of this particular conversation. Nevertheless, as she crossed the stone flags to the door leading into the passage beyond, she wondered if she would have felt differently had she been born to this environment. She had always been happy in the valley. Those summer weeks still possessed a dreamlike quality that she had never been able to duplicate anywhere else. Waking in the mornings in her little room under the eaves, hearing the woodpigeons crooning on the chimneys, smelling the pervading scents from her aunt's flower garden; all these things had imprinted themselves on her memory. But, more significantly, she associated Penwyn with her awakening from girlhood to womanhood, and the painful realisation that dreams were no substitute for reality . . .

It was a little after ten when they drove back to Pendower. Catherine would have left earlier, but Robert had shown a genuine interest in her aunt's reminiscences, and with some misgivings she went to find her uncle in the cowsheds. Mervyn Powys was uncommunicative, however, and as the local vet was with him and she was obviously in the way, Catherine soon returned to the house.

'I like your aunt,' remarked Robert, as she drove up the winding road that led out of the valley. 'She's quite a character. Is she your mother's sister? I must say, she's not very like her.'

'No.' Catherine shook her head, concentrating on the narrow road ahead. 'Uncle Mervyn is my mother's brother. But Mummy left the valley nearly thirty years ago, and unlike me, she's never wanted to come back.'

Robert shrugged. 'You can't blame her, I suppose. Life on the farm was probably pretty spartan in those days.'

Catherine nodded, changing into a lower gear as the Renault laboured up the steepest part of the pass, and then stepped automatically on the brake as some small creature flung itself across the road ahead of them.

'What the devil was that?' exclaimed Robert, gazing at her profile in the semi-darkness, and she made a helpless movement of her shoulders. 'It almost looked human to me,' he added, rolling down his window and staring towards the ditch that dipped beside them. 'What did you think it was?'

Catherine was still shaken by the immediacy of her

reaction, but she managed to say weakly: 'I thought it was human, too. It had legs.'

Robert grimaced. 'So do animals, in case you hadn't noticed.'

'No. I mean—*two* legs. I thought it was a child.'

'A child! Up here? At this time of night?'

'I know it seems crazy.' Catherine removed her moist palms from the wheel. 'Should we—should we look?'

But even as she said the words, they heard a whimper which sounded suspiciously like a sob, and without waiting for Robert's answer, Catherine thrust open her door and got out, circling the car to reach the ditch. She wished she had a torch, or a match, although it would never have stayed alight in the stiff breeze that was blowing off the mountains. Instead, she concentrated on the shifting shadows beneath the level of the road, endeavouring to distinguish a human form among the ferns and undergrowth.

'I know you're there,' she declared, annoyed to find her voice quavered a little as she spoke, and Robert at the elbow asked in a wry undertone whether she expected some imp of Satan to appear. 'I don't know, do I?' she demanded, half irritated by his complacency, and then started again, as a small figure rose up in front of her.

'Good God! It is a child!' muttered Robert disbelievingly, while Catherine stared in amazement at the small boy who moved into the shadow of the car's headlights.

'I—I'm sorry if I startled you.' The boy spoke clearly and well, she noticed. 'I'm afraid I've hurt my knee. I didn't hear the car, you see, because of the wind, and I fell getting into the ditch.'

Catherine shook her head helplessly. 'Do you realise what time it is?' she exclaimed, unable to think of anything else to say at that moment, and the boy nodded, apparently unconcerned.

'It's late, I know,' he answered. 'I missed the last bus from Pendower, so I had to walk, you see. Then I twisted my knee and——'

'But where are you walking to?' demanded Robert, but as if freezing before the unmistakable exasperation in his voice, the boy made no response, merely shifting his weight from one leg to the other and offering a mutinous expression.

'We can't leave him here, you know,' Robert added, close to Catherine's ear. 'Wherever he's going, he could die of exposure before he gets there. It's so damn cold!'

Realising she had to make the next move, Catherine gestured towards the car. 'Can we give you a lift?' she suggested, wondering how a boy of no more than ten years of age could be wandering these roads at this time of night. Who was he? Where had he come from? 'It's much warmer inside.'

'I'm not allowed to accept lifts from strangers,' the boy replied then, hunching one shoulder, but Robert stretched out a hand and caught his arm.

'Well, we can't leave you here, old man,' he declared, urging him towards the Renault. 'Come on. We can talk just as well inside.'

'No, no! Let go of me!' The boy fought like a little fury then. 'I shall tell my father about this. He'll be furious, I can tell you. He owns this valley——'

'*What!*' Catherine detained Robert's enforced abduction, grasping the boy's shoulder and turning him so that she could see his face. Her heart lurched as Rafe Glyndower's dark features were exposed to her stare; smaller, younger, perhaps a little fairer, but definitely related. 'You mean—you're Thomas?'

'That's right.' He fought back a sob. 'And you have no right to keep me here!'

Catherine gathered herself with difficulty. 'Does your father know where you are?' she demanded, knowing the answer before she voiced the question. If Glyndower's son had been discovered missing, the whole valley would have heard about it by now. 'You know he doesn't. You're supposed to be away at school, aren't you? What's happened? Have you run away?'

'Yes—no. That is—it's nothing to do with you!'

Shades of Lucy Glyndower, thought Catherine dryly. Then: 'And do you think you'll be welcome, at this time of night? I'd hazard a guess that your father will be less than pleased to see you.'

'Catherine, we can't stand here arguing the toss,'

Robert exclaimed shortly, showing uncharacteristic signs of irritation, and although she deplored his impatience, she appreciated his point.

'I wasn't going home,' Thomas was saying now, shocking her still further. 'There's a shepherd's hut not far from here. I was going to spend the night there and go home in the morning, only . . . only . . .'

'Only what?'

'Only—it's jolly dark, isn't it? I'm not afraid of ghosts, of course,' he added, holding up his head, 'but I might not find it in the dark, might I?'

Catherine felt an overwhelming surge of sympathy for him. 'You have run away, then? From school?'

The boy nodded, looking down at his toes, and over his bent head Catherine exchanged an appealing look with Robert. Thomas was only wearing a blazer over his uniform grey shirt and trousers, and Robert hadn't been far wrong when he considered the possible effects of exposure. The boy was shivering already, and a night spent in a shepherd's hut . . .

Without hesitating, Catherine came to a decision. 'Look,' she said, squatting down beside him, 'you know you can't sleep in an old hut at this time of year. That might have been all right in the summer, when the nights were warm, but now it's cold, very cold, and you could freeze to death.'

Thomas sniffed. 'You're going to take me home?'

'Is that what you want?'

'Oh, honestly, Catherine——'

Overriding Robert's exasperated ejaculation, she repeated the question, and this time Thomas shook his head. 'Not—not tonight,' he admitted unhappily, and she straightened with determination, taking his small cold hand in hers.

'Now you listen to me,' she said firmly. 'How would you like to spend the night at my cottage in Pendower, then I'll run you home in the morning myself?'

Her legs quivered at this prospect, but short of bundling the boy into the car and dumping him on his father's doorstep at eleven o'clock at night, there was nothing else she could do.

'You're crazy!' declared Robert, jerking open the car door. 'Why can't you take him home?'

'What do you say, Thomas?'

The boy hesitated. 'Do you have buttermilk?'

'Oh, my God! Not only does he hesitate, but he makes conditions!' exclaimed Robert frustratedly, but Catherine ignored him.

'I'm sorry,' she said to the child now, 'I don't have anything like that. Why? Is it your favourite?'

'No!' Thomas was adamant. 'I hate it. My mother makes me drink it.'

'I see.' Catherine raised her eyebrows helplessly, as he suddenly smiled up at her.

'I'll come with you now,' he said. 'Can I sit in front?'

With much grumbling from Robert, Thomas was wedged between them, and the remainder of the journey was accomplished mostly in a stony silence. Thomas seemed to enjoy watching the road ahead, examining the instruments on the dashboard from time to time, and making comparisons between the Renault and his father's Volvo, but otherwise there was no conversation. Catherine was glad when they reached their destination, although she was taken aback when Robert said he was going to move into the hotel.

'You only have two beds,' he pointed out shortly, as they stood in the small hallway of Catherine's cottage in Pembroke Square. 'And as you've given one away . . .' He paused, significantly. 'Unless you'd like me to share yours?'

'Oh, Robert . . .'

'I thought not.' He marched angrily up the stairs. 'Then I'll just get my case and leave you two alone.'

'Robert!' Catherine felt terrible now. 'Robert, there is the couch.'

'No, thanks.' He came down again, carrying the overnight bag he had taken up earlier. 'I prefer a proper bed, thank you.' He halted in the hall, and looked half longingly at her. 'I'll see you in the morning, shall I?'

'Of course.' Giving the boy a helpless glance, Catherine moved forward and bestowed a kiss on his cheek. 'I'm sorry.'

'So am I,' he declared shortly, and then, as if not trusting himself to say more, he swung open the front door again and slammed it behind him.

Catherine moved automatically to lock it, sliding the bolt and looping the chain into place. Then she looked down at Thomas and pulled a wry face.

'Well,' she said, 'that's that. Now, are you hungry?'

'Ravenous!' he admitted, a small smile tugging at his mouth, and with a determined shake of her shoulders she led the way into her small kitchen.

With his mouth full of cornflakes, Thomas found time to comment on his surroundings. 'Do you live here all alone?' he asked, gulping from a glass of lemonade she had set beside him. 'I mean—aren't you married?'

'No.' Catherine smiled, perching on a high stool beside the breakfast bar. This seemed to be her night for being asked that question, but somehow she didn't mind his interest. 'Are you?'

Thomas giggled. 'Of course not.' He wiped his mouth on the back of his hand, thought better of it, and hastily smudged it down his trousers before she could stop him. Then he frowned, tipping his head on one side. 'I say—I know you, don't I?'

'Do you?' Catherine made a negative gesture. 'I don't think you do.'

'Yes.' Thomas was definite now. 'You came to my house, didn't you? The last time I was at home.' He paused. 'Did my mother upset you?'

Belatedly, Catherine remembered the sensation she had had of someone observing her from the stairs when she had rushed out of the house on that never-to-be-forgotten occasion.

'You were there?'

'Yes.' Thomas bent his head. 'I'm always running away from school. Mummy was furious. So was my father, but he—sort of understands.'

'I see.' Catherine shivered, half appalled at the responsibility she had taken upon herself. 'Well, as soon as you've finished that, you'd better get upstairs to bed. You've got quite a big day yourself tomorrow.'

'Yes.' Thomas put down his spoon suddenly. 'You

will—come with me, won't you? You won't just—leave me?'

'What do you mean?' Catherine frowned.

'Well—when we get there. You won't just drop me off, will you?'

'I don't suppose I could do that, really,' remarked Catherine, with a sigh. 'Someone is bound to see us, and wonder what you're doing with me.'

'Oh, yes.' Thomas sounded relieved. 'I'm glad. I—I'm sure my father will want to thank you.'

'Are you?' Catherine was less convinced. 'Well, let's not think about that now. Come along, I'll show you where the bathroom is. I expect you want to have a wash.'

'I've got a bloody knee,' he remarked, looking down, and she sensed the pleasure it had given him to use that forbidden word. A smile tugged at the corners of her mouth, as he lifted his head again to meet her gaze mischievously, and she felt a sudden surge of emotion. He was such a charming little boy, and she wondered how anyone could bear to send him away to boarding school so young. Didn't his mother care about him? His conversation was smattered with comments about his father, but she'd noticed how little his mother's name was mentioned. Except when he'd asked her whether she had upset her . . .

Later, lying in her own bed, she wondered what Rafe Glyndower would say when she returned his son in the morning. He wouldn't be pleased, that much was obvious. If the boy made a habit of running away, he was probably heartily sick of the whole business. But if Thomas wasn't happy at school, why didn't they let him stay at home?

She thought she must have slept for a short time, despite the turmoil of her thoughts, but she awakened to the sound of her bedroom door being opened. For a moment she thought it was Robert, come to try and change her mind about their relationship, but then she remembered Robert wasn't sleeping in the house. Another visitor occupied her spare room.

Quickly, she stretched a hand and switched on the lamp beside her bed, her eyes widening in surprise when she saw Thomas shrinking back against the door. He was wearing the nightshirt she had loaned him for sleeping, and his expression revealed his dismay at being discovered.

'What are you doing?' she demanded, sitting up in bed, her hair a tangled curtain of silk about her shoulders. 'Why aren't you in bed?'

Thomas chewed unhappily on his lower lip. 'I was cold,' he mumbled. 'I couldn't get to sleep.'

'So why were you creeping in here?'

'Sometimes—sometimes Daddy lets me sleep with him,' he muttered uncomfortably. 'I—I thought—if you were asleep . . .'

'. . . you'd curl up beside me?' Catherine finished for him.

'Well—yes.'

She shook her head helplessly. He looked so thin and forlorn standing there. How could she send him back to a cold bed?

'All right,' she said, folding back the covers. 'Get in. But I warn you, if you take up too much room I'll send you back to your own bed.'

'Yes, Miss Tempest.'

With a bound he was into the bed beside her, but before she turned out the light, she asked curiously: 'How do you know my name?'

Thomas snuggled down happily beneath the covers. 'Daddy told me. I asked him who you were, and he said your name was Miss Tempest, and that he'd known you since you were as old as I am now.'

CHAPTER FOUR

CATHERINE awakened before seven the next morning to the awful realisation that never once had she considered what the school might do when they discovered Thomas was missing. She had been so concerned in saving him from his father's wrath that she had completely forgotten there were two parties involved.

Unable to rest any longer, she slid out of bed, taking care not to disturb the boy, and pulled on her candlewick dressing gown. As she fastened the buttons, a rather anxious expression clouded eyes which this morning had the opacity of smoked amber, and lifting her long hair from the neckline of the robe, she wondered what on earth she should do. She hadn't the faintest idea which school Thomas was attending, and even if she awakened him to find out, what authority did she have for ringing there and assuring them that he was safe? They might think she was a kidnapper or something awful like that, and how could she explain to strangers the unlikely events of the night before?

There was only one person she could call, she realised, though her stomach churned at the prospect. Rafe Glyndower was the boy's father, his guardian; and the sooner she contacted him the better, before an alarm was raised. She dreaded the possibility that the police might already have been alerted, and she swung on her heel abruptly and made for the door.

But before leaving the room she looked back at the remaining occupant of her bed, and for a moment her eyes softened. He looked so young lying there, arms flung carelessly above his head. So vulnerable. Surely his father would try and understand his behaviour, and not punish him too severely for what he had done. He was only a child—certainly not old enough to be treated as a recalcitrant adolescent.

It was chilly downstairs, and she turned on the radiators and plugged in the electric kettle, before returning to the hall where the telephone waited. What was she going to say? she asked herself, picking up the directory to find the number. How could she begin? How much easier it would have been just to deliver him to the door and thus avoid unnecessary explanations.

It was ironic that she was having to contact the Glyndowers again. What if Lucy Glyndower should answer, as before? She dreaded having to explain the situation to her.

Realising she was doing no good by just sitting there, anticipating the worst, Catherine picked up the receiver and dialled the number before she could change her mind. As the ringing tone confirmed that she had achieved her objective, she caught her lower lip between her teeth. What time was it? Seven? Seven-fifteen? Would anyone be up at that hour? And if the butler answered, should she ask to speak to his employer, or just explain the situation to him?

The receiver was lifted, and her mouth went dry. When Rafe's masculine voice intoned: 'Glyndower!' she almost put her receiver down again, until she had time to steady her nervous response.

'Mr—Mr Glyndower?' she asked huskily, giving herself a moment to recover, and at his impatient confirmation added: 'This—this is Catherine Tempest.'

'Catherine—*Tempest!*' He sounded astounded. Then, as if summoning belief, he exclaimed: 'Miss Tempest—you're an early caller.'

'I know. I'm sorry if I've disturbed you.' Catherine shifted the receiver from one ear to the other. 'But—but I wanted to reach you as—as soon as possible.'

'Did you?' He was clearly perplexed, but not, she thought, distressed. Obviously the school had not informed him yet of his son's disappearance. Possibly they hadn't discovered the runaway. If Thomas had left after tea, he might not be missed before breakfast.

'Yes.' Catherine pleated the skirt of her dressing gown, but before she could go on, he asked:

'Is something wrong, Miss Tempest? There hasn't been an accident at Penwyn, has there?'

'Oh, no. No,' Catherine hastened to reassure him, 'I—there hasn't been an accident at all.'

'I see.' His voice had deepened. 'Then why are you ringing me, Miss Tempest?'

Catherine hesitated only a moment, then she plunged in at the deep end. 'It's about your son, Mr Glyndower. About Thomas. He—he's with me!'

There was absolute silence for about ten seconds, and then Rafe repeated quietly: 'Thomas is with you?' A pause. 'Perhaps you'd better explain, Miss Tempest.'

Catherine expelled a tremulous breath. 'It's a long story. I—we—that is, a friend and I were driving home last evening, when we encountered him about—about three miles from Pendower.'

'I see.' She sensed he was trying to disguise the shock she had given him. 'And—he asked you for a lift?'

'Oh, no.' Catherine was quick to deny this. 'He—he didn't want to come with us at first. Robert tried to per-suade him, but he was adamant about not accepting lifts from strangers.'

'Robert?'

'A friend,' said Catherine, wondering why she should feel so guilty about admitting it. 'But when I discovered who he was, I—I realised you couldn't know he was missing, and as he was planning to spend the night in a shepherd's hut, I offered him a bed here.'

'Here? Where? Penwyn?' There was a clipped edge to Rafe's voice now, but she hardly noticed it.

'No,' she denied. 'Here—at my cottage, in Pendower.'

Another ominous silence ensued, and then he said: 'What did you mean—about a shepherd's hut?'

Catherine sighed. 'He—well, he didn't intend arriv-ing so late, and I think he was afraid you might be furious——.'

'*Might be!*'

'—so he planned to turn up this morning.'

'After spending the night in some hut?'

'Yes.'

'My God!' There was a wealth of feeling behind those words. 'Well, Miss Tempest, I suppose I must thank you for—taking him in, although I have to confess to some impatience with your reasons for doing so. Surely, it would have been much simpler, and much less inconvenient for you, to bring him here.'

'It wasn't an inconvenience,' Catherine protested quickly, and as she did so, she heard the unmistakable sound of the stairs creaking behind her. 'I didn't mind, honestly. I—just didn't want you to worry if the school should get in touch with you.'

'You knew he'd run away, then?'

'Yes.' Catherine sighed, glancing round to see Thomas slowly descending the stairs, a look of worried apprehension marring his thin features. 'He—he's here now.' She ignored Thomas's vigorously shaken head. 'Do you want to have a word with him?'

There was another pause, and then Rafe said evenly: 'If you wouldn't mind.'

'Not at all.'

Catherine got up from the seat beside the telephone and offered the receiver to Thomas, trying not to be influenced by his air of gloomy dejection. The boy came forward reluctantly, his bare toes curling in the pile of the carpet, and she turned quickly away and left him to it.

The kettle was boiling, and the kitchen was filled with steam. Opening a window to clear the air, she shivered in the moist draught from outside, warming her hands around the teapot, trying not to listen to what was going on in the hall. Presently, however, she heard Thomas replace the receiver, and realising she was holding her breath, expelled it in a gulp, turning aside determinedly and lifting beakers down from the shelves.

Thomas appeared in the doorway, incongruous in her pink nightshirt. 'Daddy's coming to fetch me,' he said, offence evident in every line of his thin body. 'Why did you phone him? Why didn't you just take me home, like you promised?'

Catherine sighed, setting down the bottle of milk she had just taken from the fridge. 'You forget,' she said, 'someone's going to notice you're missing at school, aren't they? What would have happened if the school had rung your father before I did? He'd probably have called out the police to find you.'

'Oh!' Clearly, Thomas had not thought of this either. Then he lifted his head. 'But they wouldn't have missed me before Assembly. I've missed breakfast before. They have porridge, and treacle. Ugh!' he grimaced. 'I hate porridge.'

Catherine's tension eased a little. 'Is that why you ran away?' she asked, pouring milk into two beakers.

'No,' Thomas pursed his lips. 'Can I have two spoons of sugar, please?'

Catherine made an indifferent gesture, and added the sugar to his beaker. Then she stirred the tea before pouring it. When she had pushed a cup across the breakfast bar towards him, she said: 'What time is your father coming? I have to go down and open the shop at nine o'clock.'

'You have a shop?' Thomas's eyes lit up. 'What kind of a shop?'

'I sell clothes,' said Catherine flatly. Then, prompting him: 'What time, Thomas? What time is your father coming over?'

'Oh—right away,' declared Thomas airily, shocking her so much she almost choked on her tea.

'Right away?' she echoed. 'But I'm not dressed!'

'That's all right.' Thomas was unconcerned. 'You look fine to me. I like that yellow colour, it's pretty.'

'Well, thank you, but——' Catherine ran frustrated fingers through her hair. 'I've got to get some clothes on. You—er—you drink your tea. I won't be long.'

Upstairs again she sluiced her face thoroughly, cleaned her teeth, and ran a hasty brush over her hair. Her working clothes of dark red cords and an embroidered smock were to hand, so she put them on, grimacing at her appearance as she searched for her boots.

Downstairs, Thomas was perched on the stool he had occupied the night before, apparently unperturbed that his father's arrival was imminent. It was as if, secure in the reiteration of her support, he was no longer afraid to face him, and Catherine wished she could instil the same kind of confidence in herself that she obviously instilled in Thomas.

'You look nice,' he said, as she came in, regarding her with appraising interest. 'You're tall, aren't you? I wish I was as big as you. Then no one could tell me what to do.'

Catherine pulled a wry face, and went to examine the

contents of the fridge. 'It's these boots,' she declared. 'They have a high heel. Now, what do you want for breakfast? I only have eggs, I'm afraid.'

'Do you think I could have a boiled egg, please?' he asked, his eyes sparkling, and she felt a smile lifting her lips.

'You can have two, if you like,' she declared humorously, and saw his genuine excitement at the prospect.

'Why don't you go and put your clothes on, while the eggs are boiling?' she suggested, but Thomas's reactions were not enthusiastic now.

'Can I do it later?' he pleaded. 'I'm awfully hungry, and I don't expect Daddy will get here for ages and ages.'

Catherine's eyes widened at this. 'You said he was coming right away,' she reminded him, and he shrugged his thin shoulders.

'That could mean anything,' he replied, looking so longingly at some grapes on a dish that she broke a sprig off and gave them to him. 'Thank you. And I will get dressed, just as soon as I've finished eating.'

'All right.'

Catherine gave in, realising as she did so that she was probably doing everything wrong. First, she had allowed him to stay with her, when she had known she ought to take him home, and now she was allowing him to eat breakfast in the borrowed nightshirt, when she was sure that at home he was expected to present a tidy appearance.

Still, she consoled herself, with a pang, it was never likely to happen again, and maybe he deserved a little freedom. It wasn't her responsibility to discipline him, and apart from his evident dislike of boarding school, he was extremely well behaved. He seemed a perfectly normal ten-year-old, who needed a family environment, instead of the unnatural isolation of living away from home.

Despite his nonchalance, however, Catherine saw the way he stiffened when the doorbell rang halfway through breakfast. She felt her own nerves tighten as she got up from the table and went to open the door, and she couldn't deny the impulse to glance at her reflection in the mirror hanging in the hall. It was as if she was condemned always to meet Rafe Glyndower defensively, and she swung open the door with a determined air of defiance.

He stood on the path outside, lean and dark and disturbing in a navy fur-lined parka, his hair sparkling with drops of rain tossed from the cherry tree in the garden. It was just light on a grey autumn day, and his face reflected the dourness of the weather.

'Good morning,' he said, making no attempt to enter. 'Is he ready? I've left the engine running.'

Only then did she notice the dark green estate car at the gate, its steady vibration and the open door significant of his desire not to delay longer than was necessary. For some reason this knowledge irritated her beyond reason, and with uncharacteristic complacence she said: 'He's having his breakfast, Mr Glyndower. We didn't expect you quite so promptly. And as he's not yet dressed, I'm afraid you'll have to come in and wait.'

Her eyes challenged his, tawny softness confronting ice-blue steel. She would not be intimidated, she told herself angrily. Just who did he think he was, coming here with that supercilious air? She was glad Thomas still hadn't got his clothes on. It would do Rafe Glyndower good to be thwarted for once.

It was an uneven battle. Her eyes were already wavering as he turned away, but he allowed her the victory. Without saying a word, he went and switched off the Volvo's engine, locking the door, before coming back up the path.

Mutely, Catherine stood aside, and he entered the narrow hallway, loosening his parka as he did so, bringing with him an odour of dampness and tobacco, and the warm male smell of his body. Unlike Robert, he made the hall seem small and claustrophobic, his nearness arousing an uneasy awareness inside her. Although she was a tall girl, he still topped her by a couple of inches, even in her high-heeled boots, and although he was lean, he was muscular. There didn't seem to be anywhere else to look than into his eyes in that small confined space, and the colour was rising up her face when his gaze shifted from hers to some distance beyond her.

Glancing round, she saw Thomas standing in the lighted doorway of the kitchen, his long thin legs outlined through the cotton nightshirt. He was gazing apprehensively at his father, and with a word of apology to Catherine, Rafe strode down the passage towards him.

Catherine hesitated, uncertain as to whether she should be an uneasy interloper to their reunion. No doubt Rafe Glyndower had things to say to his son that were not for her ears, and it was obvious he had no intention of delaying longer than was necessary, but this was her house, after all, and she had played some part in Thomas's flight from authority.

Thomas solved the problem for her, however. 'Did you thank Miss Tempest for letting me sleep in her bed, Daddy?' he asked, raising his voice, which was just a trifle shaky, so that Catherine could hear what he said, even if she had not overheard his father's low remonstrance. 'She—she was jolly nice to me. She let me have two eggs for breakfast.'

It was impossible for Rafe to ignore her after that. With a tight smile he glanced over his shoulder, and after a barely perceptible pause, he said: 'No. No, I didn't thank you, did I, Miss Tempest? I apologise. Naturally, I'm very grateful for what you've done.'

He didn't sound grateful, and Catherine made a mute gesture, going down the passage towards them, smiling at Thomas and saying gently: 'Don't you think you ought to go and get dressed now? It is getting late, and I do have to go to work, you know.'

Thomas hesitated. Then he nodded, brushing past her with an appealing grimace, padding up the stairs with an evident lack of enthusiasm.

After he was gone, it was worse, if anything. Rafe Glyndower stood silently in the passage outside the kitchen door, and she had to brush past him to reach the remains of her own breakfast. She had been having toast and coffee, and now she picked up the percolator and said: 'Can I offer you some, Mr Glyndower?'

He looked at her steadily for a long moment, and then, as if relaxing some control he had over himself, he nodded, shrugging out of his parka and draping it carelessly over the end of the banister. His open-necked shirt and close-fitting pants were infinitely less formal. Catherine guessed they had been pulled on in a hurry, and paused to wonder whether she had got him out of bed after all.

'This is your cottage, Miss Tempest?' he asked, as she poured coffee into a cup. 'When you said you lived in Pendower, I assumed you lived—with your parents.'

'My father is dead.' Catherine pushed the cup towards him across the bar where Thomas had been eating his breakfast, and indicated the cream and sugar. 'My mother remarried. She still lives in London.'

'I see.' He helped himself to two spoons of sugar, but no cream. 'And you work in Pendower?'

'I run a boutique,' she admitted reluctantly, unwilling to admit her commercial success to him. 'I like designing clothes. It's always interested me.'

Rafe nodded, making no attempt to drink his coffee. She was irritated to discover that it hurt her that it should be so. They were exchanging the same kind of small-talk one could hear at any social gathering, between people who had never met before, and were never likely to meet again. Surely there were more important topics to discuss than this. Like why Thomas kept running away from school, for example.

Licking her lips, she exclaimed: 'You don't have to pull your punches, you know. I know you're really furious because I kept him here. But I couldn't let him stay out all night, and he'd never have come with us if I hadn't agreed to wait until the morning before contacting you!'

If she had expected her outburst to provoke some equally emotional retort, she was mistaken. Rafe merely shrugged his shoulders and picking up his cup, he said quietly: 'I'm sorry if I've given you that impression. I was –surprised, that was all. I shouldn't have thought you and your—er—friend would want company.'

Catherine gasped, staring at him with indignant eyes. 'You think—you think—Robert and I——'

'It's nothing to do with me, is it?' Rafe retorted, turning back into the hall, his cup raised to his lips, and Catherine felt like dashing its contents all over his cold, expressionless face.

'Robert Brooke is my accountant,' she declared vehemently, not quite knowing why she felt this need to justify herself to him. 'And we are not—*friends*—in the way you understand the word!'

Rafe put down his cup then with carefully controlled movements. She noticed with some amazement that his hands were not quite steady as they guided the cup on to the bar, and she realised she had been wrong in imagining he was unmoved by what had happened. Thomas's appearance must have shocked him more than she thought, and her own attitude was not helping matters.

'I'm sorry,' he said, tugging impatient fingers through his hair. 'Your—personal affairs are not my concern, and I had no right to insinuate that they were. You'll have to forgive me, I'm not usually so ill-mannered.'

'Oh, honestly . . .' Catherine put out a hand towards him automatically, withdrawing it swiftly when her fingers encountered the taut muscle of his arm, hard beneath the dark grey silk of his shirt. She had no right to touch him, to offer him sympathy. He was just someone she had known for a brief period in her life, someone who had grown away from her, a virtual stranger after all these years. The fact that circumstances were contriving to throw them together again was neither of their faults, and no matter how disturbing she found him, she must never forget who he was, or that he was married . . .

Taking a backward step, she extended her hand politely, forcing a smile and saying awkwardly: 'Can't we just be friends, Mr Glyndower, instead of antagonists?'

'Antagonists?' He took her hand in his, and she felt a moment's anxiety at the sensation those strong fingers inspired inside her. He must never suspect he could arouse her this way, and she longed to pull her hand away from him and put the width of the room between them. 'We are not antagonists, Catherine,' he declared flatly. 'Perhaps it would be better for both of us if we were.'

'What do you mean?'

The words were torn from her, but he released her hand then and turned away, saying casually: 'Are these beams the original timbers? I seem to remember these cottages being renovated some years ago. Did you know they were once part of the Penwyth estate?'

'No. That is——' Catherine sought for coherence, '—the beams were restored, but I didn't know the cottages were once yours.'

'Not mine,' Rafe amended dryly. 'My grandfather's, perhaps.' He gained her silent permission and strolled into the low-ceilinged living room. 'And even that might be wishful thinking. They were probably struggling for survival even in those days, and selling property was always a convenient way of raising money.'

Catherine followed him into the room, hovering near the door as he walked to the lead-paned windows, to stare out broodingly on the garden at the front of the cottage.

'How long have you been living in Pendower?' he asked, with his back to her, and she moved her shoulders in an offhand gesture he could not see, before replying: 'About nine months.'

'Nine months?' He repeated her words as he turned to face her. 'So—what made you come back to Wales? Surely there are more interesting jobs available in London than in this depressed area.'

Catherine shrugged. 'I—just like it here,' she confessed. 'I always liked coming to the valley.'

'Yes, you did, didn't you?' His expression was not cold now, and contrarily, she wished it was. He was too approachable in this mood. 'Little Catherine! Who thought she could ride as well as any boy!'

Catherine said nothing. What could she say? It was too disturbing knowing his memory of those days was as good as hers.

'Tell me,' he went on, 'do you still ride? Or don't you find time now that you obviously have other commitments?'

Catherine avoided his eyes, and pretended an interest in a fallen petal from a bowl of chrysanthemums resting on the bookshelves. 'Uncle Mervyn doesn't keep any horses I could ride these days,' she averred lightly. 'Besides, as you say, I don't get much time . . .'

'I could lend you a mount,' Rafe offered quietly. 'So far I've managed to hang on to a couple of horses, and Tom's mare needs exercise.'

Catherine licked her suddenly dry lips. 'Doesn't—doesn't your wife ride, Mr Glyndower?'

There was another of those little, awkward silences. Then he said flatly: 'Is that meant as a reminder, Miss Tempest? The offer was quite an innocent one, I do assure you.'

Catherine was hot with embarrassment. 'I merely meant—that is—doesn't Thomas ride his own horse?'

'When he's at home.' Rafe inclined his head. 'But only with supervision. He's not got enough experience to venture beyond the paddock. And in any case, those occasions are infrequent, as you know.'

Catherine nodded, and then, taking all her small store of confidence into her hands, she ventured: 'It would be easier if—if Thomas—well, if he lived at home, wouldn't it?'

Rafe crossed the room slowly towards her. 'Are you offering me your opinion—or your advice, Miss Tempest?' he enquired dryly, halting before her. 'Whatever, let me offer you a piece of advice—don't get involved.'

'With—with what, Mr Glyndower?'

'With my son, with his problems—or with me.'

Catherine refused to be daunted. 'He's only a child,' she protested. 'Why can't he go to school here in Pendower? Why does it have to be somewhere he obviously hates?'

'A good question.' His hands descended on her shoulders suddenly, and her heart leapt into her throat, almost suffocating her. But all he did was move her firmly aside so that he could walk into the hall, though it took her several minutes to recover from that unexpected contact.

'Tom!' he called, and with a shivery feeling of anti-climax she followed him into the hall just as Thomas came dejectedly down the stairs. 'Are you ready?'

Thomas nodded reluctantly, then he turned to Catherine, saying eagerly: 'Can I come to your shop some time? I—I'd like to see it.'

Catherine looked at Rafe, meeting his guarded gaze with appealing eyes. 'I—well, I suppose so, Thomas,' she agreed, ignoring the ominous tightening of his father's expression. 'Next—next time you're on holiday, give me a ring, and we'll arrange something.'

'Miss Tempest is very kind, but I think she's only hum-ouring you, Tom,' Rafe said then, successfully extinguishing the spark of excitement that had kindled in the boy's eyes. 'Boutiques are not suitable places for small boys. You'd just be in the way, and you wouldn't like that.'

Catherine's lips sagged. What was that supposed to mean? That he would not approve of his son associating with her? She couldn't believe he really thought she would have no time for the boy, not after what she had said.

'Do you have a coat?' Rafe continued, thrusting his arms into the sleeves of his own parka, and when Thomas offered a mute denial, he put a hand on his blazer-clad shoulder and urged him down the passage towards the front door.

Then, he looked at Catherine again, and she steeled herself to face his cold disapproval. However, his expression revealed only polite gratitude now, and he offered her his hand in farewell.

'Thank you again,' he said formally, and at his words Thomas turned to echo his father's sentiments.

'I will see you again, won't I?' he asked, and the appeal in his voice was irresistible.

'Of course,' she said, ignoring Rafe's outstretched hand to go down on her haunches beside the boy. 'I promise!' *And let your father make what he likes of that*, she added silently.

She didn't wait to see the Volvo drive away, As soon as they were outside the door, she closed it behind them, leaning back against the panels with a fast-beating heart. She had been rude and ungracious, she realised, but she didn't care. Was he completely without feeling when it came to the boy? Didn't he care that the idea of being sent back to that school again was tearing Thomas to pieces? Had he forgotten his own childhood so soon?

Eventually, of course, she had to move. A quick glance at the broad masculine watch on her wrist confirmed her suspicions that it was almost nine o'clock, and her assistant, Mary, would be waiting at the shop.

Ignoring the untidy mess of dishes on the breakfast bar, she collected her coat and let herself out of the cottage. It was a dull misty morning, and she had never felt less like going to work. But she had the sense to realise that work was the one thing in which she could lose herself. Rafe Glyndower was right, after all. It was not her concern. And the sooner she put all the Glyndowers out of her mind, the better.

CHAPTER FIVE

CATHERINE was in the stockroom when Mary Grant came to tell her there was a visitor in her office.

'It's a man,' the other girl said, rolling her eyes expressively. 'Some man! Where did you meet him?'

Catherine was in the process of stocktaking, and she was in no mood for her assistant's humour. Taking the pencil from behind her ear, she marked down a figure on the clipboard she carried, and gave Mary an impatient glance.

'Who is it?' she demanded tersely. 'Not Colin Barstow, I hope. I told you the last time he came here——'

'It's not *him*!' Mary made a sound of impatience. 'I'd know Colin Barstow if I saw him again, wouldn't I? And it's not your tame accountant either. He doesn't even look like a salesman. I don't think I've seen him before. I'm sure I wouldn't have forgotten if I had.'

Catherine stiffened. 'Well, what does he want? Surely you asked him that. Mary, I've told you——'

'He just asked to speak to you, that's all.'

'And you didn't get his name?'

Mary flushed. 'No.'

'Oh, Mary . . .'

Catherine put down her clipboard, and gave her reflection a hasty appraisal in the cracked mirror that occupied a corner of the stockroom. She had a crazy idea who it might be, and the prospect of meeting Rafe Glyndower again filled her with unhealthy excitement. It was frightening how that man affected her.

'You look fine,' exclaimed Mary generously, hoping to divert her employer's disapproval, and Catherine cast her a look of irritation.

'All right, Mary,' she said. 'I'm not angry with you. Look, you go on checking the sizes of these jeans while I find out—what he wants.'

Mary took over the task willingly, and Catherine ran up the few steps between the lower back room and the boutique itself. The disco music which was an accompaniment to sales technique these days was turned up to deafening proportions, and guessing this was another of Mary's doings, Catherine went to adjust the tuner. As she did so, her eyes were drawn, through the open doorway, to the dark green estate car parked at the kerb.

Immediately her mouth went dry. So she had been right. Mary's description, his lack of identity, the car: it all fitted, and her palms felt as if they were glued together. Yet why was he here? At the boutique? He had left her in little doubt as to his opinion of such places, the last time they had spoken together. How long ago was that now? One week? Two? The days had run together since that disastrous weekend, and Catherine had tried not to think about the Glyndowers or their problems. Her mind leapt ahead. Had something happened to Thomas? Was that why his father was here? Had the boy run away again? Was he missing? Did they think he might have come to her? Surely, by now, they must have reached a compromise.

Smoothing down her denim skirt, she turned towards her office, the tiny cubicle at the back of the store where she did most of her paperwork. It was hardly big enough to hold her, and the desk it contained, and she dreaded the prospect of a confrontation with Rafe Glyndower there.

He was seated on the edge of her desk when she paused in the doorway, indolently flicking over the pile of stock sheets she had been checking earlier. The half-finished cup of coffee Mary had made her for her break over an hour ago stood in chilly isolation on the filing cabinet, and for a moment she felt the interloper, the intruder into his privacy.

'Yes?' she said, the word clipped and nervous, a revealing indication of her own uncertainty, and Rafe slid politely to the floor, facing her with guarded approval.

He was more formally dressed than she had seen him before. His medium-grey suit fitted his shoulders immaculately, the cut of the material an indication of its quality, and the silk tie that matched it was only a couple of shades darker than his shirt. He didn't wear an overcoat, and he pushed his hands carelessly into the waistline pockets of his trousers.

Even though she had expected to find him there, Catherine was still shocked by his appearance. Every time she saw him, she expected to find she had lost that disturbing awareness of his presence, and every time she was thwarted by the subtle attraction he exerted over her.

'Good morning,' he said, his voice no warmer than hers. 'Your assistant said I might wait in here. I'm sorry, by the way. I didn't realise you were such an astute business-woman when I spoke to you so patronisingly about employment in this area. Your—er—Miss Grant enlightened me.'

'Oh, yes?' Catherine tilted her head.

'Yes.' He shrugged. 'I should have realised, when you said you had an accountant. My apologies.'

Catherine took a deep breath, becoming aware as she did so that her breasts swelled against the thin denim of her shirt, revealing an arousal she would rather have concealed. 'What can I do for you, Mr Glyndower?' she enquired, with consequent frustration. 'I—er—I am rather busy.'

'Yes.' The word was absent, but she was aware that no small item of her appearance missed his keen appraisal. 'I expect you are.' It sounded like an accusation. 'As a matter of fact, I came to speak to you about Tom . . .'

'Thomas?' Anxiety entered her expression. 'Is something wrong? He hasn't run——'

'No, no, nothing like that.' Rafe removed his hands from his trousers pockets and adjusted the pocket flaps on his jacket. 'On the contrary, he hasn't returned to boarding school. I spoke to his headmaster, and for the present he's attending the junior school here in Pendower.'

'Oh!' Catherine could not hide the relief this information gave her, or the sense of satisfaction she felt that Rafe Glyndower was not the unfeeling machine she had suspected him of being. 'That's marvellous news!'

'I thought you'd like to know,' he remarked flatly. 'And once again, I must apologise for Tom's unnecessary intrusion into your private affairs. He told me how he apparently turned your—friend—out of his bed, and I feel that I ought to offer to pay for his night's accommodation at the hotel.'

Catherine's cheeks flamed. 'There's no need, I can assure you.'

'I disagree.' His voice had hardened. 'It's become obvious to me that had my son not entangled you in his problems, Mr—er—Brooke? Is that right? Yes, Mr Brooke would have spent the night at your cottage.'

Catherine heaved a trembling breath. 'That may be so,' she admitted, annoyed at the tremor in her voice, 'but I do have *two* bedrooms, Mr Glyndower, and—and you're jumping to conclusions again!'

'The right ones, in this instance,' he retorted grimly. 'Tom told me how—disappointed Mr Brooke was at being turned away. But you have no need to defend yourself to me. I was merely trying to make amends for what must have been a most *frustrating* experience.'

The sound of her fingers striking his cheek seemed to echo in the tiny office, resounding off the walls with ominous reverberation. Catherine had never slapped anyone's face before, and she was surprised to find her fingers stinging almost as much as Rafe's face must have done.

Of course, the minute the blow had been struck she regretted it, but it was too late then. The damage had been done, and the slender red weals were appearing like magic upon his lean tanned cheek. The horror of her actions followed quickly on remorse, however. This was her uncle's landlord she had assaulted, the man who held her family's future in his grasp. Dear God, why had she allowed his words to provoke her, when it meant little to her what he thought of her?

'I'm sorry,' she burst out impulsively, wishing the floor would simply open up and swallow her. 'I—I'm sorry.'

'Are you?' he queried dryly, lifting his hand and running exploring fingers over his burning skin. 'Why? Have you changed your mind about what I said?'

'*No!*' He was being deliberately cruel now, and her breast heaved with the turmoil of her emotions. 'I—well, you can think what you like of me. I don't care.' She glanced behind her half nervously, and was reassured to find the shop was still empty. 'I—I don't think we have anything more to say to one another.'

'Don't you?'

Still he made no move to go, and the seconds stretched into minutes as he continued to regard her with a mixture of admiration and contempt. If Mary appeared now, she would have food for gossip for a month, Catherine worried anxiously, wishing desperately that she had considered before behaving so recklessly.

At last, when her nerves were taut and her blood was singing in her ears, Rafe said: 'Actually, I do have something else to ask you.'

'Yes?' She was abrupt, nervous fingers seeking a strand of honey-brown silk, straying from the coil at her nape. 'If—if it's about my uncle, then I can tell you that he's still as morose as ever.'

'It's not about your uncle,' he declared, his hand falling to his side, exposing the marks which were fortunately fading a little. 'It's to do with you.'

Catherine stiffened, her nails curling painfully into her palms. 'If it's about my invitation to Thomas, you needn't worry. I shan't try to get in touch with him——'

'Damn you, let me finish!' he snapped, aroused at last. 'It's nothing to do with Thomas, or your uncle—or my *wife*, or anyone else in the valley.' He paused, recovering his composure. 'I wondered if you would do me the favour of riding the mare I told you about. She's an admirable creature, but she needs a firm hand, and I think you'd manage her easily. I could stable her with your uncle for the winter. I'd provide the fodder, of course, if you could find the time . . .'

Catherine's lips parted in astonishment. '*Me?* Ride your mare?' And although her heart leapt at the chance of being able to ride again, she stared at him in disbelief. 'Why on earth would you want me to ride your mare?'

Rafe looked down at the toes of his suede boots for a moment, then he looked back at her. 'I've told you—she's a spirited animal. She needs exercise. I'd like you to take on that responsibility.'

Catherine moved restlessly. 'But now that Thomas is home——'

'He's too young. I explained the situation.'

Catherine shook her head helplessly. 'I—I don't know that I'll have the time . . .'

'Make time,' he suggested crisply. 'To—please me.'

'To placate you, you mean,' she retorted, and he moved his shoulders indifferently.

'If it pleases you to believe I need placating,' he essayed smoothly. 'The reasons are unimportant. I want you to do it.'

'*Why?*'

The word was wrung from her, but Rafe was already moving towards her, forcing her to step aside from the doorway. 'I'll arrange to have the mare sent down to Penwyn,' he said, and as she shrank back against the wall to allow him passage, he added: 'Don't look so worried. I deserved the rebuke. For the second time I've been guilty of verbal interference in your affairs. I should apologise, not you.'

Catherine gazed up at him, trying to distinguish his real feelings behind the guarded mask of his face. The dark blue eyes, which a moment before had flashed fire, were now as bland as ever. He had himself in control again, and she wondered why it was so necessary for him to exercise such restraint.

Her heart lurched at the possibility that occurred to her. Did he find her attractive? Was that why he maintained such formality in her presence? It was a tantalising thought; tantalising because, like that son of Zeus who was so tormented, Rafe Glyndower was far out of her reach.

The impulse to find out surged within her, only to be subdued by common sense. It would be easy to flirt with him, to use the weight of her attraction against him, but the memory of Thomas's trusting little face deterred her. She had never allowed herself to become entangled with a married man; she had always despised girls who ignored the vows of matrimony and treated all men the same. She was not a conceited girl, but she had been aware of her attraction for the opposite sex for some years now, and she had little doubt that given enough encouragement, most men felt compelled to prove their masculinity. Her silky mass of honey-coloured hair had a sensual appeal all its own, and her air of independence invariably instilled them with a desire to tame her, but so far her forays into the emotional field had been few and far between. Rafe Glyndower was different. Hadn't it always been so? And she ought to be grateful he respected her sufficiently not to take advantage of his position.

Unaware, a little of her feelings had showed themselves in her eyes, however, and her pulses raced when, almost unwillingly, his hand lifted to stroke hard fingers along her jawline. Her chin lifted to escape that tenuous caress, but his touch remained, burning her skin.

'Do you forgive me?' he demanded, and she was shocked to hear the emotion in his voice after the silent reassurance she had just given herself.

'Please . . .' she whispered, hardly aware of what she was saying, and almost savagely, his hand was withdrawn.

'Yes,' he grated. 'Thank you for your time!' And without a backward glance he strode out of the shop.

Limply, Catherine sought the sanctuary of her desk, and she had barely had time to compose herself before Mary Grant put her head round the door. Her immediate appearance prompted the anxiety of wondering exactly where she had been hiding herself while Rafe was here, an anxiety which was not allayed by her words.

'Has he gone?' she asked, excitement bringing a husky squeak to her voice, and Catherine guessed she knew full well he had. 'Wasn't he gorgeous? How did you get to know him?' She paused, to give her next words full effect. 'I—er—I didn't realise your uncle's family was on such friendly terms with Lord Penwyth!'

Somehow Catherine managed to stifle the gulp of astonishment that escaped her, but it was not so easy to find words to hide her dismay. 'You—must know that was not—*Lord* Penwyth,' she ventured, as the other girl eased herself into the office with a conspiratorial tapping of her forefinger against her nose, and Mary pulled a wry face.

'As good as. It was Rafe Glyndower, wasn't it? His son. And from what I hear, he makes all the decisions at Penwyth now. The old bloke's virtually senile, isn't he, since that stroke he had a couple of years ago.'

'Where did you get all this information?' exclaimed Catherine, appalled. 'And how did you—know who it was?'

Mary shrugged. 'I told you. I didn't think I'd seen him before, but there was something familiar about him. Then I remembered. He opened the chapel fête, two Christmases ago. I never forget a face, not a face like his anyway.' She hesitated. 'Why did he want to see you? Was is something to do with your uncle?'

In ordinary circumstances, Catherine knew, Mary would never have had the audacity to ask such a question, but they were both aware of the subtleties of this situation. For some reason, Mary considered she was free to say what she liked, and Catherine would have given a lot to know exactly what she was thinking.

However, she was not about to satisfy her curiosity. If the girl thought she knew something, she could come right out and say it. Catherine was not going to make things easy for her.

'It was a—business matter,' she stated now, making a pretence of studying the stock lists on her desk. 'Did you finish checking those jeans?'

When no reply was immediately forthcoming, Catherine was forced to lift her head, her lips tightening at Mary's knowing expression. The girl was watching her closely, and irritation took the place of apprehension.

'Well?' she prompted, controlling her colour with great difficulty. 'Did you?'

'Did I what, Miss Tempest?'

'Did you finish checking those jeans, as I asked you to do?'

'Oh—oh, yes.' Mary nodded absently. Then she came forward to lean against her employer's desk, saying astonishingly: 'You don't have to worry, you know, miss. I won't tell anyone.'

Catherine pushed back her chair then and got to her feet with trembling indignation. 'You won't tell anyone *what*, Mary? If you've got something to say, then say it, I've got nothing to hide.'

Mary hesitated, torn between the obvious desire to state her suspicions, and the possible outcome of admitting that she had been eavesdropping.

'A—about you and Mr Glyndower, miss,' she conceded at last, the words coming out with a rush. 'I mean—well, he's married, isn't he, and I don't suppose his wife knew he was here visiting you.'

The pencil Catherine had been holding snapped between her fingers, and she thrust it impatiently aside. Then, choosing her words carefully, she said: 'You surprise me, Mary, you really do. I didn't realise you were so small-minded. Is it so inconceivable that Mr Glyndower and I should have a business relationship? He is my uncle's landlord, you know, and he has every right to stable horses at Penwyn, if he so desires.'

'Stable horses . . .' Mary was at sea, and Catherine took advantage of her opportunity, realising with fervent relief that whatever else she had learned, Mary could not have heard the slap she had administered. If she had, she would have said so, used that as her argument right away. But it was terrifying to realise how easily a relationship could be misconstrued.

'Yes, stable horses,' Catherine continued now. 'One horse, at least. Mr Glyndower has asked me if I'll exercise his son's mare for him. The animal needs exercise, and the boy, Thomas, is not yet old enough to handle her himself.'

She had some misgivings about admitting this, but after all, she was bound to be seen about the valley sooner or later. Surely, if she volunteered the information, without giving anyone the opportunity to find out for themselves, it would allay suspicion, not arouse it.

Mary was looking a little sulky now, as if sorry at being deprived of a secret. But she had one last thing to add.

'Well, if I was his wife, I wouldn't like it. Him coming here, asking you to do him favours—it's not natural, is it? I mean, why can't he exercise his own horse, or sell it, if the boy's not old enough?'

Catherine schooled her features. 'That isn't really our business, is it, Mary?' she retorted tautly. 'Now, if you don't mind, we'll get on with our work.'

Her aunt rang that evening, almost as soon as she got home from the boutique.

'Do you know about this horse of Glyndower's that Owen's having to make room for?' she asked without preamble, and Catherine expelled her breath on an uneasy sigh.

'Oh, Aunt Margaret!' she exclaimed. 'I was going to come out to the farm and see you about that this evening.'

'Well, I shouldn't,' remarked her aunt dryly. 'Tempers are too frayed at the moment, as it is, and I think you might have thought twice before burdening us with more work.'

'But I haven't!' Catherine sank down wearily on to the bench beside the phone. 'Aunt Margaret, I'm going to look after the horse myself. And, if you've seen Glyndower, you must know he's going to provide its feed.'

'But whatever possessed you to take on such a responsibility?' her aunt exclaimed impatiently. 'You know how your uncle feels about the Glyndowers. This is like—like rubbing salt into old wounds!'

Catherine pushed back her hair with unsteady fingers. Put like that, it did sound thoughtless. 'I'm sorry,' she said. She always seemed to be apologising these days. 'I'm sorry, I didn't think.'

'No.' Her aunt sounded as if she agreed with her. 'Well, I hope you know what you're doing.'

'Aunt Margaret, you know the stables at Penwyn are never used. The roof leaks, I know that, but it's only in one place, and I'm sure I can find a stall that's dry enough and warm enough for one animal.'

'Maybe so. But who's going to muck it out?'

'I will,' declared Catherine firmly, wishing she had had more time to prepare for this. But Rafe Glyndower had not given her any choice, and in any case, Aunt Margaret knew he was entitled to stable his horses anywhere on the estate.

'Well . . .' her aunt brought the call to a close, 'you've done it now. I just hope you won't regret it.'

'So do I,' murmured Catherine fervently, as she replaced the receiver.

Afterwards, it was incredibly difficult to concentrate her attention on anything else. The reasons why Rafe should have involved her in his affairs didn't make sense, and it would have been just as easy for him to stable the mare with the local riding school, and let them take charge of it. Aside from this, there were other people, friends of the Glyndowers, with daughters only too eager to ride anything on four legs, without asking the niece of one of his tenants, a girl who had already interfered in matters which should not have concerned her.

Which reminded her of Thomas, and what Rafe had told her about him, bringing with it a reassuring feeling of gratification that perhaps she had played some small part in persuading his father to change his mind. She wondered how he was settling down in his new school. Was he happy now? He was living at home, of course, which was bound to make a difference, and at weekends he would have the company of his parents. She guessed his mother might resent this at first, creating, as it did, the need for someone to take care of him on those occasions when she and her husband wanted to go out, but no doubt she would employ a nanny, or someone in a like capacity, to take the less appealing aspects of a small boy's upbringing off her shoulders.

Catherine sighed, emptying the contents of a tin of spaghetti bolognaise into a saucepan. She couldn't be bothered to prepare anything more interesting this evening, and as she watched the coils of orange pasta bubble over the heat, she reflected that if Thomas was her child, she wouldn't need a nanny to take care of him. She liked children, and he was an adorable little boy. Her own childhood had been devoid of the friendship of brothers and sisters, and she guessed part of Thomas's problem was the fact that he was an only child.

She turned abruptly away from the hotplate. It was nothing to do with her. She must stop involving herself in other people's problems, particularly those of the Glyndowers. She was quite sure that if Lucy Glyndower had wanted another baby, she would have had one. Perhaps she had been advised not to have any more children after Thomas was born. She was very small. Her hips were probably very narrow. Maybe she wasn't built for childbearing. Or maybe she just didn't like the inconvenience . . .

Inconvenience! Catherine ran an exploring hand over her own flat stomach. She would not have found it inconvenient to have Rafe's child. To imagine his seed growing inside her brought a wave of heat rushing over her body. It was useless to deny it. Once, when she was a child of eleven, he had kissed her, and she had never forgotten that. He had been sixteen at the time, and he had pushed her, more roughly than usual, down the ladder from the hayloft, where they had been having their lunch with Owen. She had slipped down several steps and fallen painfully on the barn floor. Owen had only laughed, and gone charging off, with the callous insensitivity of a nine-year-old, but Rafe had picked her up and apologised, and then, on impulse it seemed, bestowed a light, restoring kiss on her parted lips. Afterwards, he had never mentioned it again, but she had never forgotten . . .

The smell of something burning brought her out of her reverie. Her hasty rescue of the spaghetti did not remove its acrid aroma, and she grimaced at the browned mess in the bottom of the pan. It was ruined, and she felt in no mood to open another tin.

The ringing of the telephone was a welcome interruption, but as she went to answer it she paused to wonder who her caller might be. She hoped it wasn't her uncle, or Owen, phoning to make their objections known. She didn't think she could stand any more opposition today.

When she picked up the receiver, however, it was Robert's amiable tones that greeted her, and her own response was that much warmer because of the depressing slant of her thoughts.

'I didn't know I was such a popular person around Pendower,' he remarked, in answer to her obvious pleasure at hearing from him. 'The last time I was there, I recall, I was made to feel very much the outsider.'

'Oh, Robert! Don't be silly.' Catherine was prepared to overlook the friction which had characterised their last weekend together. 'You know you're always a welcome caller.'

'Do I?' Robert sounded less convinced. 'However, in this instance, you may revise your opinion. When are you planning on coming up to town?'

'To town?' Catherine frowned. 'Why? Is something wrong? I heard from Sarah the other day, and she seems to be coping pretty well.'

'Oh, she is.' Robert was enthusiastic. 'You couldn't have found yourself a better manager. Unfortunately, it's nothing to do with Sarah's management.'

'Unfortunately?'

'Yes. Managers can be replaced, but leases can't. At least, not always.'

'Leases?' Catherine hesitated. 'You don't mean that old chestnut's reared its head again?'

'I'm afraid so.' Robert was apologetic. 'Don't you read a newspaper in that backwoods town? Old Haughton died last week. I've been warned by his solicitors that the new executors of the estate may not be prepared to renew the lease when it comes due at the end of the year.'

'Oh, *no*!' Catherine couldn't believe it. After the day she had had, the last thing she needed was to hear that her Hammersmith boutique was in danger of being closed. She shook her head disbelievingly. 'Robert, what am I going to do?'

'That's what I'm here for,' he declared encouragingly. 'As a matter of fact, we do have an alternative.'

Catherine hunched her shoulders. 'What alternative?' she asked dully, a headache beginning to make itself felt behind her temples. 'Robert, why didn't you ring me this morning? Don't you know it's not good to give people bad news in the evening?'

Robert snorted. 'Wait until you hear *all* I have to say before flexing your muscle! The alternative shouldn't be overlooked. It's a double-fronted unit in Chelsea. Two floors, with a flat above, and plenty of room for storage.'

Catherine gasped. 'Robert! Are you out of your mind? Property in Chelsea costs the earth, and you know it. The shop we have now is only viable because the rent was fixed some time ago. I couldn't afford to open a store in Chelsea, particularly not that size!'

'You could if you closed down the Pendower shop,' argued Robert smoothly. 'Concentrate all your energies on one boutique. Increase the amount of garments you design yourself. Employ your own seamstresses, instead of contracting the work. You could do it—you have the ability.'

Catherine sank down weakly on to the bench seat. 'You can't be serious! Robert, what you're suggesting is—is——'

'Ambitious? All right, I admit it. So what? It was ambitious to open a boutique in the first place, and even more ambitious to start again in a place like Pendower.'

'But the Pendower store is making money,' she protested. 'Young people buy my clothes. It doesn't seem to matter that money is in short supply. Girls still spend every penny they can spare on clothes.'

'I know that.' Robert sounded impatient. 'But remember, one of the reasons they come to you is because your clothes are just that little bit different. Teenagers always go for the unusual. Those mock-suede skirts you designed have been tremendously successful, and Sarah's put an order in for another dozen. And those boots, with the leather fringes——'

'You're not suggesting I open my own shoemakers, are you, Robert?' she demanded dryly, and then went on, without waiting for his reply; 'I don't think I want that kind of business. Honestly! I mean, I'm sorry about this trouble over the lease, but I can't see me ever opening another shop in London.'

'Why not?' Robert sounded angry now, and she had to admit he had some justification. 'What about Sarah? Don't you care about her? If the Hammersmith shop closes, she'll be out of a job. And why? Because you have some sentimental urge to indulge yourself in nostalgia. Really, Catherine! I don't know what's the matter with you. Since going to live in Pendower, you seem to have lost touch with reality!'

Catherine sighed. The words 'I'm sorry' trembled on her lips, but were not spoken. After all, she was only one of Robert's clients. Just because he thought himself emotionally involved was no reason for her to feel guilty, when the decision was all hers. She was sorry about Sarah Fairfax, of course. She was a good worker, and a loyal employee. But she could easily get another job, and Catherine would see she didn't suffer financially. And besides, it wasn't altogether definite that the lease would not be renewed.

'So you won't be coming up to town to look at the property?' Robert said now, his voice tight with resentment, and Catherine agreed. 'When will you be coming to London, then?' he added, taking another line. 'Your mother phoned me the other day and asked whether I'd heard from you lately. I think she'd like to see you, too.'

Catherine moved the receiver into her other hand, flexing her fingers in mild impatience. 'I'll let you know,' she said, and as she said the words, she realised that in one thing at least, he was right. She was losing touch with her life in London, and that could be a mistake.

CHAPTER SIX

Rafe walked into his wife's bedroom, as she was changing for dinner. Their apartments were in the west wing, well away from the other occupants of the house—a situation Lucy had arranged, when Thomas was a baby in the charge of a nurse, and inclined to cry occasionally during the night. She had never had any time for him when he was a baby, disliking his baby smell, and avoiding his moist, clutching fingers, and she had not changed much since he had grown older. She was prepared to suffer his presence when he was home from school, but Rafe knew she could hardly wait for him to leave again, and she never involved herself in any of the difficulties he experienced. He was a necessary encumbrance, the price she had had to pay to become the next Lady Penwyth, but aside from that, she had no affection for the boy. He set her nerves on edge, and Thomas, aware of her censure, was more than usually clumsy in his mother's company. In consequence, she was always screaming at him, a circumstance which terrified him so much that he invariably ended the scene in tears. It was the main reason that Rafe had agreed to Lucy's suggestion that Thomas be sent away to school. He had convinced himself that nothing could be worse for the boy than her hysteria, but in this, it appeared, he had been wrong.

Now, she looked round from her seat at the dressing table and regarded him without pleasure. She was almost ready, just putting the finishing touches to her make-up, the dress she was to wear that evening laid out in readiness on the bed.

'Must you barge in here without knocking?' she exclaimed, testily, turning back to her reflection with thinning lips, and Rafe moved his shoulders in an indifferent gesture.

'You are my wife, Lucy,' he reminded her, strolling

across to the dressing table and regarding her through the mirror. 'And I do have certain—rights, you know.'

Lucy's eyes widened. 'You don't intend to exercise them now, I hope,' she declared distastefully, and Rafe's mouth assumed a mocking curve.

'No, thank you,' he replied, deliberately cutting. 'As I haven't exercised that right for the past two years, I doubt the sight of you—even in that flimsy underwear—could cause me any discomfort.'

'You're coarse, Rafe!' she asserted jealously, getting to her feet and reaching for her gown. 'Just because I haven't the appetites of one of your back street harlots, it does not give you the right to insult me. I haven't denied you my bed. You're welcome to join me any time you wish. But I know I can't satisfy you, and I see no reason why I should have to curb your lust! You know I don't enjoy sex. I never have. But I'm prepared to——'

'Oh, shut up, Lucy, will you?' Rafe had heard this argument a dozen times before. 'I didn't come here to argue with you. Not about sex, at any rate. I just wanted to say that I wish you'd consulted me before arranging this dinner party.'

'Like you consulted me before taking Thomas away from St Matthew's, I suppose?'

Rafe sighed. 'That's different, Lucy, and you know it.'

'How is it different? You know how I feel about having Thomas at home all the time. He's too old—and he's a nuisance. And because he was disobedient enough to run away half a dozen times, you're *punishing* him by letting him have his own way!'

'This is his home,' Rafe remarked dryly. Then, realising that their son was yet another subject on which they would never agree, he went on: 'But to get back to tonight: why did you feel it was necessary to invite Norcroft's crew? Aren't John Norman and his wife enough? Must we appear to be in cahoots with the whole damn business?'

'You're too sensitive, Rafe,' Lucy retorted smoothly, stroking satisfied fingers through her cap of dark chestnut hair. Then she turned sideways. 'Do you like this dress? Do you think it suits me? I bought it yesterday in Pendower, of all places. A little boutique in the High

Street, run by that friend of yours—Miss Tempest.'

Rafe's features revealed none of the sudden apprehension he was feeling. 'Did you?' he remarked, without expression. 'I wouldn't have thought a boutique was the kind of place you would frequent.'

'Well, I wouldn't—ordinarily,' returned Lucy, enjoying her moment of triumph. 'But Laurence told me you had taken the mare down to Powys's place, for the — er—*young lady*—to ride, and I wanted a second chance to see for myself what it is about her that you so obviously admire.'

Rafe's fists balled in the pockets of his dark blue velvet evening jacket. 'What did you say to her, Lucy?' he enquired, with admirable restraint, but his wife did not answer him, merely smoothed the skirt of the lemon silk sheath and surveyed her reflection with evident satisfaction.

Rafe disciplined his emotions. He had no intention of letting her see that her words had in any way disconcerted him, and realising he could not force her to speak, he turned abruptly towards the door.

However, once she saw that she was in danger of losing his attention, Lucy became talkative. 'I asked her how Juniper was getting along, of course,' she said innocently. 'I explained that you'd originally bought the horse for me, but that I didn't care for riding, and how expensive it is these days to hire a stablehand.'

Rafe wrenched open the door. He could imagine how Lucy had explained the situation, and he could also imagine Catherine's reaction. He was amazed the mare had not been returned forthwith, thus destroying any further attempts his wife might make to humiliate her.

'Are you angry with me, darling?' Lucy's silky tones were irritating, and he was briefly tempted to humiliate her in the only certain way he knew. But right then, the idea of touching his wife was abhorrent to him, and without hesitation he walked into the corridor.

She followed him, however, and now she was on the defensive as she added vindictively: 'I'm not jealous, Rafe—you know that. I don't care how many women you have. That's of no interest to me. Just so long as they're not known to me . . .' She paused. 'I think I have the right to ask that.'

Their guests arrived within minutes of one another. First to come were the Warrenders, a retired Naval officer and his wife, old friends of Lord Penwyth, and Rafe's godparents. He was glad Lucy had had the good sense to include them. At least their friendship was genuine.

The Normans came next. Patricia Norman was Lucy's age, and they got along well together. Rafe had no quarrel with her husband, but his involvement with Norcroft was always present in their conversations, and lately John talked of little but the geological reports, which seemed to confirm his belief that there was lead in the valley. With them came the two men Rafe had least wanted to see, Norman's geophysicist, Malcolm Forrest, and his assistant. Until that evening Rafe had not been introduced to either man, but now he stared at the second man with unconcealed disbelief.

'Mappin!' he exclaimed, before Norman had had time to introduce them. 'Jeff Mappin! My God! Why didn't you let me know you were involved in all this?'

Jeff Mappin grinned and shook the other man's hand warmly. A tall man, almost as tall as Rafe himself, with unruly russet-coloured hair and hazel eyes, and more weight about him than he could have wished, he had changed little since their university days together, and his voice was wry as he ventured: 'I didn't like to, Glyn. I understood we weren't altogether welcome here.'

Rafe shook his head, and John Norman took the opportunity to intervene. 'I gather you two know one another,' he remarked, attracting his wife, and Lucy's, attention. 'Well, that's a relief! At least I have one man in Penwyth who won't be driven off at gunpoint!'

'Oh, John . . .' It was Lucy who spoke then, looking at the newcomers with interest, asking to be introduced.

Rafe performed the introduction, though not without some misgivings. However, Jeff seemed to find his wife charming, and confided afterwards that he thought his friend was a lucky devil.

'All this—and Penwyth, too?' remarked Rafe, in a wry undertone. 'Oh, yes. Lucky indeed!'

Lucy had supervised the menu for dinner, and in consequence everything was superbly served. Mrs Jones, the mother of the girl who came daily to the Manor, helped out on these occasions, and it was due to her ministrations that the food was always well cooked and piping hot. Lucy was a good supervisor, but in practical matters she was less successful, and it took the experience of someone like Mrs Jones to put her plans into operation.

During the meal, the talk turned inevitably to the explorations being carried out farther up the valley. It was Lucy who led the conversation into these channels, and Rafe guessed she wanted to display her own enthusiasm for the project.

'It's a lengthy business, Lucy,' John Norman replied, in answer to her query as to the extent of their findings so far. 'My geologists are always cautious about committing themselves too soon. We've taken a number of core samples back to the laboratory for analysis, but so much depends on the area of the find. We have to decide whether it would be economically feasible to develop the site.'

'I understand you were responsible for Mr Norman hearing about the axe-head that was found, Mrs Glyndower,' Jeff added, with interest. 'How did you know what it portended?'

'I didn't.' Lucy exhibited her girlish laugh. 'As a matter of fact, I had a much more selfish idea.' She looked about her, well satisfied that she had the attention of everyone in the room, with the possible exception of her husband. 'Just recently, I'd read about a similar find in Yorkshire—oh, not a lead mine, or anything, but an old Roman spear, that had suddenly appeared in a stream near Richmond. The spear was sold at auction for quite a considerable sum, and I thought perhaps I might make a little money that way.'

Polite laughter rippled round the room, and Patricia Norman assured her that she would have done the same. 'It's amazing how these things suddenly come to light after hundreds of years, isn't it?' she exclaimed. 'One wonders why they've never been found before.'

'It's not so surprising really,' Jeff observed. 'The earth

is constantly on the move. Cracks appear, for no apparent reason. Fissures, worn by years of erosion, suddenly open up. Like graves, expelling their dead, they spew out the history of the area.'

'Rather an unfortunate choice of terms, Mappin!' declared Commander Warrender tersely, pushing his plate aside. 'That was a delightful dessert, Lucy. Peaches really are my favourite fruit.'

'What he means is, the brandy went down very well,' remarked his wife dryly. 'But it was a delicious meal, as usual, Lucy. You really have superlative taste.'

Lucy smiled, content to receive the praise without any of the effort, and then suggested they adjourned to the drawing room for coffee and liqueurs.

Rafe found Jeff beside him as he poured Commander Warrender a generous measure of cognac. The other man refused his offer of the brandy, saying wryly: 'The wine we had at dinner was enough for me. I've got to work tomorrow.' And then added: 'But I would like to talk to you, Glyn.'

'Of course.' Rafe crossed the floor to hand the glass to Commander Warrender, and then after ascertaining what the ladies would like to drink, came back to where Jeff waited. 'What can I do for you?'

Jeff sighed, glancing round at the mellow panelling of the room, admiring the distinctive blend of ancient and modern in its decoration. 'I gather you and your wife share conflicting interests about this business,' he remarked softly, and Rafe cast him a mocking smile.

'You gather correctly,' he agreed, unscrewing the cap from a bottle of *crème de menthe*. 'And believe me, if I had any choice in the matter, Norcroft would never have been allowed to set foot in the valley.'

'So I heard.' Jeff's tone was dry. 'Do you wonder I didn't try to contact you before this!'

Rafe laughed then, his blue eyes warm with amusement. 'Why should I feel aggressive towards you? You're only doing your job. Believe me, Jeff, if I'd known you worked for Norcroft, I'd have made a point of finding out.'

'Well, thanks.' Jeff gave a relieved grin. 'But it was your wife who invited us up here, wasn't it?'

'Yes.' Rafe carried two narrow glasses of the green

liqueur he had just decanted across to the ladies, and ignoring Lucy's inquisitive stare, returned to his previous position. 'Tell me, Jeff, are you married? I seem to remember you were engaged to some girl who worked at Guy's, weren't you?'

Jeff pushed his hands into his trousers pockets, his expression reminiscent. 'Cecily? Oh, yes, we were engaged. But it didn't work out.'

Rafe frowned. 'No?'

'No.' Jeff chuckled. 'There was this girl at the lab. where I worked. A real—swinger, you know what I mean? Well, I guess I got careless. Anyway, Cecily found out and . . .' he snapped his fingers, 'that was that.'

'I'm sorry.' Rafe offered wry sympathy. 'And there's been no one else?'

'Lots of them,' retorted Jeff humorously. 'But I'm not married, if that's what you mean. Not yet. Although I have to confess to considering it more seriously lately.'

'Oh, yes?' Rafe raised his own goblet of brandy to his lips, and Jeff nodded reflectively.

'Yes. I'm not getting any younger, I realise that. I'm thirty-three, you know.' Then he grinned, adding with a grimace: 'Of course you do. We're the same age, aren't we? Well, anyway, I think I'm getting too old to play the field. The idea of settling down appeals to me.' He laughed. 'My God! Imagine Mappin saying that! I must be getting old. Or else it's seeing all my friends with wives and families . . .'

'Yes.' Rafe cradled the crystal goblet between his fingers. 'Or maybe it's just the result of ageing hormones!'

'Hey! Do you mind?' Jeff looked indignant. 'You don't sound as if you care.'

Rafe considered the liquid in his glass. 'Let's say I have reservations . . .'

'About what?'

'Rafe! Rafe!' Lucy's complaining tones brought an escape from a direct answer. 'Darling, must you monopolise Mr Mappin all evening? What are you talking about so earnestly? Can't we all share your confidences?'

'Glyn and I were just idling over old times,' declared Jeff smoothly, relieving the awkward moment, although his eyes revealed his own lack of understanding. He paused. 'As a matter of fact, I was just admiring your taste in decoration. Where did you find these lampshades? They're beautiful!'

Fortunately he had chosen a subject close to Lucy's heart, and she spent the next quarter of an hour describing the difficulties she had experienced in matching the shades with the heavy damask draperies at the long windows. It meant Rafe was relieved of the necessity of explaining himself, although later in the evening Jeff did contrive to have another word alone with him.

'I'm staying at the local pub,' he said, as Malcolm Forrest and the Normans made their farewells to Lucy. 'You know the place—the Bay Horse? Why don't you come down one evening and have a drink? I'd like for us to have more time to talk.'

Rafe nodded. 'I'd like that, too, Jeff,' he agreed, smiling, in control of the situation once more, and Jeff looked pleased.

'Your wife's been telling me you have a son,' he said. 'I'd like to meet him. What a pity he didn't join us this evening.'

Rafe's mouth thinned. 'Yes—well, I'm afraid Tom was sent to bed an hour before you arrived. Lucy doesn't believe in involving children in late-night parties. Besides,' his tone was wry, 'he disgraced himself at teatime by stuffing himself with fruit cake, and then trying to speak when his mouth was full.'

'I see.' Jeff looked sympathetic. 'What a shame!'

'Yes.' Rafe hesitated. 'I'll bring him over to the site to meet you, if you like. He'd enjoy the outing. He doesn't get many treats, poor little devil!'

Jeff grimaced. 'I'll look forward to it,' he said. 'And don't forget about that drink.'

'I won't,' Rafe promised, and Jeff shook his hand before going to bid his hostess goodnight.

Rafe poured himself another glass of brandy. He was drinking too much, he reflected dourly, but tonight he felt he needed it. He'd have the devil's own headache in the morning, no doubt, but at least he might get some sleep, a commodity which seemed in short supply these days.

Their guests had gone by eleven, Jeff gaining Rafe's promise to visit the site within the next few days before leaving. Lucy went straight towards the stairs as Rafe bolted the heavy door, and turning, he guessed she was as aware of his alcoholic state as he was and eager to escape from it. He let her go. He had no desire to rekindle their earlier relationship, which had been a one-sided affair at best. Her emotions were very shallow things. He doubted she had any depth of feeling for anything other than material interests. She did not love him. She did not love their son. All she craved was wealth and security.

Climbing the stairs, Rafe turned in the direction of his father's rooms. The old man seldom left them these days, avoiding guests with whom he found it difficult to communicate, spending his days reading or working out chess problems on the board that was constantly at his side. The stroke which had partially paralysed him had also given him an excuse to escape from the problems that beset him, and Rafe guessed he was happier now than he had been for years. His mind did wander, and from time to time he suffered losses of memory, but his son was shrewd enough to realise that these failings were most usually evident when some decision was required of him.

When Rafe entered his father's bedroom, he found old Lord Penwyth sitting up in bed, a book propped carelessly on his knees. The lamplit room had an air of warmth and isolation, and for a moment Rafe wished he had such a place to retire to. Morgan had made up the fire earlier, and now the glowing embers of the logs in the grate cast rosy shadows on the ceiling. The bed, a four-poster, was enveloped by its warmth, and the old man lying against the lace-edged pillows had no need of the shawl about his shoulders. There was an aroma of tobacco, however, and Rafe looked suspiciously towards his father. He had been warned about smoking in bed, but the old man seldom took anyone's advice, least of all Lucy's.

Lord Penwyth was seventy, and looked older. He had married for the second time in his late thirties, his first wife having died in childbirth. The child had died too, but Rafe's mother had succeeded in producing a healthy son. The fact that she also had predeceased her husband, was no small sorrow to him and her death had indirectly precipitated the stroke which had paralysed him. Without her steadying influence, he had begun to drink too much, leaving more and more of the estate's business in Rafe's hands, until that terrible afternoon when his horse had thrown him, and he had suffered the attack. Rafe knew his father had not wanted to recover. With the only woman he had ever loved dead, he had not wanted to live. But, as always, fate did not decree to order.

Now, the old man looked up at his son's entrance, his lined features breaking into a smile as he saw the identity of his visitor.

'Have they gone?' he asked, and Rafe nodded, crossing to the hearth to warm his hands over the embers.

'Warrender came up to see you, didn't he?' he asked, supporting himself with one arm along the mantel, as the heat made his head swim, and Lord Penwyth put his book aside.

'Yes, he came,' he agreed. 'He said Lucy had invited some of those chaps from the mining company. You didn't tell me that. I understood only Norman and his wife were invited.'

Rafe pulled a wry face. 'Does it matter? As it happens, I knew one of them—a fellow named Mappin, Jeff Mappin. He and I were at Oxford together.'

'Hmm.' His father hitched the shawl more securely about his shoulders. 'Is that why you're in your cups? Because this Mappin fellow is an old drinking partner?'

'In my cups?' Rafe shook his head. 'What an expression, Father! And no, I can't blame Jeff for the state I'm in. He's a much sober—soberer character than I am.'

Lord Penwyth exhibited his impatience. 'Then you should have more sense!' he declared, revealing no trace of senility at the moment. 'Drink never did anybody any good, and I should know.'

Rafe grimaced. 'I'm not drunk, Father, I know what I'm doing. It's you I worry about. Have you been smoking in here?'

'Stop trying to change the subject,' declared Lord Penwyth shortly. 'Rafe! For God's sake, don't let her break you, boy! She's not worth it.' He muttered irritably to himself. 'She will, you know, if she gets the chance. Just like she's trying to break Tom's spirit.'

Rafe's mouth tightened and he straightened away from the mantel. 'I'll look after Tom,' he declared, focussing with difficulty. 'Are you all right? That's what I came to find out.'

Lord Penwyth sniffed. 'I'm well enough. Well out of the way, I always think. I don't envy you, boy. I don't envy you at all.'

'No.' Rafe looked at the old man half impatiently. 'I sometimes think you're well enough to handle your own affairs.'

His father lifted a protesting hand then, however, resting back against his pillows and shaking his head. 'Oh, no.' he demurred. 'It's in your hands now, boy. Your hands. Just take it easy. We'll make it—we always do. There've always been Glyndowers in the valley, and there always will be.'

Rafe wished he could feel as sure. Maybe as long as his father was alive perhaps, but after that . . .

With a feeling of weariness he moved towards the door, only to be halted again by his father's voice. 'Rafe . . .'

'Yes.' He stood by the door, his fingers on the knob.

'I heard something today. About you and some girl in the valley.'

Rafe stiffened. 'What?'

His father frowned. 'Is it true, then?'

'Is what true?' Rafe was abrupt, disturbed by his father's words, and unable to hide it.

'They're saying that you've given her the mare. It's an expensive present from someone who doesn't have two halfpennies to scratch himself with.'

Rafe smothered an oath. 'My God!' he muttered. 'Do the people in the valley have nothing else to do than make up stories of this kind?'

'It's not true, then? Morgan said it was. He said the mare had been moved to Penwyn.'

Rafe heaved an angry sigh. 'That's true,' he declared. 'I am stabling the mare of Penwyn for the winter, but that's all.'

Lord Penwyth studied his son's dark features. 'You don't have to defend yourself to me, boy,' he said quietly. 'I just thought I should warn you, that's all. If it should get to Lucy's ears . . .'

'It already has,' retorted Rafe, rapidly sobering as the implications of what his father had said shifted the numbing mist from his brain. 'But thank you, anyway.'

'Is it Powys's niece?' enquired Lord Penwyth shrewdly, and his son stared at him.

'How do you know about Powys's niece?' he demanded, but his father had obviously decided he had said enough.

'Powys's niece?' he echoed absently now. 'Who is Powys's niece?'

'You know, you old devil!' grated Rafe exasperatedly, and then left the room knowing the futility of arguing with his father in this mood.

In his own room, he made no attempt to undress, however, flinging himself into the armchair by the window, staring out blankly at the wind-tossed garden his mother had cultivated. He was tired, deathly so, but he knew that his mind was too active to allow his body to rest. Was it true, then? Had his offer of the mare become a talking point in the valley? Or was it simply the servants at the Manor who had been talking among themselves?

Gritting his teeth, he got to his feet again, and paced restlessly across the room. Never, at any time since his marriage, had he found himself in such a situation. His affairs with women had been few and far between, but inevitable, bearing in mind Lucy's coldness and his own natural appetites. On those occasions when he had needed a woman, it had not been difficult to find one, but not in the valley, *never* in the valley.

And it was not like that now, he argued with himself. His association with Catherine Tempest had been governed by circumstance, and his offer of the mare had been an instinctive thing, born of his desire to compensate her for his own boorishness. And yet...and yet . . .

The door that led into Lucy's bedroom mocked his uncertainty. Clenching his fists, he strode towards it, reaching for the handle with reluctant determination. But his fingers slid from their objective without ever achieving it. The idea of entering Lucy's room, of invading her bed, filled him with self-disgust. He was simply not capable of using her right now. He didn't want Lucy. Lucy would not satisfy this feeling of dissatisfaction inside him. She didn't have it in her to satisfy any man. She was a shell, that was all, a beautiful shell, without any soul. *God*, didn't he know that? Hadn't he learned it in those first frenzied weeks of their marriage, when he had fought not to believe it? When his mother's death had been enough for his father to bear, without the added burden of learning that his son had made a disastrous mistake? He wondered what would have happened if Tom had not been conceived. Would he eventually have got a divorce? Or would his own pride have demanded him not to admit his failure? After all, he had loved Lucy, or he thought he had. And in any case, Tom had been conceived, and after that . . .

With a heavy sigh, he tugged his tie from around his neck, and shrugging out of his jacket and shirt, went into the adjoining bathroom. Warm water was soothing against his heated skin, and after cleaning his teeth, he went back into the bedroom.

Stripping off his trousers, he threw them carelessly on to a chair and slid naked between the sheets. It was good to relax his body, good to feel the smoothness of clean linen against his flesh, but he tossed and turned for hours before oblivion came to claim him.

He met Jeff for a drink a couple of nights later. He had hesitated before driving down to the pub, realising that sooner or later Jeff would realise the hollow sham that his marriage represented, but he could hardly avoid the fellow. They had been good friends for a number of years, and there was no reason to suppose that Jeff suspected anything was wrong. Nevertheless, Rafe had some misgivings when he entered the bar, acknowledging the landlord's greeting with a casual gesture, to find Jeff waiting for him, propped lazily against the bar.

'Glad you could make it.' Jeff was as amiable as ever. 'What'll you have? A beer—or a Scotch and soda?'

'Scotch is fine,' Rafe replied evenly, and helped himself to some nuts off the bar as Josh Evans hurried to serve them.

'So . . .' Jeff initiated the conversation, 'you're the local lord of the manor around here. I'm surprised you come down here to drink with the peasants.'

His grin robbed his remark of any sting, but Rafe grimaced at him. 'Leave it alone, will you, Jeff?' he ordered quietly. 'How are things at Penwyn? Making any progress?'

'Some. I've got to go back to the lab next week to carry on with the tests, but I should tell you, they're pretty positive.'

'That there is lead?'

Jeff nodded. 'It looks like it. Whether there's enough to warrant a full-scale mining operation is another matter.'

'What do you mean?'

'You can guess. Lead is nearly always combined with other elements, and the amount of rock we would have to move to get at it might determine whether it's worthwhile or not. I mean, there are no roads around here—not worth speaking of, anyway. We'd have to have some means of transporting the ore. Rail, maybe, although I doubt it.'

Rafe scowled into the glass Josh had set before him. 'I see.'

'And your feeling—is what?'

Rafe shrugged. 'You know that, too. I don't want it, but I can't refuse it.'

'There are worse things. Coal, for instance.'

'Don't play devil's advocate with me, Jeff. I do know the score.'

'Okay.'

Jeff shrugged and Rafe half turned towards the door. As he did so, however, he suddenly sucked in his breath, and Jeff turned to see what had caused his reaction. Rafe, his jaw muscles stiffening, was forcing a polite smile to his lips, and Jeff looked curiously at the girl who had come to stand by the bar. Above average height, and slim without being excessively so, she was one of the most attractive young women he had ever seen.

Rafe, for his part, was steeling his emotions. It was almost two weeks since he had seen Catherine Tempest, but he was appalled to discover that he recalled every tiny detail of her warm, disruptive beauty. She saw him in almost the same moment, and although he sensed her desire to avoid his gaze, after she had asked Josh if he had seen her cousin, she was forced to turn politely to Rafe and his guest.

It was then he became aware of Jeff's interest, of the curious look on his face, and the speculative light in his eyes, a detail which was not extinguished when Rafe was obliged to introduce them.

'I was just looking for Owen,' she said, after shaking hands with Jeff. 'If you'll excuse me, my aunt's looking for him,' and she left again, as abruptly as she had appeared.

'Well, well . . .' Jeff expelled his breath on a whistle as the door closed behind her. 'Some girl, hmm?'

Rafe nodded, reluctant to take part in any discussion of that kind, but Jeff was persistent.

'So you know her,' he murmured reflectively. Then, more insinuatively: 'How well, I wonder?'

'What the hell do you mean?' Rafe knew he was over-reacting, but seeing Catherine again had unnerved him. Jeff's amused stare was a little too knowing, and he resented the feeling of being baited.

'Nothing,' Jeff said now, shrugging his shoulders. 'Want another drink?'

'It's my turn,' retorted Rafe shortly, summoning the barman, and by the time their drinks were served the awkward moment had passed.

Their conversation moved into less personal channels, as Jeff outlined his career up until that point. There were people they both knew that they could talk about. Jeff had kept in touch with many more of their contemporaries than Rafe had done, and it was interesting hearing how his fellow-undergraduates had fared.

It was only towards the end of the evening that the conversation shifted in another direction, and as before, it was Jeff who instigated it.

'That girl,' he said idly, fingering his glass, 'the one who came in earlier. Who is she really? She doesn't look like one of the village girls, somehow.'

'She's not.' Realising he could not avoid an answer, Rafe explained. 'Her uncle is the tenant at Penwyn.'

'Our Penwyn?'

'Yes.'

'Dear God!' Jeff uttered a short laugh. 'Of course—I've seen her. I saw her a few days ago, actually. She rides, doesn't she? When she isn't falling off.'

'What do you mean?' Rafe was abrupt suddenly, and Jeff sighed.

'Don't look like that! I'm only kidding. She did fall off, though. Quite near to where we were working, actually. I don't think she hurt herself, though. She picked herself up pretty quickly, and rode off.'

'She was riding near the drilling site?'

'Yes.'

'She had no right to be up there!'

'Oh, come on . . .' Jeff was indignant. 'She's old enough to look after herself.'

'The horse she was riding was mine.'

'Oh, I see.' Jeff snorted. 'You're more concerned about the bloody horse than the girl.'

'I didn't say so.' Rafe wished he hadn't said that.

'It sounded like it.' Jeff frowned. 'So how long you known her?'

'Oh—years.' Rafe tried to sound offhand. 'When I was a boy, I used to spend a lot of time at Penwyn.'

'With her?'

'And her cousin.'

'Oh, yes,' Jeff nodded. 'She's very attractive.' He paused. 'Do you think she'd recognise me again?'

Rafe stiffened. 'I suppose so.'

'Good.' Jeff lay back in his chair. 'I'd like that.'

Rafe regarded him dourly. 'Hell, Jeff——'

'What?' Jeff raised his eyebrows. 'Go on, tell me what you want to say.' He shook his head. 'I'm not a fool, you know, Rafe.'

Rafe rose to his feet. 'She's a—friend, that's all. I wouldn't like to see her—hurt.'

'And that's all?'

'What more could there be?'

Jeff got slowly to his feet. 'Quite a lot, I should say,' he remarked dryly. 'Judging by the aggro in your voice. Shall we have another?'

CHAPTER SEVEN

IT had rained solidly for several days, and Catherine had had little opportunity for exercising Juniper. The fields around Penwyn were waterlogged, and the Llanbara had flooded the lower meadow. It was cold, too, with a raw wind blowing off the mountains, and even the mining team had retired to a laboratory in Cardiff to assess the results of their findings.

Eventually, however, Catherine had known she must ride, in spite of the weather. The stables needed cleaning out, too, and she knew better than to expect either her uncle or Owen to help her. In any case, she told herself, she needed the exercise, despite the bruises she still possessed from the fall she had had, but the long dark evenings were no encouragement to go out once she got home from the boutique. It was all too tempting to curl up by the fire with a book, or her accounts, and put all thoughts of Rafe Glyndower and his mare out of her mind.

After Lucy Glyndower's visit to the shop, she had thought of returning the mare to its owner, but reason had prevailed, and she was glad now she had not let the other woman intimidate her. Probably Lucy had expected her to act impulsively, but Catherine wanted to avoid any more involvement with Rafe Glyndower. If she had acted in the heat of the moment, she would have said something to him that night she encountered him at the Bay Horse, but in any case, he had not been alone, and seeing him there had unnerved her enough as it was. Besides, did it really matter why he had offered her the mare, or whose mare it was? Before the rain blanketed the valley in a fine mist, she had enjoyed the freedom that riding gave her, and she had no right to object if Lucy chose to acquaint her with the real facts of the matter. Nevertheless, it had hurt to feel she was being *used*, and these days of rain had acted like an abrasive on feelings already raw and sensitive.

She was drenched by the time she got back to Penwyn, but after attending to the mare, she refused her aunt's offer of a meal.

'I think I'd better get home and take a bath,' she replied, in answer to her aunt's invitation. 'I'm soaked to the skin, and I need a change of clothes.'

'Gillian could lend you something to wear,' pointed out Aunt Margaret reasonably. 'And the water's hot. Why do you always rush away back to that cottage these days? You used not to.'

Catherine sighed, lifting her hands to squeeze the moisture out of her hair. 'Oh, Aunt Margaret,' she said, 'you know why. Owen doesn't want me here, and I never seem to see Uncle Mervyn. They blame me for what's happened, I'm sure of it. They don't seem to understand that there are always two sides to every argument.'

Her aunt frowned. 'I know, I know. But I like to see you, and I know Gillian does. Couldn't you put up with Owen for our sakes? I've made a rabbit pie. You're welcome to share it.'

Catherine hesitated, but to refuse would have been unkind, and with some misgivings she agreed to stay. However, soaping herself in the steamy atmosphere of the ground floor bathroom, she wondered if she had done the right thing. Owen could be so unpleasant, and she felt too vulnerable to withstand his censure.

A tap at the door brought her head round with a start. 'Yes?' she called, then, realising she had not bolted the door, added: 'Don't come in, Owen. I'm in the bath.'

'It's not Owen, it's me,' declared Gillian, putting her head round the door. 'I've brought you some clothes. Will these do?'

Catherine relaxed, nodding as the other girl exhibited a pair of jeans and a dark blue sweater.

'The jeans are mine, only I can't wear them at the moment,' remarked Gillian humorously, indicating the swelling mound of her stomach, 'but the sweater's Owen's. None of my jumpers are good enough to lend anyone, and I'm sure he won't mind.'

'Won't he?' Catherine was not so sure. 'Well—thanks, anyway, Gill. They're fine.'

'Don't you wear a bra?' Gillian asked inquisitively, picking up the wet garments to take away for drying, and Catherine admitted that she didn't, always.

'It depends what I'm wearing,' she replied, reaching for the towel, but Gillian didn't take the hint.

Instead, she hovered near the door, kneading the wet clothes between her hands until Catherine's impatient gaze made her ask what she was obviously longing to know: 'Have—er—have you seen any more of—of Mr Glyndower?'

Catherine subsided abruptly into the water. 'What do you mean?'

Gillian shrugged a little nervously. 'You know—the squire!'

'I know *who* you mean,' declared Catherine evenly. 'I just don't know *what* you mean.'

'Oh, come on . . .' Gillian made a sound of disbelief. 'We know you've been seeing him. His car was parked outside your shop for fully an hour last week!'

Catherine gasped. 'Where did you hear that?'

'Isn't it true?'

'No. That is—yes, I mean he—*was* there. But it wasn't last week.' Catherine was annoyed at the way she was handling this, and stopped a moment to control her babbling tongue. 'It—was a couple of weeks ago, actually. When—when he came to ask me to look after the mare. That's the only occasion he's ever been to the shop.'

Gillian looked sceptical. 'Is it?'

'Yes.' Catherine was firm. 'Now, if you don't mind, I'll get dressed.'

It was incredibly difficult going into the dining room after that conversation. She had little doubt that Gillian had discussed the matter with Owen, and she dreaded the kind of pointed questions he might ask. What if he asked if Rafe had ever been to the cottage? How could she answer him? How could she defend herself without revealing Thomas's part in all this? And somehow she sensed even Lucy Glyndower did not know about that.

In the event, Owen said little. Whether her aunt had

warned him beforehand, Catherine couldn't be sure, but his comments were confined to the state of the weather, and the possibility of snow before Christmas.

Talking of Christmas made Catherine realise it would be her first Christmas at Pendower. If she stayed. She guessed her mother would invite her home for the festivities, but somehow she had no desire to spend Christmas in London. On the other hand, she could not spend the day alone at the cottage, which left only Penwyn as an alternative. Unless she invited Robert down for a couple of days. She could do that, and she had no doubts that he would come. But was it fair to him to keep him dangling like this? Knowing their relationship could never develop beyond its present limitations?

When the meal was over, Owen surprised her still further by inviting her to join Gillian and himself for a drink at the Bay Horse. 'We can go down in your car,' he suggested, and Catherine was only too willing to agree. The bar of the Bay Horse would be crowded at this hour of the evening, and there would be less opportunity for awkward questions.

She borrowed her aunt's hacking jacket to put on over the sweater and jeans, and obediently climbed into the back of the Renault when Owen asked if he could drive. Gillian was obviously more comfortable in the front, and she sighed enviously when Owen pulled away.

'This is better than that old banger of ours,' she exclaimed, touching the moulded dashboard. 'Isn't it, Owen? Why can't your father get a new car?'

This was a moot point, but to Catherine's relief her cousin did not make the obvious retort. 'We'll get a new car sooner or later,' he responded, more intent on seeing how quickly the Renault would accelerate than on his wife's conversation. 'Hey, this is great, isn't it? How fast will it go? Seventy? Eighty?'

'In that area,' agreed Catherine, before adding dryly: 'But not on these roads.'

'Yes. Slow down, Owen.' Gillian seemed to realise the dangers to herself more than any of them, and with a resigned shrug of his shoulders, her husband applied the brakes.

They almost skidded on to the parking area in front of the Bay Horse. Despite the appalling weather, the small car park was full, and they had to cruise around for several minutes looking for an empty space. Eventually, Owen thought he saw one at the far side of the park. There was just room for them to squeeze in between the last car and the hedge, he assured Catherine, but her worst fears were realised when the offside wheels slumped into the ditch which had been hidden by the rain and the darkness, and an ominous grinding sound indicated something infinitely more serious than a puncture.

'Owen!' It was Gillian who voiced all their apprehensions. 'You idiot! You've landed us in the ditch.'

With great difficulty, she opened her door and scrambled out, followed closely by Catherine. The little car was tipped sideways into the ditch, its rear wheel turning freely, but when Owen joined them on the bank, all his earlier amiability had fled, and he viewed his error with resentful indignation.

'How was I to know there was a ditch there?' he muttered, scuffing his heel, but Gillian was ready for him.

'You should!' she declared. 'You've spent enough time at this pub in the past! Oh, Catherine, I'm so sorry! What are you going to do?'

'I suggest we go inside,' said Catherine reasonably, putting her hand on Gillian's arm. 'There's no point in getting soaked all over again. Come on. We can talk about it over a drink. I could surely use one!'

As expected, the bar was crowded, but Owen, urged on by his wife, forged a path to the bar, and came back with two gin and tonics and a pint of bitter for himself. Swallowing half his drink with one gulp, he surveyed his cousin with sheepish eyes, and Catherine made an effort not to show the annoyance she was feeling.

'Do you think it'll be all right?' asked Gillian, and they all knew to what she was referring. 'I mean—if we can get it out of the ditch?'

Catherine shook her head. 'I don't know. I heard a sort of grinding sound, like metal bending or something. I have the feeling the chassis's twisted.'

'You would say that, wouldn't you?' muttered Owen

with a scowl. 'It wasn't my fault. I was only trying to park the damn thing.'

'I haven't said it was your fault, have I?' asked Catherine evenly. 'I'm only answering Gill's question. I don't think I'll be able to drive it home tonight, that's all. And in any case, how do you suggest we get it out of the ditch? No garage mechanic is likely to turn out in this weather, is he?'

'We could get a tow.'

'I think not.' Catherine sipped her drink with controlled deliberation, and then turning to Gillian added: 'Are you all right? That's the most important thing.'

'Me?' Gillian patted her stomach reassuringly. 'Oh, yes.' Then, realising how indifferent her husband had been, she remarked acidly: 'Not that Owen cares—the way he drives.'

Catherine licked her lips and looked helplessly about her, wishing herself anywhere but here. If only she had insisted in returning to the cottage after her ride, instead of accepting her aunt's invitation to supper. If only she had not agreed to accompany Owen and Gillian to the pub. If only she had not let Owen drive. *If only . . .*

They had attracted some attention, and Catherine being a virtual stranger was attracting more than most. Several pairs of eyes appraised her, and her own shifted uncomfortably towards the bar and Morris Evans's friendly face. The barkeeper raised his glass to her and as he did so, another vaguely familiar face was turned in her direction. It was the young geophysicist Rafe Glyndower had introduced to her, Jeff Mappin. She recalled his name quite easily. She guessed he must be staying at the pub, and on impulse she excused herself from Owen and Gillian and made her way towards him. Perhaps he would give them a lift back to the farm, she thought. Anything to avoid the inevitable recriminations which would ensue if they had to walk home.

It was only as she neared the man, however, that she realised he was not alone. As before, Rafe Glyndower leaned at the bar at his side, and an unreasonable sense of panic gripped her. Were they friends? Was Rafe Glyndower associating with the enemy now, so to speak? Or was this just another coincidence?

Rafe had turned at her approach, and now he rested his back against the bar, elbows supporting himself. In dark grey trousers and a matching knitted sweater, he was achingly familiar, and recalling that scene in her office, Catherine couldn't prevent the wave of emotion that swept over her. She was intensely conscious of the shortcomings of her appearance, Gillian's jeans a little too short in the leg, and Owen's sweater outlining the roundness of her full breasts. And the worn hacking jacket was no competition for his own leather jerkin.

'It's—Miss Tempest, isn't it?' It was Jeff Mappin who spoke first, greeting her enthusiastically, not at all put out by this unexpected interruption. 'So we meet again. Is there something we can do for you?'

Catherine flicked a nervous glance in Rafe's direction before replying: 'I—er—I came down for a drink with my cousin and his wife.'

'Is that right?' Jeff looked sideways at Rafe. 'What a pleasant surprise.'

Catherine forced a smile, and obliged to acknowledge Rafe, she added: 'Good evening, Mr Glyndower.'

'Good evening, Miss Tempest.' He was chillingly polite, she noticed. 'I expect you're surprised to see us together again. You may assure your uncle I don't make a habit of fraternising with the opposition, but Jeff and I were at university together.'

Her deepening colour was an irritation, but she managed to say sharply: 'It's nothing to do with me, Mr Glyndower,' before burying her nose in her glass.

Jeff chose to intervene at that point, saying casually: 'So where are your cousin and his wife? Aren't they with you?'

'Oh, yes.' Catherine glanced uncomfortably towards Rafe once more. 'As—er—as a matter of fact, I came to ask you a favour.'

'Me?' Jeff sounded surprised, and she saw the way Rafe's lids descended, hooding his eyes with disturbing intent. 'What can I do for you?'

'It's my car,' murmured Catherine reluctantly, unwilling to discuss her problems in front of Rafe, but unable to see any alternative. 'Owen, he—well, he's managed to park it in a ditch. I think something's broken—underneath. I don't think it's fit to drive anyway.'

'You mean he crashed it?' demanded Rafe grimly, and she gazed at him defensively.

'No, not exactly.' She hesitated. 'It was an accident, that's all. He was trying to fit in on to the car park, and it—well, half turned over.'

Rafe's mouth thinned. 'What was he?—drunk or something?'

'No.' Realising she was defending herself to his companion, and not to the man whose help she had sought, she turned to Jeff once more. 'There's nothing can be done about it tonight, Gillian's pregnant and we have to get back to the farm, and I wondered if——'

'I'll drive you back to Pendower,' said Rafe, before Jeff could answer her. 'Jeff can see your cousin and his wife home.'

'Now wait a minute . . .' Jeff broke in indignantly. 'If Miss Tempest needs a ride back to Pendower, I can take her.'

'It's not necessary, really.' The last thing Catherine wanted was to ride all the way back to Pendower with either of them. 'I can stay the night at the farm, and borrow Uncle Mervyn's Land Rover in the morning.'

'I've said I'll drive you home,' declared Rafe, his eyes dark with impatience, and she gazed helplessly down into her glass. 'Jeff doesn't know these roads as I do, and on a night like this . . .'

'I know the roads pretty well by now, Rafe,' Jeff protested. 'I don't mind driving her home.' He grinned. 'On the contrary, I'd enjoy it!'

Rafe's lips tightened. 'Might I remind you, she's had one unpleasant experience this evening. I shouldn't like to risk her having another.'

Jeff looked indignant. 'Are you suggesting——'

'Don't be a fool!' Rafe's lips curled. 'You know what I mean. These roads can be treacherous, and with the Llanbara flooded . . .'

Jeff looked at Catherine. 'I suggest we let Miss Tempest decide,' he said, and there was a certain tightness about his own expression now.

'Oh, really . . .' Catherine didn't want to get caught up in any more arguments. 'I could stay at the farm . . .' Then she weakened before the anger in Rafe's eyes. 'But— if Mr Glyndower doesn't mind . . .'

'Okay.' Jeff's annoyance was tangible. 'Then at least let me buy you another drink before you leave. What will you have?'

Catherine accepted another gin and tonic, and was half relieved to hear Owen's voice behind her. He shouldered his way into their small circle, and then, realising who it was his cousin was talking to, effected a note of apology.

'I'm sorry, sir,' he said, looking awkwardly into his now empty glass. 'I was just about to tell Catherine here that I've found someone to pull her car out of the ditch.'

Catherine frowned. 'Who?'

'Lewis Edwards,' conceded Owen reluctantly, ident-ifying one of the labourers from Meredith's plantation. 'He says his Land Rover will have it out in no time——'

'I understood the chassis was suspect,' observed Rafe then, and Owen cast his cousin a look of impatience.

'We don't know that, sir,' he explained. 'In the rain and all, it was impossible to tell.'

'Then I suggest you leave it where it is until the morn-ing,' remarked Rafe, exerting the assurance of his position. 'You have no objections, I'm sure, Powys, and Miss Tempest has already made other arrangements.'

'What other arrangements?'

Owen was suspicious and Catherine said hastily: 'Mr Mappin is going to take you and Gillian home, and—and Mr Glyndower is going to run me back to Pendower.'

'I see.' There was a wealth of meaning behind those words, but Rafe's tone was smooth, as he added:

'I'll arrange with the garage to have the car shifted in the morning. I think that would be safer, don't you? Just in case there's any serious damage.'

Owen's protests were silenced, but Catherine did not mistake the resentment in his gaze. He thought she had betrayed them yet again, and it was useless trying to make him see that he was to blame.

Gillian came to join them, and Jeff bought them all a drink. Clearly both Owen and his wife were discomfited in the presence of the squire, and Catherine couldn't wait to leave. She drank her second gin and tonic in the swiftest possible time, and then asked politely if they could be going soon.

'I have a busy day tomorrow,' she said, realising her explanations were an attempt to justify herself in Jeff Mappin's eyes. She had liked him, and in other circumstances . . .

'I hope we meet again,' he said, as they were leaving, making his intentions very plain, and Catherine nodded before bidding him and her relatives goodnight.

It was still pouring with rain when she and Rafe emerged from the inn, and he asked her to wait in the shelter of the porch while he brought the car to the door. It took only a couple of minutes before the green Volvo drew to a halt beside her, and Rafe thrust open the door from inside and bade her join him.

In spite of the coldness outside, it was warm in the car, and Catherine guessed he had not been long at the pub. There was the faint aroma of tobacco and damp leather, and the more distinguishable perfume that Lucy used. It reminded her of his wife and her visit to the boutique, and made her draw back even farther into her corner.

As if aware of her withdrawal, Rafe glanced her way as he left the car park and turned the Volvo on to the Pendower road. 'I'm sorry if my company is abhorrent to you,' he said, 'but I meant what I said about these roads.'

Catherine expelled her breath on a sigh. 'I know you did,' she conceded. 'It—it's a dreadful night, isn't it?'

'I've seen worse.' His tone was abrupt. Then, brusquely: 'I've embarrassed you. I'm sorry. But I couldn't let Jeff take that chance, not when he's already driven up from Cardiff this afternoon.'

'He has?' Catherine was surprised. 'I didn't realise.'

'No—well, he wanted to get back, and—my wife invited him for dinner.'

'And you came down to the pub afterwards, for a drink,' she murmured, and he nodded.

'Yes.'

Catherine peered blindly through the streaming windows. 'Do you think the road is flooded?'

'It wasn't an hour ago. I doubt if the river's that high. But there may be water coming down off the top, and I'd hate you to end up in the ditch a second time.'

'Would you?' Catherine turned to look at him profiled in the dashboard lights. 'I'd have thought that might please you.'

'Why?'

His voice grated, and she shook her head. 'I slapped your face.'

'We both know why.'

'Yes.' She bent her head. 'Because—because you assumed too much.'

Rafe said nothing in response to this, and she turned her head to the windows again. They were climbing the winding pass out of the valley near the very spot where Thomas had darted across the road in front of her and Robert. At least he would not be out on the road tonight, at the mercy of the elements as they were.

The silence was oppressive, and taking another tack, Catherine asked: 'Have you known Mr Mappin long?'

Rafe hesitated. 'About fifteen years, I guess,' he said at last. 'Why? Do you find him attractive?'

Catherine gasped. 'I—he seems very nice. I—I hardly know him.'

Rafe moved his shoulders in a dismissing gesture. 'Will you go out with him, if he asks you?'

Catherine stared at him. 'Why should you assume he might?'

Again there was no answer, and a tightening core of tension balled inside her. He took too much upon himself, she thought resentfully. It was nothing to do with him whom she liked or whom she went out with. Those days of the lord of the manor being able to direct the private as well as the working life of his tenants were dead and gone, and he had no right to question her like this.

Recklessly, she said: 'Did your wife tell you she came to the boutique last week? Oh, yes, I'm sure she must have. She bought a dress, and you must have seen it.'

Rafe's long fingers spread and flexed on the wheel. 'Yes.' he agreed quietly, 'she told me.'

'Did she also tell you what she said to me?' Catherine's

dark brows arched interrogatively. 'That the mare was her horse, not Thomas's? And that you were desperately short of stablehands?'

Rafe's breath whistled in his throat. 'You didn't believe her.' It was a statement, delivered with hard emphasis. 'You know she was lying.'

'Was she?' Into her stride, Catherine was not so willing to let him off the hook. 'How do I know that?' She paused. 'You may be the one who's lying, for all I know.'

Rafe's fists clenched on the wheel now. 'I can't force you to believe me, of course.' he said roughly. 'I have no proof.' He glanced sideways at her. 'You must make up your own mind.'

'Yes.' Catherine chewed on her lower lip, and then, choosing her words carefully, she added: 'Did you know your car was seen outside the boutique?'

Another silence, and then he said heavily: 'Does that worry you? You should know by now, nothing ever happens in Pendower without everyone knows about it.'

Catherine digested this. 'And it doesn't worry you?'

'Damn it, of course it worries me!' he snapped, his patience shredding. 'I don't like the idea of being a topic of discussion, a source of gossip for the people in the valley! But it's done now, and I can't better it.'

Catherine slumped lower in her seat. 'I see.'

'Do you?' His voice was still harsh. 'What do you see, I wonder? What do you really know about me, or my life?'

Catherine sniffed. 'All right, all right. I'm sorry if I've been the cause of some—embarrassment to you, but—well, I didn't ask you to come to the shop.'

'No, you didn't.' His tone was flat. 'I haven't forgotten that either.'

There was something in his voice now that stirred unwilling emotions inside her, and almost instinctively, she stretched out her hand and touched the sleeve of his jacket. 'I'm sorry, Rafe,' she murmured huskily, her fingers curving over the taut muscles. 'It was kind of you to offer to drive me home, and I'm just being a bitch. I'm sorry.'

'For God's sake, Catherine——' He wrenched her hand almost convulsively from his arm, and she shrank wretchedly into her corner, as the lights of Pendower appeared ahead of them.

Pembroke Square was only a stone's throw from the market place, and in no time at all the Volvo was dipping its lights before the cottage.

Eager to escape from the car, Catherine sought for the handle, and she had thrust the door open and climbed out almost before the vehicle had stopped. Holding on to the door, she bent to make an enforced statement of gratitude for his having run her home. But his seat was empty, and she straightened to find him facing her across the roof of the car. She stood there for several seconds, just looking at him, with the rain pouring down on them, his expression strained in the light from the street lamps, and then she managed to say tremulously: 'You don't have to wait, you know. I—I have my key.'

Rafe shook his head, and on trembling legs she made the circuit of the car to where he was standing, on the pavement in front of her gate. Fumbling in her bag, she brought out the key, and showing it to him, added: 'Th-thanks again. And—and goodnight.'

Without answering, Rafe took the key from her unresisting fingers and walked up the path to her door. Inserting the key in the lock, he swung the door open, and then said quietly: 'Can I come in?'

Catherine's mouth was dry. It was difficult to say anything. Instead, she went ahead of him into the hall of the cottage and switched on the light. The almost harsh illumination streamed out on to the path, and Rafe, stood there, bathed in its radiance.

'Well?' he said, and she moved aside automatically, so that he could step into the narrow hall.

CHAPTER EIGHT

THE door closed behind him, and finding her breathing suddenly difficult to control, Catherine went ahead of him into the living room, switching on the lamps and quickly drawing the russet-brown curtains across the windows. The fire she had tended before she went out was still smouldering in the grate, and she opened the flue to allow the cold air from outside to draw it away. As she attended to her duties, she was conscious of Rafe behind her in the doorway of the room, watching her, his back propped against the frame.

'Would you—er—would you like some coffee?' she asked, straightening, and after a moment he made an assenting gesture.

'Thank you. Can I do anything?'

Catherine licked her dry lips. 'You—you could feed some logs on to the fire,' she offered. 'When—when the flames are strong enough.'

Rafe inclined his head, and she went towards him, halting uncertainly until he had moved out of the doorway to allow her to pass through.

In the kitchen, her fingers were all thumbs. She stripped off her aunt's jacket, and while the percolator was bubbling, she cast an unsatisfactory glance at her reflection in the polished chrome. Strands of fine hair were curling on her forehead, and the long coil of honey-brown hair was an untidy curtain about her shoulders. She didn't have time now to secure it properly, but she gathered it all together and wound it round her hand before holding it at her nape and pressing in a couple of hairpins.

When she returned to the living room, the fire was blazing warmly, fresh logs spitting sparks into the wide chimney. In the lamplight, the room had a disturbing intimacy, a feeling which was enhanced by Rafe stretched lazily on the couch before the fire, staring broodingly into the flames. He had shed his leather jacket, and the opened neck of his shirt revealed the strong brown column of his throat and the gold medallion that glittered there.

He rose to his feet, however, as she entered the room with the tray, taking it from her willing fingers and setting it down on the hearth rug. Then he waited for her to sit down before reseating himself.

'Oh, please——' Catherine gestured awkwardly, feeling more in control of the situation while she was on her feet. 'Do sit down. I—er—I'll pour the coffee.'

'You can do that just as well from the couch,' he pointed out quietly, and as she sought for some excuse to escape his nearness, he regarded her between narrowed lids.

Realising he had given her no real reason to avoid him, she felt obliged to do as he suggested. But it was with some misgivings that she came round the end of the couch and perched precariously on the end as she bent to the tray.

Rafe came down beside her, his weight depressing the cushions. 'Will—will you take cream?' she ventured chokily, and he asked for sugar with no cream. He seemed to have deliberately seated himself near her, and when she sat back to drink her coffee, her elbow brushed his arm. Immediately she shifted slightly to avoid the contact, drinking her coffee far too hastily, and almost scalding her mouth in the process. Was it only her nerves that sensitised the silence between them? Why couldn't she think of something to say? Thomas! Yes, that was it. She would ask him about Thomas. He at least was a harmless subject.

But even as her lips parted to say the words, she felt his fingers at her nape, removing the hairpins, allowing the heavy weight of her hair to fall silkily about her shoulders. Then, when her heart was drumming in her ears, his fingers moved from her neck to trace an invisible line across her shoulder and down the quivering length of her arm.

'Why do you fasten your hair in a knot?' he demanded, in a low voice. 'I like it much better loose—like it is now.'

Catherine put down her cup and drew a steadying breath. 'You—you have no right to—to touch my hair——'

'I know that.'

'—and—and aren't you worried that someone might see your car outside? I mean—I mean, it would be far more damning for someone to see it there at—at this time of night——'

'I know it.' But he wasn't looking at her face. His attention was all concentrated on the hand he had captured and was presently stroking with his tongue.

'Oh, God, Rafe——' Her cry was desperate, as she tried to drag her hand from his grasp. 'You mustn't . . .'

'On the contrary . . .' He lifted his eyes, and her pulses raced at the raw emotion she saw there. 'I *must*—or go quietly out of my mind.' And his hand at her nape propelled her mouth to his.

It was like drowning, she thought fatalistically, trying futilely to keep her head. In spite of her opposition, his lips were parting hers without effort, and the plundering urgency of his mouth had a suffocating sweetness. She felt herself sinking back against the cushions, his weight crushing her breasts, the wine-dark intoxication of his kiss silencing her conscience. For so long she had kept even thoughts of him at a distance, but now all that was real was his touch and his nearness, and the male scent of him that acted like a stimulant on her already heated senses.

'Catherine,' he groaned, his mouth moving from hers to the hollow beneath her ear, while his hand slid beneath the concealing sweater to the swollen fullness of her breast. 'Beautiful,' he murmured, pushing the offending woollen aside, his tongue finding the tautness of her nipple and caressing it eagerly. 'Beautiful . . .'

'Rafe . . .' His name was less an appeal for his withdrawal than a protest of embarrassment that he should see her thus, but his eyes mocked her reluctant denial.

'I'd like to see all of you,' he muttered huskily. 'Don't stop me . . .'

It was a devastating, intimate experience, made the more so by her own increasing awareness of the length of his lean body beside hers. With his leg thrown across her, she could not avoid the knowledge of the hardening muscles of his thighs, and while there was a wild delight in knowing she could arouse him this way, she could not deny a certain apprehension as to his intentions. How did

regard her? Did he think she was a liberated woman of
he world? A free-thinking emancipationist with the experience of other affairs behind her? Had he any idea how
inexperienced she was? Did he realise, for example, that
no other man had ever been this close to her, that no
other man had even been permitted the intimacy of kissing
her as he was doing?

But when his mouth sought hers again, reason was
stifled. Whether it was the isolation of this room like some
suspended moment in time when everything and every-
body ceased to exist but their two selves, she didn't know,
but she felt her hands reaching for him, curling into the
hair at his nape, holding him closer. This was more real,
more exciting, more pervasive than any of the fantastic
dreams she had had about him, and infinitely more disturbing. She had not known how he might make her feel,
how wanton her emotions could be, or suspected the
aching longing he was arousing in her loins, a yearning for
fulfilment that that only he could assuage.

Her hands slid from around his neck, parting the buttons
of his shirt so that the hair-roughened skin of his chest
rubbed abrasively against her breasts. It was an in-
flammatory experience, but when her hands moved lower,
eager to explore further, Rafe made a tortured sound of
protest, and dragged himself away from her to sit on the
side of the couch.

'God!' he muttered shakily, raking back his hair with
unsteady hands. 'What do you think you're doing to me?'

Catherine froze. Then she pulled her sweater into place
with trembling fingers. 'I'm sorry,' she said, unable to
disguise the tremor in her voice, 'I—I thought that was
what you wanted.'

'What I wanted?' He stared at her with tormented eyes.

'Well, wasn't it?' Somehow she had to sustain her composure here, but it wasn't going to be easy when every
nerve in her body was crying out for a satisfaction it had
not attained. 'I—I thought you said——'

'I know what I said,' he interrupted her harshly. 'But
I'm not an animal! I'm a thinking, reasoning human
being!'

Catherine's tongue appeared momentarily. 'You—you

don't want me, then?' The words stuck in her throat.

'Want you?' He clenched his fists on his knees. 'God! Of course I want you—I can't hide that. But, unlike the men you're probably used to associating with, I find I can't—*use* you. You're not like the other women I've——' He broke off in disgust. 'I'm sorry, I'm doing this badly. I'm afraid I don't go in for this sort of thing.'

'I see.' With controlled movements Catherine swung her feet to the floor, and got up from the couch. 'You think I do.'

He looked up at her. 'I didn't say that.'

'You didn't have to.' Her lips tightened. 'But, unlikely as it may seem to you, I've had very little experience with men.'

Rafe made a dismissing gesture. 'You don't have to humour me, you know.' He shook his head impatiently. 'I may be old-fashioned in some ways, but I have heard of the pill.'

Catherine's jaw trembled, as he got to his feet to face her. 'You—you prig!' she got out jerkily. 'You—you sit there——'

'I'm standing now.'

'—and—and tell me you've heard about the pill! As if I was some kind of—of female stud! That—that unlike the other men I've known—*known*, mark you, in the biblical sense, of course, you can't—can't *use* me!'

'It was meant as a sign of the respect I have for you,' he protested quietly, but Catherine was not listening to him.

'What's the matter?' she taunted. 'Aren't I good enough for you? Don't I have the right background? Is laying a shopgirl not to the taste of the next Lord Penwyth——'

'Catherine, for God's sake——'

'What makes you so sure I'd—I'd have let you—*use* me?' she demanded. 'I'm not an instrument, to be—to be used to satisfy any man's cravings, least of all yours!'

'Catherine, listen to me——'

'No. Why should I?' She turned her back on him, striving desperately to retain what little self-respect she had left. 'You come in here without invitation, you drink my coffee, you share my fire——'

'—and try not to abuse your hospitality!' he muttered savagely. 'God, Catherine, do you think I wanted to let you go?'

Almost against his will, he moved behind her, his hands closing on her hips, drawing her back against the swollen muscle between his legs.

'Does this feel as if I want to let you go?' he demanded, his breathing harsh and laboured. 'My God, do you know what holding you like this does to me?' His lips brushed her hair. 'We're alone here, and God knows, I don't want to leave you. I want to hold you—and love you—and sleep with you——'

'No!' Catherine knew she dared not let him go on. Whatever happened now, she could never be sure she had not instigated this, and in any case, with the return of sanity, she knew he was right. He would have no respect for her if she gave in to the emotions that were tearing her to pieces. Wanting wasn't enough. There had to be more than that. And he had no more to give.

'Catherine . . .'

His hoarse whisper was seducing, weakening her resistance, inciting the desire to surrender, but somehow she managed to pull herself away from him. 'Don't touch me!' she choked, steeling herself for his protest, but it never came. It was as if that phrase held some special message for him, and with a stifled imprecation he left her, snatching up his jacket as he crossed the room, striding out of the house without another word.

With his going, a terrible emptiness possessed her. While he was there, in the room with her, even when they were arguing together, she had felt fully alive, for the first time in her life. But now she was alone, and she had never known such a sense of deprivation.

Sinking down on to her knees on the hearth before the fire, Catherine wrapped her arms protectively around herself, as if that small gesture might ward off the sense of despair she was experiencing. She should never have let him come here, never have allowed him into the house. The desperation she was feeling right now made a mockery of her earlier anxieties about her car. It seemed such a small problem, compared to her feelings for Rafe, feelings which had crystallised in those minutes when he had held her in his arms. Until then she had been able to fool herself that she was imagining the way she felt, there had been nothing on which to base the belief that she loved him. That was no longer true. Lying in his arms, she had been unable to deny the depth of her emotions, and knowing he belonged to another woman was the cruellest kind of torture. Her mind was tormented by images of him and Lucy together. Could he turn from her to his wife without hesitation? Would he—*use* Lucy, as a palliative, an assuagement, without fear of the complications any other relationship might bring? He had wanted her—she acknowledged that. But that could mean anything, particularly with a man who undoubtedly was no amateur when it came to making love . . .

She slept badly, waking fitfully throughout the night, listening to the rain drumming on the windows, and the wind soughing through the trees in the gardens of Pembroke Square. The morning was not much brighter. The local radio station had news of roads being blocked by fallen branches, and the Llanbara had flooded some cottages in the valley.

Listening to the newscaster's words, Catherine couldn't deny a certain anxiety as to whether Rafe had made it home safely. What if the road had flooded? What if he had been stranded? Surely he would not have spent the night in the car, without any heating to ward off the cold.

Washing her breakfast dishes, and feeding her toast to the birds, she forced herself to think sensibly. Rafe Glyndower was not her concern. He never had been. And just because, in a weak moment, he had succumbed to a purely physical attraction, did not mean she had any right to worry about him. She must put what happened yesterday completely out of her mind. It might even be better if she returned Juniper to the stables at Penwyth. That way, she would have less reason to spend time at the farm, or run the risk of encountering Rafe again.

She had to leave for work earlier than usual, because she had to walk. It was fortunate the wind had dropped a little, or her umbrella would have been of little use to her, and Mary Grant gazed at her in surprise as she approached along the High Street.

'Where's your car?' she asked, as inquisitive as usual, and Catherine had to admit that Owen had ditched it the night before. 'So how did you get home?' Mary pressed her, eager to know all the facts of the case, and with some misgivings Catherine said that Owen had run her home in the Land Rover.

'Oh, poor you!' Mary grimaced. 'I've seen that smelly old thing about the town. Does he ever clean it?'

'Does it matter?'

Catherine was short with her, but she couldn't help it. The last thing she needed was Mary's inconsequent chatter, and the girl went off to make some coffee with a barely-concealed air of injustice.

The telephone rang almost before Catherine had had time to gather herself. It jangled noisily in her small office, aggravating the slight ache that was making itself felt behind her temples, and she reached wearily for the receiver.

'Yes? Catherine Tempest speaking.'

'Miss Tempest?' The voice was unfamiliar to her. 'This is Blake's Service Station here. We've got your car here for repair.'

Catherine gulped. 'You have?' She hadn't thought anyone would have known about it yet.

'Yes.' The man went on: 'Mr Glyndower contacted us first thing this morning, so naturally we got on to it right away.'

Naturally! Catherine's mouth was dry. 'Well—thank you.' She hesitated. 'Do you—er—can you tell me what's wrong with it?'

'Yes, miss. I've examined the vehicle, and I'm afraid I have some bad news for you. The exhaust system has been damaged beyond repair, and unfortunately the angle of the ditch caused it to fracture the brake pipe, too.'

'Oh, damn!' Catherine rested her elbow on the desk, supporting her head with one hand. 'So what does that mean?'

'It means a new exhaust system, and a new brake pipe, Miss Tempest.'

Catherine sighed. 'And—can you do it?'

'Oh, yes, we can do it. The exhaust system presents no problems whatsoever. If it was only that we could have it done for you by tomorrow at the latest, maybe even this afternoon. But the brake pipe might take longer. We'll have to send for one of those, you see, and that could take two or three days.'

'Oh, well . . .' Catherine really had no choice in the matter 'Please—go ahead. Do what you have to.'

'Very good, miss. I'll let you know how long it will take later in the day.'

'Thank you.'

Catherine replaced the receiver with a heavy heart, although at least the call had dispelled her anxieties about Rafe. He must have returned home safely, and with his usual attention to detail he had not forgotten his promise to contact the garage. It was chilling really, realising that after all that had happened he could still behave with detachment.

Mary came back with her coffee, raising her eyebrows at the telephone. 'That wasn't David Maxwell, was it?' she probed. 'I've told him not to ring me at work, but you know what boys are like.'

'No, it wasn't David Maxwell,' agreed Catherine resignedly. 'It was the garage in Penwyth, letting me know the damage that's been done to the Renault.'

'Oh?' Mary looked intrigued. 'I didn't realise you'd called out the garage last night.'

Catherine opened her mouth to explain, and then closed it again. 'A new exhaust system, and a new brake pipe,' she volunteered after tasting her coffee. 'Hmm, this is just what I needed.'

She did play with the idea of calling Rafe and thanking him for his assistance, but it was quickly squashed. For one thing, his wife probably knew nothing about the previous evening's events, and for another, she had no intention of allowing him to speculate that perhaps she had regretted the way the evening had ended. That information was strictly classified, and no one must ever know exactly how much Rafe had hurt her.

She had only a sandwich at lunchtime, poring over some invoices in her office while Mary went to meet her latest boy-friend. She could hear if anyone came into the shop, and as lunchtime was not normally a busy period, she was surprised when she heard the sound of someone moving about among the racks of dresses.

Putting her sandwich down, she came out of the office, and then frowned when the shop appeared to be empty. She could have sworn she had heard someone, and she went to check that the till had not been tampered with, turning down the audio-equipment at the same time.

A rustle of material brought her round with a start, then her lips parted in amazement as she gazed at the boy confronting her. 'Thomas!' she exclaimed, her nerves tightening at the awareness that he might not be alone. 'Thomas, what are you doing here?'

'You said I might come,' he reminded her, his smile so like Rafe's that weakness overwhelmed her. 'You don't mind, do you?'

Catherine looked beyond him to the street outside. But there was no Volvo parked at the kerb, and her breathing eased a little. 'But what are you doing here?' she protested. 'Aren't you supposed to be in school?' She hesitated. 'You haven't run away again, have you?'

'No!' Thomas was scornful. 'I wouldn't run away from here. I like this school. And I don't have to *sleep* there.'

'That means a lot to you?' Catherine raised her eye-brows.

'Yes.' Thomas pursed his lips. Then he sighed, looking around at the kaleidoscope of colour represented by the clothes that filled the long dress racks, and the small, cir-cular displays. 'I like your shop, Miss Tempest. You sell some pretty clothes.'

Catherine chose her words with care. 'But what are you doing out of school?' she persisted gently. 'Is this your lunch hour? Are you supposed to leave the playground?'

'Oh . . .' Thomas expelled his breath noisily. 'No. We're not allowed to leave school until it's time to go home.'

'Then——'

'But school's over for today. For this week, actually.' He sighed. 'You know that awful storm we had last night? Well, it brought down the old elm tree near the school, and it crashed on to the roof.'

'Good lord!' Catherine was appalled, imagining the disaster that might have occurred had the children been in school at the time.

'Yes. Well, when Daddy brought me to school this morning——'

'Daddy brought you to school?'

'That's what I said,' Thomas nodded. 'Yes, when he brought me to school this morning, Mr Forrester didn't really know how bad the damage was. But I think it's pretty bad, because there's water pouring into one of the classrooms, and there are slates off the roofs of others.'

'I see,' Catherine nodded slowly. 'So . . .'

'So—we all have to go home.'

Catherine tried to contain her patience. 'But how are you getting home, Thomas?'

'I 'spect Daddy will come for me again.'

Catherine pushed her hands into the pockets of her cords. 'But not here.'

'No, to the school, silly.' Thomas swung round on his heel, unaware of her disconcertment. 'But Mr Forrester had to make all the telephone calls, so I thought I might come and see you.'

'But does anyone know where you are?' Catherine asked in dismay.

'Well, yes, Miss Mayhew does. She said I might walk along to see you. I said you were my aunt, you see.' He sounded unconcerned. 'Don't look so worried. The school's just at the end of the High Street.'

'I know where it is.' Catherine chewed anxiously on her lower lip. 'I—well, it was very nice of you to come and see me, Thomas, but I think you ought to go back now and wait for your father. I mean, it wouldn't do for him to worry about you, would it?'

'He won't,' declared Thomas nonchalantly. 'He knows you. He likes you, I know he does. He'll come here for me.'

'No.' Catherine didn't think she could stand that. 'No,' she said again, trying to ignore Thomas's disappointed little face. 'I—er—I have to go out. Now. I—I was just leaving, as a matter of fact. Maybe—some other day . . .'

'But there might not be another day,' Thomas protested.

'Why can't you go out after I've gone? Surely it's not so important. Daddy won't mind, honestly. And he'll be here at any minute, anyway. I thought you'd be pleased to see me.'

Catherine drew an unsteady breath. 'Thomas, you don't understand. I— well, I am delighted to see you, of course, and you know you're welcome to come here at any time, but today I really do have to go out.'

Thomas's face drooped. 'Why? Where are you going? I know you don't have a car because I heard Daddy telling Mr Blake at the garage that your car had broken down.'

Catherine couldn't prevent the faint smile that curved her lips. 'Broken down?' she echoed. 'Well, I suppose you could say that.'

'What happened really? Did you have a crash?'

Thomas was morbidly interested, but Catherine shook her head. 'No. My cousin parked it in a ditch, that's all. And now the exhaust's broken, and it needs a new brake pipe.'

Thomas nodded. 'I liked your car, it was nice. I'd like to be able to drive. Oh, not a Renault, of course. I'd like a Rolls-Royce, or a Jaguar. My grandfather Redvers has a Rolls-Royce. I rode in it once, but he was always saying for me to sit down, and not to fiddle with the controls, and to keep my feet off the seats. He's an awful snob!'

'Now, really, Thomas . . .' Catherine put out a protesting hand. 'You shouldn't talk like that about your grandfather.' She looked apprehensively towards the door as a car sped along the High Street, but it wasn't a green Volvo, and she relaxed a little. 'I expect anyone with a car like that would want to take care of it.'

'Daddy says that cars can only take you from A to B. He likes a fast car, but he doesn't worry about muddy feet, or stop me from turning on the radio or switching on the wipers.'

'Well, I expect your father is more used to a boy of your age,' declared Catherine evenly, realising that this conversation was stretching out of all proportion. 'Thomas——'

'I like my grandfather Penwyth best. He's much more

fun, when he's all there.'

'*Thomas!*'

'Well, it's true.' Thomas was defensive. 'Sometimes he just sits and mutters to himself, and doesn't notice me. I think it's when Mummy's been grumbling at him. He and Mummy don't really like one another.' He grimaced. 'As a matter of fact——'

'Thomas, this has nothing to do with me.' Catherine looked round helplessly. 'Thomas, I really ought to be going . . .'

'Can I see your office?' Ignoring what she had just said, he skipped across to the back of the shop, peering inquisitively into her small den. 'Ooh, isn't it tiny? Daddy's study is heaps bigger than this.'

'Yes, well, your father's study is something else,' agreed Catherine patiently. 'This is only a small shop.'

'Why do you call it Her—Hera——'

'Heraklion?' Catherine supplied, and he nodded. 'Well, because the first garments I designed were after I'd spent a holiday in Greece, and I guess I was influenced by the Greek style.'

'You made all these clothes?' Thomas sounded impressed, but Catherine quickly disillusioned him.

'Oh, no, I didn't actually *make* any of them. I designed a few. You know—drew a picture of what I wanted. But mostly I buy the clothes I sell from fashion warehouses. Not only in this country, but in France, and Italy, places like that.'

'You go to these places?'

'Sometimes,' she nodded. 'And sometimes my assistant in London goes.'

'You have another shop in London?'

'For the time being,' she agreed dryly, remembering Robert's forebodings about the lease. 'Look, Thomas——'

But even as she said these words, she heard someone else come into the shop, and her throat went suddenly dry. Almost in slow motion, she turned, and then felt the warm colour flood into her face at the sight of Lucy Glyndower standing impatiently in the middle of the sales floor. Thomas had seen her, too, but instead of running to her as Catherine had expected, he hung back, half behind her, his lips pursing and unpursing as if he expected trouble.

'What's going on?' Lucy's succinct enquiry fell coldly on the air. 'What is Thomas doing here? Did you fetch him from the school? You had no right to do so, you know. It's not at all convenient for me to waste my time searching for him.'

Catherine was taken aback. Casting a doubtful look down at the boy, she wondered if her initial suspicions of the story he had told her when he first appeared in the shop had been justified. But even if they were, had she the heart to betray him, to explain to his mother that she had had no part in his disappearance from the school?

However, Thomas took the onus from her. 'I came to Miss Tempest's shop on my own,' he declared bravely. 'And—and Miss Mayhew knew where I was.'

'Miss Mayhew told me some cock-and-bull story about you visiting your aunt!' retorted his mother coldly. 'When I told her you didn't have an aunt in Pendower, she had to think again.'

Thomas's confidence faltered. 'I—I thought Daddy would come to collect me,' he murmured innocently, unknowingly saying the one thing which would infuriate his mother most.

'Oh, did you?' Lucy snapped, crossing the floor and grasping his arm with biting fingers. 'I suppose you, like everyone else in the valley, know of your father's weakness for silly little shopgirls!' Her eyes raked Catherine with contemptuous malevolence. 'Or perhaps *little* is the wrong word to use!' Her lips curled. 'You're not the first, Miss Tempest, and I doubt you'll be the last!'

'Mrs Glyndower, *please*——'

'Please? Please what? Are you ashamed that I know of your relationship with my husband?'

'There is no relationship, Mrs Glyndower.' Catherine twisted her hands together, gesturing eloquently towards the boy. 'Please. Thomas——'

'Why shouldn't Thomas hear about it, too? He thinks his sainted father can do no wrong. Well, perhaps now he'll think differently.'

Thomas's face had crumpled. 'Let go of my arm!' he

cried, trying impotently to pull himself away from her. 'I don't care what you say about Daddy. I love him. I love him, do you hear? Better than I love you!'

Lucy slapped him then. In all honesty, Catherine had to admit she was driven to it, but the blow was harder, more vicious, then it need have been, and Thomas rocked on his heels, his dazed expression mirroring the shock he had received.

'Mrs Glyndower!' Catherine had to protest, but Lucy was already dragging her son after her, out of the shop, and there was nothing she could do to stop them. Just for one second Thomas turned to gaze at her before the Volvo pulled away, and then the throbbing rhythm of the disco music filled her head, matching the painful throbbing of her temples.

CHAPTER NINE

She rang Aunt Margaret that evening to let her know that she would not be over for the next couple of days, explaining about the repairs to the Renault, and asking her if she would ensure Juniper was fed. Her aunt was not unwilling, apologising for Owen's carelessness, and promising that she would look after the mare.

'He's pretty shamefaced, I can tell you,' she said, in answer to Catherine's assurance that she didn't blame him for what had happened. 'Will the repairs be very expensive?'

Catherine hadn't really given the matter a lot of thought, but now she conceded to herself that it might prove very expensive indeed. Particularly as the insurance company would deprive her of any bonuses after this.

'Don't worry about it, Aunt Margaret,' she said, realising they had enough on their minds at the moment without having to worry about garage bills, and her aunt thanked her again before ringing off.

During the next couple of days, she tried not to think about Penwyth or the Glyndowers. She refused to contemplate Rafe Glyndower's reactions to his wife's recriminations, or to consider Thomas's feelings towards her after hearing the accusation his mother had thrown. The whole affair was like some terrible nightmare, and one afternoon she found herself seriously considering Robert's suggestion of closing the Pendower branch, and using all her resources to finance a larger shop in London. She could do it, and it would certainly solve all her problems. But even now, the thought of actually leaving the district was like a knife turning in her stomach.

She was scrambling some eggs for her evening meal when the telephone rang. After her thoughts of the afternoon, she would not have been surprised to find Robert telepathically at the end of the line, but to her surprise it was Jeff Mappin.

'I'm spending the evening in Pendower, and I wondered if we could have dinner together,' he said, without too much preamble. 'That is, if you don't have a previous engagement, of course.'

Catherine hesitated. 'I don't have a previous engagement,' she admitted at last. 'But it is rather short notice.'

'My fault,' said Jeff ruefully. 'I've been with my boss for most of the afternoon, and I didn't know until the last minute whether I'd be expected to eat with him.'

'Oh, I see.' Catherine teased him. 'So I'm just a stopgap, am I?'

'Hell no!' Jeff sounded genuinely shocked. 'I wanted to call you yesterday, but I was afraid you'd think it was too soon. I mean, I'd hate you to think I was taking advantage of the situation. But when Mr Norman said he had to go back to Cardiff tonight, I couldn't resist calling you. On the offchance . . .'

'Well, I'm—flattered, of course——'

'Don't say that. It sounds as if you're going to refuse me. Couldn't you—well, couldn't you make it?'

Catherine ran doubtful fingers over her hair. 'I'd have to change . . .' she began reluctantly, not at all sure she ought to go out with him, yet drawn to him because of his association to Rafe, but that was all Jeff needed.

'You'll come?' he exclaimed. 'Oh, marvellous! Look, it's seven o'clock now. How about if I pick you up in, say—twenty minutes?'

'Make it half an hour,' said Catherine, giving in. 'Do you know how to get here?'

'Well, I know the address,' he answered eagerly. 'It's here in the phone book in front of me. But if there are some special instructions you want to give me . . .'

She was ready when he came to the door, not risking any awkward moments in the house. Her dress of apricot-silk chiffon swirled in full pleats about her knees, and with it she wore the dark pigskin coat she had treated herself to for the winter. Its mink collar framed her warm features, her hair smoothly coiled into a knot at the back of her head. Jeff was obviously impressed, and she wondered what he had expected after the jeans and hacking jacket she had worn to the pub.

They ate at the largest hotel in Pendower. The food was hot and plentiful, and what it lacked in variety it more than made up for in flavour.

'This is nice,' remarked Jeff, with some satisfaction, raising his wine glass to her. 'My luck must be changing. I wondered what the devil you'd say when I telephoned you.'

Catherine smiled. 'You're too modest. I'm sure you're never short of female company.'

'How about you?' He gave her an interrogative glance. 'Is there no man on your horizon? No hearty Welsh half-back, just waiting to transplant my teeth?'

Put like that, Catherine had to laugh, albeit a little selfconsciously. She wondered what he would say if she told him she was hopelessly in love with a married man. More than that, if she told him the man's identity . . .

'I'm a career woman,' she said, covering her glass with her hand when he would have refilled it. 'And I have to to have a clear head for work tomorrow.'

'You don't look like a career woman,' declared Jeff, filling his own glass. 'You're far too attractive. You're much more the type to get married and have a brood of kids around you.'

'Do you think so?' Catherine tried to keep her tone light. 'Isn't that rather an old-fashioned concept?'

Jeff shrugged. 'Maybe. People still seem to do it, though.'

'I read somewhere that the family unit is a very delicate framework, liable to crack with the least pressure.'

He shook his head. 'That sounds a very cynical analysis.'

'You don't agree with it?'

'Not particularly.'

'Then why aren't you married?'

He chuckled. 'Good question.'

'You haven't been?'

'No. I once contemplated it, seriously I mean. But it didn't work out?'

'Her fault or yours?'

'You don't pull your punches, do you?' He grinned. 'Mine, actually. I used to have a roving eye.'

'Used to have?'

He shook his head. 'Well, anyway, I've seen enough of the seamier side of marriage to know that some of what you say is true. Even so, there are thousands of couples living quite satisfactory lives, bound by that old-fashioned institution.'

'Yes,' Catherine nodded, her tongue making a circle of her lips. 'I know.'

'Tell me,' Jeff rested an elbow on the table and leaned towards her, 'how well do you know Rafe Glyndower?'

His question was unexpected, and it took all her self-composure to stifle the gasp that rose to her lips. 'I—Rafe?' she said, playing for time. 'Oh, not very well.'

'But you have known him a long time haven't you?' He paused. 'I wondered if you'd based your opinion of marriage on his.'

'No!' She stared at him across the candlelit table, eyes wide and defensive. 'I—why do you say that?'

Jeff's eyes narrowed. Then he shrugged. 'I don't know. I just wondered, I guess.' He drank a little of his wine, and then added: 'I mean, he and Lucy are such opposites, aren't they?'

'I really don't know Mrs Glyndower,' replied Catherine stiffly, wishing she could change the subject. 'Mmm, this steak is delicious, isn't it?'

'Then why aren't you eating more of it?' inquired Jeff dryly, and now her face did flush with embarrassing colour. Immediately he was contrite, saying apologetically: 'Don't take any notice of me, Catherine. I've had a frustrating afternoon, and I guess my social graces have exhausted themselves—I'm sorry. I always seem to say the wrong thing.'

Catherine tasted her wine. 'Don't worry about it,' she murmured, putting the glass aside. 'Tell me about your work. What exactly does a geophysicist do?'

It was an innocuous topic, and successfully saw them

through dessert and coffee, so that it was quite late in the evening before Rafe's name was mentioned again. Then it was Catherine herself who inadvertently brought the Glyndowers into the conversation, replying to Jeff's inquiry about her car by volunteering the fact that she had been unable to ride for the last couple of days.

'I should have thought the weather would deter you anyway,' he replied. 'It's been so damp and cold. Pneumonia weather! Did you know Rafe had succumbed?'

'To pneumonia!'

The horrified words were out before she could prevent them, and Jeff regarded her shocked face with a kind of resigned recognition before reassuring her. 'No, not pneumonia,' he said heavily. 'Just 'flu, I guess. Whatever, he looked pretty sick the last time I saw him.'

Catherine hesitated, trying to make her next words casual. 'Which was when?' she ventured. 'Er—when did you last see him?'

'Yesterday evening.' Jeff's voice was dry now. 'I had dinner at the Manor.'

'Oh.' Catherine swallowed the remainder of the brandy in her glass with a gulp. 'And—and how was he?'

'I told you—he looked lousy to me. Not that he would give in to it. Lucy said she'd asked him to go to bed, but he'd refused. Anyway, I should think the boy—Thomas, do you know him? Yes? Well, I should think he was pretty relieved his father was up, if you know what I mean. He's a nice kid, I like him. He's a lot like Rafe. But his mother—well, I think she should have had a career, not a family. She has no time for that boy, and not only that, she makes it painfully obvious. God, if I was Rafe, I'd feel like strangling her sometimes, the way she speaks to him.'

'To—Rafe?'

'No.' Jeff grimaced. 'To Thomas.' He flicked a speculative look at her. 'But you knew that, didn't you?' He sighed. 'I think you know a lot more than you're admitting. Hell, I should have guessed. An attractive girl like you, unmarried——'

'No! No, you're wrong.' Catherine swallowed convulsively. 'I—there's nothing between—between Rafe and me.'

'No?' Jeff sounded unconvinced, but he shrugged his broad shoulders. 'Well, perhaps not physically.'

'What do you mean?'

'Let me tell you something.' Jeff summoned the waiter and when Catherine refused a drink, he ordered himself another brandy. 'We were students together, you know, Rafe and I—at Oxford. I guess it must be almost fifteen years ago now.' He shook his head. 'Anyway, there was this woman——'

'I—I don't think this has anything to do with me,' Catherine began uncomfortably, but Jeff silenced her with a squeeze of his hand on hers.

'No, listen to me,' he begged. 'This woman, the female in question, she was the wife of one of our professors.' He smiled reminiscently. 'She was quite something—tall and slim and willowy. Years older than us, of course, but not at all the sort of creature you'd expect to be married to someone like Professor Donnelly.'

'What has this to do with me?'

'Let me tell you. As you may have expected, she took a fancy for Rafe——'

'Oh, Jeff——'

'—but he wasn't interested.' He laughed softly. 'Oh, she tried her best—you know, making sure they kept bumping into each other, always attending the same university functions, making it patently obvious what she wanted. The rest of us—*boy!* We'd have jumped at his chances, but we might as well not have existed as far as Mrs Donnelly was concerned.'

Catherine pressed her lips together. 'So what are you saying? That Rafe—really was in love with her?'

'Hell, no! I guess he may have been tempted to give her what she wanted. Who wouldn't be? But she was married, and so far as he was concerned, it was no contest.'

'And?'

'Well, I'm just trying to illustrate what an honourable bastard—oh, sorry!—I mean, that's the kind of man he is.'

Catherine looked down at the table. 'So?'

'Hell, Catherine, you know what I'm trying to say. It's he who's married now. Don't you see that?'

Catherine's face flamed. 'I think you're letting your imagination run away with you, Jeff. Either that, or the brandy has gone to your head.'

'Brandy never goes to my head,' retorted Jeff heavily. Then he stretched out a hand and lifted her chin. 'So what are you saying, Catherine? That the field is clear? That I can joust for the lady's colours?'

Catherine pulled her chin away from his hand. 'I think we ought to be leaving,' she said. 'Like it or not, I do have a job to do in the morning.'

They drove back to the cottage in Jeff's B.M.W. 'Nice car,' said Catherine, as her fingers lingered on the metallic paint. 'The fruits of a bachelor existence, hmm?'

Jeff took her by the shoulders and bent to kiss her lips. 'Why do I get the feeling you don't envy me?' he demanded cynically, when he lifted his head. 'Your lips are cold. Are you going to offer me something to warm us both up?'

'Not tonight.' Catherine shook her head. 'I could only offer you cocoa, and I'm sure that's not what you have in mind. But thank you for a very—edifying evening. I enjoyed it.'

'Did you?' Jeff sounded unconvinced. Then: 'Will you tell Rafe?'

She drew away from him abruptly. 'What makes you think I'll be given an opportunity?'

Jeff opened his car door with an exaggerated sigh. 'Let's say it's an informed opinion.' He levered himself behind the wheel. 'Goodnight, Catherine. Go and make your lonely mug of cocoa. I'm going to take something stronger to help me sleep!'

The garage rang the following morning to let her know her car was ready. Catherine arranged to collect it that afternoon, and realised as she rang off that she now had no excuse to stay away from Penwyn. As soon as Owen knew she was mobile again, he would expect her to attend to the mare, which meant her running the risk of meeting

Rafe again. She would rather not see him, she had decided, in the wee small hours of the morning. In spite of her instinctive reaction to Jeff's revelations, she knew it would be easier not to see him, even though the knowledge of his being ill filled her with dismay.

How could anyone be so foolish she asked herself that morning, labelling a carton of shirts that had arrived from the wholesaler. Unwilling to meet the man for whom she cared desperately, yet unable to move far enough away so that there was no possibility of them ever encountering one another again. It was like living on the knife-edge of temptation, walking a precarious path between two impossible solutions.

She took the bus to Penwyth that afternoon, getting off in the village and collecting her car from the service station. Mr Blake, the proprietor, was very deferential, pointing out the various adjustments which had been made, and assuring her that she should have no further trouble. Even his bill seemed modest after what she had expected, and she speculated that perhaps she would not have to use the insurance after all.

Driving out of the yard, she hesitated before turning back to Pendower. She knew she ought to call at the farm and see how everyone was faring, but censuring herself for a coward, she drove back to town. She would come out to the farm in the morning, she promised herself, remembering it was Saturday, and therefore her free day this week. She had a part-time assistant who helped in the boutique on Saturdays, and she and Mary took it in turns to have the day off.

The telephone was ringing as she arrived home that evening, and she felt slightly guilty when she recognised her aunt's voice. Had someone seen her in the village? Someone who had taken the trouble to report it to her aunt?

'Why didn't you call this afternoon?' Her first words seemed to confirm this belief, but before Catherine could think of a reply, her aunt went on: 'I hope you know I've had Mr Glyndower sitting in my kitchen for over two hours. He expected you to come, and I must say, so did I.'

Catherine sank down weakly on to the cushioned seat beside the telephone. 'Rafe Glyndower?' she echoed faintly. 'You've had him——'

'—for two hours, yes.' Her aunt sounded harassed. 'I didn't know what to say to him, and Mervyn—well, you know what he's like at the moment.'

Catherine tried to gather herself. 'But what did he want?'

'I don't know, do I? To see you, I suppose. Something to do with the horses, I think. He knew your car was ready for collection, and I suppose he expected you to call and see your own family.'

'Oh, Aunt Margaret . . .' Catherine put a bewildered hand to her head, 'I don't know what to say.'

'No more do I.' Her aunt's voice was dry. 'I just hope you know what you're doing, girl, getting involved with a man like him. I mean, it's not as if he was a single man, is it? People will talk. They're talking already——'

'Oh, Aunt Margaret!'

'Is that all you can say? Did you know he was here? Is that why you didn't call?'

'No! *No!*' The silent protest was almost violent in its denial. If she had *known* he would be there . . .

Yet would she have called, knowing that? Could she have faced him in her aunt's kitchen, acted as if that scene the other evening had never happened? Aunt Margaret knew her so well. She had known Rafe a long time too, and even though she called him *Mr* Glyndower these days he was still the boy who had helped with the haymaking, and shared their supper on more than one occasion. Might she have seen behind the masks of politeness they would both have been obliged to adopt? Might doubt have hardened into real suspicion?

'Well?'

Realising her aunt was still waiting for her answer, Catherine quickly made the denial. 'Honestly,' she said, 'I didn't have any idea. He—he's never come to the farm before.'

'Not in recent years,' agreed her aunt dourly. Then, as if wishing to be done with the matter, she added: 'I wish you had come. I had a nice apple pie for you to take home for your supper.'

Catherine sighed guiltily. 'Can you keep it until tomorrow? It's my day off, and I thought I'd come over in the morning.'

'Come for lunch,' invited her aunt generously, and Catherine had agreed and hung up before considering the possible repercussions of Rafe's visit. There was still Owen and her uncle to face, but with a stiffening of her spine, she refused to let them deter her.

It was a frosty night, the sky clear and star-studded as she went to empty her pedal bin into the dustbin. Shivering, she turned back towards the cottage, and then almost jumped out of her skin as a man's tall figure loomed from the shadows at the side of the house.

'Catherine?'

The husky tones were disturbingly familiar, and it was incredibly difficult to answer him calmly. 'What are you doing here?' she demanded. 'Scaring the life out of me? Why didn't you go to the front door and ring the bell like anybody else?'

Her voice was sharp, but she couldn't help it, though she felt a trace of remorse as Rafe replied: 'I did, but no one answered. I could see the kitchen light was on, so . . .' He shrugged. 'I'm sorry if I frightened you.'

Catherine was shivering now. Her smock dress was made of wool, but it was very fine, and the elbow-length sleeves left her forearms bare.

'I—I—what do you want?' she asked, remembering their previous encounter, and telling herself that it mustn't happen again. 'It's too cold to stand here chatting together.'

His back was to the light, and she couldn't see his expression, but she saw the way his shoulders hunched as he pushed his hands into his coat pockets. 'Aren't you going to invite me in?' he countered quietly, and she felt her determination faltering.

'I—no!' she said at last, firmly. 'I—don't think that would be a very good idea.'

He inclined his head briefly in a kind of acknowledgement. Then he said: 'I thought I might see you this afternoon, at Penwyn, but you didn't call.'

'No, I know. That is—Aunt Margaret rang a few minutes ago.' Catherine caught her lower lip between her teeth, to stop them from chattering. 'Is this something urgent? Wouldn't it have been easier to ring?'

'I wanted to talk to you,' he replied simply. 'I didn't realise you would still be angry with me.'

'Angry with you?' Catherine made a sound of exasperation. 'Rafe, you're crazy coming here!'

'Just desperate,' he replied steadily, and with an exclamation of protest she brushed past him into the cottage.

'You—you'd better come in,' she muttered unwillingly, and after a moment's hesitation he followed her into the kitchen, closing the door against the cold night air.

Turning to face him, she was shocked at his pallor. Jeff had not been exaggerating when he had said Rafe looked ill, and she had to twist her fingers together to prevent herself from touching him. His fur-lined grey parka seemed to rob his face of any trace of colour, his dark hair lapping the collar at the back. He unzipped the neckline of the parka in the warmth of the kitchen, but he made no other move towards staying, and she knew she ought to feel relieved.

'So?' she said, moving her shoulders awkwardly. 'What did you want to talk to me about?'

'You're looking well, Catherine,' he said without answering her question, and her nails dug into her palms.

'You're not,' she retorted, and as if to justify her statement, Rafe groped for a handkerchief then to trap the sneeze that erupted from him.

'It's a cold, that's all,' he told her brusquely, irritated by this show of weakness. 'I—you got your car?'

Catherine nodded. 'Yes, thank you.' She hesitated. 'I never thanked you for arranging that.'

Rafe made a gesture of dismissal, before continuing: 'Did your aunt tell you how long I waited?'

Catherine bent her head. 'She—she said you waited quite

a while.' Then, looking up, she added impatiently: 'Don't you think that was a foolish thing to do? Owen has no love for you. He'll enjoy relating the story—with certain embellishments of course.'

'It can't hurt you,' he retorted stiffly, but Catherine could not let it end there.

'It could hurt you! And your family,' she declared, and saw the expression of defeat that crossed his face.

'I know that,' he muttered, long fingers massaging the back of his neck. 'But I had to see you.' His lips twisted. 'Which shows what a bloody fool I am, doesn't it?'

'Oh, Rafe . . .'

The torment in his face was too much for her. Almost involuntarily, she covered the space between them, and unable to resist the temptation, took his face between her two hands and put her mouth to his.

It was heaven feeling him close to her again, his lips parting against her mouth. He made no move to hold her or enfold her, or compel her in any way to stay close to him, but their lips said it all. They exchanged short, urgent kisses that quickened their breathing and inflamed their senses, until they both knew the dangerous line they were treading.

At last Catherine came down off her toes, her hands still lingering at either side of his face, her tongue appearing to savour the taste of his lips. Rafe's eyes were dark with emotion, and the pulse that beat at his jawline revealed the erratic pounding of his heart, though he still made no move to detain her.

'Is this why you wanted to see me?' she breathed, one finger brushing the thick length of his lashes, delighting in the shy intimacy, and he closed his eyes for a moment against the warm invitation in hers.

'I intended to ride with you,' he said at last, opening his eyes again. 'I was sure if you came to Penwyn, you would take out the mare, and I thought it would give us a chance to talk.'

Catherine gazed up at him helplessly. 'But you're not fit to go riding!' she protested, her fingers dropping to the zip on his parka and propelling it slowly downwards. 'You know you're not. And—and I thought—the last time you were here——'

Rafe lifted an unsteady hand to his temple and pushed back the heavy strands of dark hair she had disordered. 'I spoke to Jeff today,' he said, his voice low, and deeper than usual because of his cold. 'He told me you had dinner together last night.'

Catherine's hands fell to her sides. What else had Jeff told him? she wondered, remembering the slant of their conversation. What ideas had Jeff put into his head, that had not been there before? He had not seemed a man of particular sensitivity, and her skin crawled at the possibility that perhaps he had intimated that she was ripe for an affair.

Taking a step back from him, she said coolly: 'Yes, I did have dinner with your friend. He rang me yesterday evening and suggested it, and I saw no reason to refuse.'

'No.' Rafe was watching her intently. 'I thought he might contact you. He finds you very attractive.'

Catherine's nerves stretched painfully: 'Really?' She made an offhand gesture. 'How interesting!'

As if sensing her withdrawal, Rafe took a sudden step forward. 'What's the matter?' he demanded. 'Have I stepped on someone's toes? I'm sorry, but I had to tell you that I knew.'

'I don't see that it matters,' declared Catherine tautly. 'Jeff Mappin has nothing to do with us. Or has he?'

Rafe frowned. 'I don't think I understand——'

'What else did Jeff say to you? Did he regale you with all our conversation, or just part of it?'

'Catherine——'

'No, I mean it. I'd like to know. You see, he had some crazy idea that—that I was involved with—with you!'

'And aren't you?' Rafe asked quietly, his tortured expression almost her undoing, but she managed to maintain an indifferent tone.

'Not—not perhaps to the extent you both imagine,' she retorted jerkily. 'And you have to admit, it is strange that you should come looking for me today, exactly twenty-four hours after my conversation with him!'

Rafe exhaled heavily. 'It doesn't occur to you that I might have—come looking for you today, as you put it, because I wanted to find out for myself exactly what happened between you and Jeff?'

'What happened?' Catherine echoed. 'Nothing happened.'

'And I'm expected to believe that, aren't I?'

She frowned. 'Of course.'

'So—what do you believe? What do you think Jeff told me?' He regarded her half defeatedly. 'Do you think I put him up to asking you out? To find out for myself whether you—slept around?'

'No!' Catherine knew she did not believe that. 'But he—I—he said you were an honourable man. He said you would never jeopardise your marriage.'

'Did he?' Rafe's facial muscles tensed. 'That was good of him.'

Catherine sighed. 'I didn't have to be told, Rafe. I—I knew.'

'Did you?' Rafe gave a resigned shrug. 'So, if you believe that, why did you let me come in?'

Catherine turned away, shaking her head. 'I don't know.' She stretched out a hand and traced the pattern of the formica on the breakfast bar with a restless finger. 'I didn't intend to.'

There was silence for a moment, and then Rafe said quietly: 'Do you want me to go?'

She turned then, staring at him helplessly. 'I—why, *no.*' It was a painful admission, made the more so by the realisation of what he might make of it. 'You must know how I feel. I haven't exactly kept it a secret.'

Rafe took the steps that brought him to stand right in front of her. 'You're saying—you're willing to let me stay here, knowing there's no future in this, for either of us?' he demanded thickly.

Catherine drew a deep breath, not immune to the attraction of his nearness. 'I—suppose I am.' Her heart was pounding rapidly as she looked at him. Then, with great daring, her hands slipped beneath his parka to slide it off his shoulders. 'You—you don't need this on, do you? It—it's very warm in here . . .'

CHAPTER TEN

THE parka dropped to the floor behind him, but for several seconds afterwards Rafe made no move towards her. Then, when her nerves were stretched like violin strings, he pulled her to him, his mouth seeking hers with compelling urgency, his hands sliding possessively down her back to her hips.

He kissed her many times, hard passionate kisses, that demanded and got her fullest response. Her hands were in his hair, at the nape of his neck, holding him closer, and without the limitations of self-restraint upon him, Rafe made no attempt to hold back from her. Every muscle in his body was straining towards her, male and aggressive, penetrating the thin layers of her clothing, bruising in its hardness. His hands arched her body to his, his mouth devouring hers, plundering the sweetness within, until the blockages in his nasal tubes left him cursing and panting for breath.

'God, Catherine,' he groaned, pressing his face into the silken curtain of her hair. 'I shouldn't be holding you like this, infecting you with my germs!' But she only trailed her lips along his cheek and temple until his own need overcame his scruples, compelling him to take what she so eagerly offered.

At last she drew back, saying softly: 'Let's go into the living room, shall we? We'll be more comfortable in there, and your temperature must be sky-high!'

'I'm all right,' he protested, resting his forehead against hers, unperturbed by its burning touch. 'Catherine, I have to tell you something.'

'What?' Immediately a sense of apprehension filled her, and the eyes that gazed so anxiously into his revealed all her inward perturbation.

'Oh, love,' he muttered, his voice shaken with emotion, 'don't look at me like that. I know you probably think I'm all kinds of a bastard really. I mean, coming here, kissing you, wanting to make love to you——'

'Please, Rafe——' She didn't think she could bear it if he walked out on her now. 'It's my decision——'

'I know that.' He bent his head and caressed her lips gently with his own. 'I just wanted you to know that— had circumstances been different——'

'Rafe!'

'—had the estate not been involved——'

'Honestly, Rafe, you don't have to say any of this!'

'I do!' His voice was harsh with feeling. 'Catherine, what I'm trying so incompetently to tell you is—I love you! That's right—I love you. And were it not for my father and Tom, I'd give everything I possess to divorce Lucy and marry you.'

'Rafe——'

'That's all I wanted to say. I know it doesn't mean much——'

'Oh, Rafe!' She moved closer to him, pressing her face to the rough wool of his sweater, feeling the hot wetness of tears against her cheek. 'You didn't have to say anything. I—I know what Penwyth means to you, and—and Tom——'

'You have to know the truth,' he insisted, lifting her chin so that he could see her face. 'Oh, don't cry for me, Catherine.' His tongue erased an errant tear from her cheek. 'I'm not such an honourable fellow, am I? Do you know how I felt when Jeff told me he'd spent the evening with you? I wanted to wring his bloody neck! That's the kind of honourable fellow I am. I was jealous—God, how I was jealous! It was all I could do not to drive straight down to the shop and ask you what the hell you thought you were trying to do to me!' He shook his head self-deprecatingly. 'That's some hold you have on me, love. And I don't honestly know whether I can wait as long as it may take.'

'Wait?' Catherine looked puzzled.

'To live with you,' he said, breaking off to cough violently. 'I'm sorry—this filthy cold. Why did it have to happen now?'

'How did it happen?' she asked, smoothing his hot forehead with her cooler fingers. 'Oh, you're burning up. You ought to be in bed!'

'Yes . . .' His thick lashes veiled his eyes. 'I must go.'

'You can't! That is——' Catherine pressed her lips together helplessly. 'Stay here. I have a bed you can have.'

'Oh, yes.' His voice was dry suddenly. 'You have two bedrooms—you told me. What makes you think I won't do as my son did, and share yours?'

Faint colour invaded her cheeks. 'I can't stop you,' she breathed, her hands sliding beneath his sweater to loosen the buttons of his shirt. 'And I wouldn't try.'

'You're crazy!' Rafe groaned, though his fingers probed the fine bones of her shoulders as if he could not let her go. 'Oh, God, you don't know what you're saying.' He shook his head despairingly. 'And I can't let you take that risk. Not—not without any precautions.'

'Surely that's my decision,' she murmured, tugging his shirt free of his pants and smoothing her palms over the burning skin of his back. 'What you have to decide is whether you're prepared to leave your car outside the cottage all night.'

Rafe hauled her to him, his taut body no less aroused in spite of his fever. 'Do you think I can debate that now?' he demanded. 'With your hands on my body destroying every sane thought in my head?'

Catherine pulled herself back from him. 'Then think about it,' she exclaimed. 'Think about how you'll feel tomorrow. Will you regret it then?'

His hoarse laugh was hollow. 'Very probably,' he agreed, and as Catherine's eyes clouded, he added: 'But not for the reasons you imagine. I can handle my life. I can handle Lucy. It's you I care about.'

'But I——'

'Look, somebody—some, shall we say, do-gooder is going to come to you and warn you about me—either that, or abuse you for getting involved with a married man——'

'I don't care.'

'I do.' Rafe sighed. 'I don't want that for you. I don't want our relationship—*sullied* in that way.'

'Oh, Rafe! You can't protect me. I'm an adult human being, I know what I'm doing. I know what's involved.' Catherine stroked his lips with her own. 'If anyone says anything to me, I shall tell them that you weren't fit to drive home. And no one could deny that's the truth,' she added dryly, touching his feverish skin. 'Come on, I'll show you where you can sleep.'

Her bedroom looked attractive in the lamplight, the green and cream embroidered coverlet turned back to reveal the lime green sheets. There were plain cream walls, and the long gold-coloured curtains at the windows cast mellow shadows. She was glad she had turned on the radiator earlier. Now the room was comfortably warm, and Rafe looked about him appreciatively.

'This is your room,' he said, tugging off his sweater. 'I like it.'

Catherine hesitated in the doorway. 'The bathroom's here,' she said, indicating the second door which opened off the small landing. 'I—I'll go get you a drink.'

'Wait——' Rafe stretched out his hand and caught her wrist, pulling her towards him into the bedroom. 'Help me to undress before you go . . .'

The ringing of the telephone was a harsh intrusion, but Catherine struggled out of his arms to answer it. 'It—it might be important,' she breathed huskily, realising if she didn't answer it, and her aunt heard that Rafe had been seen here . . .

'Don't be long,' Rafe murmured, loath to let go of her hand, and she paused a moment to bestow another kiss on his parted lips.

As she went downstairs she heard Rafe go into the bathroom, and a ripple of excitement slid along her veins. He was actually here, in her house, using her bathroom, sleeping in her bed . . . Just having him here, even if it was to be a fleeting experience, was worth all the backlash it might provoke. And surely, when you loved someone . . .

To her astonishment, it was her mother at the other end of the line. 'Catherine!' she exclaimed, offence evident in every syllable. 'Have you forgotten you have a mother?'

'Oh, Mum . . .' While her nerves were crying: *Not now, not now!* 'Mum, you know how it is.'

'No, I'm afraid I don't know how it is,' declared Mrs Hartley coldly. 'Do you realise it's almost three months since I heard from you?'

'Is it? Is it that long?' Catherine cast a doubtful glance up the stairs, as she heard Rafe go back into the bedroom. 'Well, I'm sorry.'

'Being sorry is not good enough, Catherine. I spoke to Robert the other day, and he tells me you're thinking of closing down the Hammersmith shop.'

'Did he?' Catherine sighed. 'Did he tell you why?'

'Something about a lease, wasn't it?'

'That's right. If the lease isn't renewed, we'll have to close.'

'But Robert also said that he had suggested an alternative, and you'd turned him down.'

Catherine sank down wearily onto the bench seat. 'Opening a bigger shop would have entailed closing the Pendower branch,' she explained resignedly, 'and I don't want to do that.'

Her mother sounded impatient. 'Well, I can't understand you, Catherine, I really can't. Opening the Pendower branch was quixotic enough, but now I hear you're considering making it the only branch.'

'Not through choice, Mum. Didn't Robert explain about the lease?'

'I suppose he did. What I can't understand is why you should want to live in a dead-and-alive hole like Pendower!'

'Pendower isn't like that!' Catherine glanced over her shoulder impatiently. 'Oh, Mum, is that the only reason you rang?'

'No.' Her mother was short. 'I rang to find out why you've crossed your father and me off your visiting list!'

'Graham is not my father, Mum.'

'Oh, I see. You're making him the excuse, are you? Just because you two don't always see eye to eye——'

Catherine pushed back the weight of her hair with a weary hand. 'That's the understatement of the year, Mum, and you know it,' she declared. 'But in any case, I don't have a visiting list, and you've certainly not been crossed off it. I—just haven't been up to town lately.'

'It's some man, isn't it?' Heavens, was her mother reading her mind? 'I thought it might be, and then after I'd spoken to Margaret——'

'You've spoken to Aunt Margaret?' Catherine's lethargy fled. 'What did she say?'

'This and that.' Mrs Hartley could be obtuse when she liked. 'She told me about Mervyn and how this business of the mine is progressing. Apparently he's taken it very badly.'

'Yes.' Catherine could hardly contain her impatience.

'Gillian has the baby soon, doesn't she? That must be a worry for them. What with maybe having to leave the farm and all.'

'Yes.' Catherine's fingers tightened round the receiver.

There was a pause, and then her mother went on more slowly: 'She also told me there was some talk about you in the village.'

'Oh?' Catherine hoped her words were not too revealing of her feelings. 'Really?'

'Yes, really.' Mrs Hartley's tones were clipped. 'You needn't try to pretend with me, Catherine. You know to what I'm referring.'

Catherine expelled her breath unevenly. 'What if I do?'

'Oh, Catherine!' Her mother's aggravation was evident. 'Lord Penwyth's son! And he's *married!* Have you taken leave of your senses?'

'I don't think that's anyone's concern but our own,' replied Catherine quietly, although she could not prevent the tremor in her voice. 'Aunt Margaret had no right to gossip.'

'But people do, Catherine. All the time. And how did you get to know him, anyway? When I was a girl, we were lucky if we saw his father riding by.'

Catherine hesitated, then she said quietly: 'Do you remember those summers I spent at Penwyn when I was a little girl?'

'You mean you got to know him then?'

'Yes. He used to come to the farm a lot, until he went away to university.'

'Good lord!' Mrs Hartley sounded genuinely shocked. 'No wonder you were always so keen to spend your summers with your uncle and aunt. And I thought you liked the outdoor life.'

'I did.' Catherine defended herself. 'You don't imagine

Rafe—that is, oh——'

'You might as well go on,' put in her mother dryly, and with a sigh she continued:

'What I mean is—well, he was a lot older than I was. There was nothing between us then.'

'But how did you meet him again?'

Catherine glanced up the stairs, but her bedroom door was closed, and reluctantly she explained: 'Uncle Mervyn asked me to speak to him about the mine. Our—our relationship—well, he thought Rafe might listen to me.'

'But he didn't.'

'He couldn't. Oh, it's a long story. I'll tell you some time.'

'How about tomorrow?' suggested her mother brusquely. 'I think you owe us a visit. Come for the weekend. It's the least you can do.'

'I can't, not tomorrow.' Catherine licked her lips as her mother made a sound of annoyance. 'You don't understand. I have a horse to care for. Oh—not my horse,' she hastened to add, 'Rafe's. He—he's loaned it to me, and I've promised Aunt Margaret I'll go over to the farm in the morning.'

'Come after lunch, then.' Her mother was relentless. 'At least then you'll have the whole of Sunday. Until the evening, of course.'

Catherine closed her eyes, praying for inspiration, but no reasonable excuse presented itself.

'Well?'

Her mother was waiting, and with a gesture of resignation she complied. 'All right, I'll be there some time tomorrow. But I'll have to leave again on Sunday afternoon. It's a long drive back in the dark.'

'Good.' Mrs Hartley was pleased. 'You can tell me all your news then.'

'Yes,' agreed Catherine submissively, but as she replaced her receiver, she wondered how much more her mother would want to know.

With the call over, she went towards the stairs again, her fingers trembling as they trailed up the banister. She was nervous now, as nervous as a kitten, and she wished with all her heart that her mother had not chosen this particular evening to ring. What was that expression? *In cold blood?* That was how she was feeling. Her blood was cold. It had cooled sitting in the chilly atmosphere of the hall, that had never fully benefited from the heating in other parts of the cottage, and it was getting colder than ever as she mounted the stairs. The full implications of what she was doing were filling her mind with doubts and uncertainties, and what had seemed right and necessary in the heat of Rafe's lovemaking was taking on a different image in the harsh light of deliberation.

She halted on the landing, torn by the conflicting emotions inside her, and then, taking a deep breath, she went towards the door of her room. It was slightly ajar, and as she pushed it wider, her eyes took in the lamplit intimacy of the scene. Rafe had discarded the rest of his clothes and they were strewn with careless abandon on the basket chair by the window. His suede boots lay on their sides in the middle of the carpet, and as her gaze swept compulsively up over the tumbled bedding, she saw the upper half of his naked torso, brown against her green sheets.

But he was *asleep!* Blinking, she stared at him, all her earlier emotions rekindled at the sight of him, realising his weakness had overwhelmed him. He was breathing through his mouth, the hectic signs of his fever colouring his pale cheeks, and even as she ventured nearer the bed, he twisted restlessly, turning to bury his face in the pillows.

He partially discarded the covers as he did so, and she moved hastily forward to replace them again. She tried not to look at his muscular body, not to give in to the feeling of anti-climax that was gripping her. He was unwell, she had known that. Who knows, he might never have come here at all if he had not been running a high temperature. But that didn't prevent the wave of frustration she felt towards her mother for destroying the tenuous chance that had been hers.

Tucking the covers more securely about him, she turned out all but the bedside lamp, and left the room. Downstairs again, the fire needed tending, and she fed it some logs before making herself a cup of Horlicks. She needed something to make her sleep, she thought, curling up on the couch in front of the fire, wondering if ever any would-be mistress had suffered such an experience.

The idea of watching television didn't appeal to her, and she put her book aside after reading one page more than three times without understanding a word she had read. The awareness of the man upstairs disrupted all coherent thought, and she spent some time just gazing into the fire, wondering what her mother would think if she could see her now.

It was nearly eleven when she eventually went up to bed. She was carrying a hot water bottle, the electric blanket on her bed of little use to her in the spare room. However, her nightshirt was in the room that was now Rafe's, and besides, she wanted to turn out the lamp, so she tentatively entered the main bedroom once again.

As before, Rafe had kicked the covers aside, and adopting what she hoped was a detached air, she went to cover him again. Almost compulsively, her hands lingered on his shoulders, but she drew back in surprise when she felt how cold he was. With a worried frown, she bent over him, spreading her fingers on his forehead, less worried about waking him than reassuring herself of his condition.

He was still burning up with fever, and biting her lip she seated herself on the side of the bed, looking down at him anxiously. There was no way she could ensure that he kept the blankets over him, unless she did as she had intended all along, and shared the bed with him.

Without giving herself time to change her mind, she undressed, slipping the folds of her nightshirt over her head before drawing back the covers and sliding into the bed beside him.

It was a strange experience, and as she turned out the lamp it crossed her mind that no girl could ever have had a less romantic start to a relationship. Yet, as she felt the muscular length of him beside her, vulnerable now as he had never been awake, a curious sensation of contentment gripped her. And when Rafe moved, imprisoning her beneath the encircling weight of his arm, she turned towards him and gave herself up to the thrill of spending the night in his arms.

There was a moment when he drew back, when her nearness half aroused him from his inertia, and he muttered something about her keeping away from him. But then, even in the darkness, he seemed to sense who it was he held in his arms, and with a groan of satisfaction he drew her closer, and slept again with her hair beneath his head.

Catherine had not expected to sleep at all. She was not used to sharing a bed with anyone, and the circumstances were so unusual, she had assumed she would spend a wakeful night. Yet she did sleep, marvellously soundly, not needing an electric blanket or a hot water bottle, and the grey light of morning had filled the room before she opened her eyes.

Immediately she turned to look at Rafe. He was still asleep, and her lips twitched with wry tenderness. She wondered how he would react when he discovered what she had done, and then dismissed the thought in awareness that the feverish colour had gone from his cheeks. Gently, so as not to disturb him, she touched his forehead, and found that it was much cooler than it had been the night before, almost normal in fact. The crisis point must have passed some time in the night, and now he would begin to recover.

But even as this realisation came to her, she remembered her thoughts of the night before. Would he have come to the cottage, would he have stayed, if he had not been mildly delirious with the fever? And if not, how would he feel to find she had shared his bed, whether he liked it or not?

Moving carefully, she managed to get a leg out of bed, levering herself from under his detaining arm, tugging her hair gently from beneath his cheek. Then, cold and shivery on the bedside rug, she gave in to the temptation she had known ever since she opened her eyes to find him beside her. She bent and put her mouth to his parted lips, lingering longer than she had intended at the sensuous response she aroused.

When she finally forced herself to draw away, he was already stirring, and gathering up her dressing gown, Catherine hastened into the bathroom. With the door locked, she rested against it, closing her eyes, realising she had had no cause for alarm the night before. She had only to see Rafe, only to touch him, for her blood to overheat madly, and race like a blistering torrent through her veins.

She cleaned her teeth, and washed her face and hands, and then emerged again on to the landing. There was no sound from her room, but she couldn't resist looking inside, and tentatively, she put her head around the door.

The bed was empty. The covers had been thrown aside and Rafe's clothes were missing from the chair by the window. Arched brows narrowing in surprise, she turned, a frown tilting down the corners of her mouth, and as she did so, two strong hands descended on her shoulders. Wrapped in her own peculiar misery, she had not heard him ascending the stairs, but when his hands slid intimately over the sides of her breasts to her waist, drawing her back, she could not prevent herself yielding against him. He bent his head to put urgent lips against her nape, then after stroking her ear with his tongue, he sucked in his breath with sudden impatience.

'Why didn't you wake me?' he demanded, turning her in his arms until she was facing him.

'I—I didn't realise you wanted to be up,' she protested obtusely, and the compression of his mouth revealed his awareness of her fabrication.

'You know what I mean,' he declared, shaking her gently, so that the lapels of her gown parted slightly to reveal the provocatively unbuttoned neckline of her nightshirt. 'Do you realise what time it is? Like it or not, I have to go now. I have an appointment with Marland in less than an hour. It's almost half past ten!'

'It can't be!' Catherine was appalled.

'I assure you it is.' Rafe's eyes darkened as they lingered on the rapid rise and fall of her full breasts. 'God! I don't want to leave you, but——' He released her abruptly. 'I must.'

Catherine swayed a little as he let her go. 'I—I'm sorry,' she ventured. 'I don't normally oversleep——'

'You don't normally sleep with me,' he retorted, destroying once and for all her hopes that perhaps he had not been aware of her presence in his bed. 'But you'll be happy to know I feel a hundred times fitter this morning, even though I could flay myself for what happened last night.'

'Wh-what happened?' Catherine's lips parted, and his hands went towards her, only to be withdrawn again.

'Nothing!' he declared harshly. 'That's what I mean. I've ruined your reputation, for a good night's sleep!'

Catherine felt weak with relief. 'I—I don't mind——'

'No. But I do.' Giving in to an impulse stronger than himself, he hauled her close to him again, seeking her mouth with his own and reducing her in seconds to a clinging supplicant. 'You see!' he groaned. 'I can't leave you alone.'

Catherine's shaky laughter was barely audible. 'I—I was afraid it was the—the fever,' she confessed, when his expression darkened ominously. 'Oh, Rafe—darling! I love you!'

He was not proof against such endearments, and her breasts swelled beneath the probing caress of his hands as he slid her nightshirt from her shoulders. But although his embrace was urgent, it was also all too short, and with a strangled sound he pulled her gown back into place.

'Not now,' he muttered, stroking back the damp tendrils of hair from her forehead with his thumbs. 'Tonight. I'll come back tonight. And I promise I'll remain conscious this time.'

'No.' Catherine felt wretched, but she had to shake her head. 'I can't see you tonight.'

'Why not?' Rafe's expression revealed his lack of comprehension. Then his eyes narrowed. 'You have another engagement?'

'In a manner of speaking.' Catherine gazed helplessly up into his face. 'Oh, darling, don't look like that. Do you remember that call I had yesterday evening? Oh, yes, of course you must.' She hastened on, in no way reassured by his attitude. 'Well, it was from my mother——'

'Your mother?'

'Yes. Do you remember her? I think you met her once when she came to fetch me home from Penwyn.'

'Go on.'

'Well, it was she who called. I'm afraid I've neglected her lately, and she—she insisted I drove up to London this weekend, to stay with her and my stepfather.'

'I see.' Rafe was studying her features intently. 'So you're going to London,' he affirmed heavily. 'This weekend.'

'Yes, oh, yes.' Disregarding his earlier withdrawal, she pressed herself against him, delighting in the freedom to touch him at will. 'I don't want to go, you know that. But she is my mother——'

'Of course.' Rafe disengaged himself with taut composure. 'It's probably just as well. I may not be free until late this evening.'

Catherine's lips quivered. 'And of course, Lucy may not allow you to escape two nights running,' she declared bitterly, stung by his acceptance.

Rafe turned to her then, the violence of his mouth on hers destroying the crippling doubts that his detachment had evoked. 'How do you think I feel, knowing your friend Robert is in London?' he demanded, when they were both breathless. 'And I don't like the idea of you driving all that way alone. I'd take you myself, only I'm expected to have lunch with Marland, and God knows what time I'll be able to get away.'

Catherine smiled up at him now, secure in the knowledge of his feelings for her. 'I'll be okay,' she insisted, stroking the shadow of beard on his jawline. 'You need a shave. I'm sorry, I don't have a razor.'

Rafe forcefully put her away from him and went halfway down the stairs. 'I've got to go,' he muttered, raking back his hair with an unsteady hand. 'When will you be back?'

'Sunday evening.' Catherine leant over the banister, unaware as she did so of the shadowy hollow of her cleavage exposed to his gaze. 'Why? Will I see you then?'

Rafe's impatience with himself was half humorous. 'Go and get dressed,' he advised huskily. 'Until tomorrow . . .'

'But you haven't had any breakfast,' she protested, as he reached the hall, and he pulled on his parka with wry determination.

'I'll survive,' he assured her, walking to the door. 'Drive carefully.'

'You, too,' she called, but all she heard in reply was the slamming of the door after him.

CHAPTER ELEVEN

CATHERINE awakened on Sunday morning with a distinct feeling of apprehension hanging over her. She couldn't at first ally it to the strangeness of her surroundings, and then she remembered where she was and what had happened the night before.

It had been late in the evening before she arrived at her mother's house. The drive had been accomplished without incident, except that she was tired at the end of it, but she had not left Penwyn much before teatime. Oversleeping on Saturday morning had meant it was almost lunchtime before she arrived at the farm, and after accepting her aunt's invitation to share the midday meal with them, it was well into the afternoon before the stables were mucked out and Juniper exercised. She could have asked Rafe to make some other arrangement, but she hadn't wanted to. Ordinarily, she loved these chores, and it was almost a week since she had ridden. But the prospect of the long drive ahead of her had soured the day somewhat, and not even the rumour going around that there was not enough lead in the valley to warrant a full-scale exploration could entirely lift her mood. Nevertheless, it was good to see her uncle showing a little more enthusiasm for his lunch, and actually entering into the conversation from time to time. She would have liked nothing better than to stay at Penwyn for the rest of the day, knowing that Rafe was only a couple of miles away at the Manor.

Her welcome in London, on the other hand, was another matter. Her mother was waiting for her with unconcealed impatience, pouncing on her the minute she arrived, demanding to know why it had taken her so long to get there.

'I knew you didn't want to come,' Mrs Hartley declared, sniffing expressively, 'but I never thought you'd keep me waiting and worrying all day and night as well.'

Catherine sighed. 'Mum, I told you I had to go to Penwyn——'

'To attend to some horse—yes, I know.' Her mother emphasised the connotation. 'It seems to me that animal means more to you than I do.'

'Oh, Mum!' Futilely, Catherine tried to explain how she had slept in on Saturday morning, and in consequence had wasted half the day. 'I didn't do it deliberately. I'm sorry I'm late, and I'm sorry you've been worried, but I'm here now, and—and it's lovely to see you.'

Her apologies hadn't worked, though, and her stepfather had added his recriminations to those of her mother. 'Young people today,' he intoned, 'they don't care. They leave home, leave their parents, live their own lives without thought for the people who've cared for them, looked after them, expected some degree of loyalty from them. You left home——'

'I am twenty-five, Graham!' Catherine pointed out wearily. 'Not a child any longer. And if my apologies aren't good enough, there's nothing else I can do.'

'You don't know how your mother's looked forward to you coming,' he exclaimed. 'Talking over old times . . . Women's talk!'

'But——'

Before Catherine could defend herself, however, her mother broke in. 'And you'll be leaving straight after lunch tomorrow, won't you? Hardly worth the journey, was it? What with Robert coming for lunch tomorrow, and church in the morning.'

Catherine knew what was coming next, and her stepfather voiced what she had feared. 'Why don't you stay over until Monday? Surely that assistant of yours can manage for one day. You can give her a ring and let her know you won't be coming in. Monday's not such a busy day I'm sure.'

And that was why this morning she felt such a towering weight of depression. There seemed no way she could escape from the inevitable, and in spite of her own feelings, she knew she would not disappoint her mother now. After all, it was weeks since she had seen her, and months since she had stayed here. It wasn't so much to ask, not if she could ignore the hard core of anxiety that gripped her every time she thought of Rafe.

She contemplated phoning Rafe while they were out, but baulked at the prospect of possibly reaching Lucy Glyndower first. If only she had asked him to ring her! But she had had no intention of staying on when she left Pendower. She did ring Mary Grant, however, and explained the situation to her.

'No problem,' Mary assured her confidently. 'Stay till Tuesday, if you like. I can cope.'

'Oh, no!' Catherine was glad her mother wasn't around to hear that. 'I'll be back tomorrow evening. I'll see you Tuesday.'

'All right.' Mary was unperturbed. 'Enjoy yourself.'

'Thank you.' Catherine's tone was wry. 'I probably won't, but don't let that worry you.'

Mary laughed. 'No?' She paused. 'As a matter of fact, I was surprised to hear you were in London,' and her casual remark set Catherine's nerves on edge once again. 'I mean, I heard a green Volvo was seen outside your cottage yesterday morning. Or is that who you're with in London? I promise I won't tell.'

'I'm at my mother's house!' Catherine retorted, her pulses racing even so. 'Honestly, it's impossible to do anything in Pendower without it becoming a subject for conjecture!'

'You knew that before you came here,' observed Mary dryly. 'And I'm being generous. Some people might suggest that it had been there all night.'

Catherine made some brief response, then rang off as soon as she decently could. But after the receiver was replaced, the implications of Mary's gossip struck her with devastating force. She had known there would be talk; how could they avoid it? But somehow, the anticipation and the realisation were two very different things. It wasn't her reputation exactly, although it wasn't pleasant anticipating the comments which might be made about her, it was more the realisation of how their relationship could be interpreted. Without knowing how Rafe felt about her, it was so easy to see what might be construed, and she had no means of defence. She could not go around telling people that he loved her. No one would believe her in any case, she thought hollowly. Unlike Lucy, she would be deemed 'the other woman', the interloper, the destructive element that was tearing their marriage to pieces. It would be useless arguing that the destructive elements had been at work long before she came on the scene. People were arbitrary in their judgments. They only dealt in facts. And the fact was, she had it in her power to arrest their relationship before anything irrevocable happened.

She was taut and on edge when Robert arrived for lunch. His kiss became a perfunctory thing when she turned her face aside, and he was hard put to it to maintain his good humour when her stepfather offered him a drink before the meal.

'Just sherry, of course,' Mr Hartley essayed meaningfully. 'Can't afford anything stronger these days, the cost of living being what it is, and so on. A civil servant's salary goes nowhere.'

'Perhaps if you contributed less to that organisation of yours, you'd be better off,' Catherine was stung to reply, aware that his remarks were directed at her. He had never truly forgiven her mother for advancing her enough cash to convince the bank of her viability, and the success of her business ventures was a sore point with him. It didn't seem to matter that she had since repaid her mother, with interest. He seemed of the opinion that she owed them something, and while Catherine would never see her mother in difficult straits, she refused to offer money which would ultimately find its way into the party treasury.

'Isn't this nice?' her mother interposed before her husband could make any cutting response. 'All of us together again for Sunday lunch.' She turned to Robert. 'We see too little of both of you these days. I think it's about time you called a halt to all this nonsense.'

'Mum!' Catherine was horrified, particularly after their

conversation two evenings ago, and even Robert looked slightly uncomfortable.

'I'm afraid I have no influence with your daughter, Mrs Hartley,' he declared regretfully. 'Like you, I wish she'd give up this crazy idea of living in Wales, but she seems determined to ruin herself.'

'I trust you mean—financially?' Catherine enquired, steeling herself not to lose her temper. 'In which case, you couldn't be more wrong. The Pendower boutique is doing famously.'

'Are you going to visit Sarah while you're here?' Robert changed the subject abruptly, and when she made no reply, he went on: 'I think you should. There are matters that require your attention.'

'What matters?' Catherine's fingers curled into her palms. 'Sarah knows her job as well as I know mine. She hasn't asked for my assistance.'

'You should look at the books.' Robert was persistent, and she felt her patience shredding in the complex turmoil of her thoughts.

'That's what I pay you for, Robert,' she retorted now, wondering how she had ever imagined she could come here without getting embroiled in this kind of conversation. 'Have you heard any more about the lease? Or was that just another of your little ploys to—bring me to my senses?'

'It's—possible the lease will be renewed,' conceded Robert huffily, and her lips parted in disbelief.

'You mean—you mean you've known this without telling me?' she exclaimed angrily, throwing off her mother's warning fingers, and Robert adopted an air of injured dignity.

'I didn't think you were particularly interested, the last time I broached the subject,' he responded, shifting beneath her intent gaze like an insect on a pin. 'So long as the status quo is maintained, you're prepared to rest on your profits, however small, like—like a laurel wreath!'

Catherine gasped. 'That's not true——'

'It is true.' Robert gained confidence from her

shocked expression. 'Why, only the other day, Sarah was saying to me that she'd like to expand, to move into a larger store. She's not afraid of the responsibility it might entail.'

'Oh, really, you two! Stop it!' Mrs Hartley was clearly wishing she had never started this altercation, but Catherine wasn't listening to her.

'Well, here's something else for you to think about,' she asserted coldly, crumbling the roll on her plate without regard for its edibility. 'I'm thinking of selling the Hammersmith shop, with or without the lease, and I'll find another accountant to handle my affairs in Pendower!'

Of course, afterwards, she regretted her own recklessness. It had been born of the uncertainty of her association with Rafe, and her mother's coy references to a relationship with Robert. She felt torn in half a dozen directions, not really knowing which she ought to take. Thomas's innocent little face kept imposing itself upon her mind, and the realisation of his involvement in all this could not be ignored. And Robert? He was not to blame for the complexity of her problems, nor Sarah a brunt for her own inadequacy. She had made a mess of her life; was she now to make a mess of theirs?

In spite of her boorishness, Robert stayed most of the afternoon, talking to her mother and parrying her stepfather's efforts to interest him in his nationalist policies, and when it was time for him to leave, Catherine accompanied him into the hall.

'I wanted to apologise,' she said, closing the glass door which shut them into the privacy of the lobby. 'I haven't really thought of selling the shop. But—well, I'm a bit—chewed up at the moment. Maybe I need a holiday, to get things into perspective again.'

Robert's withdrawn expression gentled. 'It's okay,' he said, after a minute. 'I should have told you about the lease. I guess we've both got problems. Only you could solve mine, whereas I can't solve yours, can I?' Catherine shook her head, and he sighed before continuing: 'Your mother told me, you know. When she rang and invited me for lunch today, she said she was worried about you.'

'Oh, no!'

'Don't worry.' Robert grimaced. 'It's nothing to do with me, and I shan't say anything to anybody. But, if you need any help . . .'

Catherine twisted her hands together. 'Thanks.'

'My pleasure.' Robert touched her cheek lightly, before running down the steps to where his car was waiting. 'Look after yourself. I'll be in touch.'

It was hard, contemplating going back into the living room to face her mother and Graham Hartley. The prospect of the evening loomed ahead of her, fraught with more questions, more reproaches, more accusations. She had little doubt that her mother would use the time to do everything she could to persuade her to leave Pendower and return to London, and she didn't know if she was strong enough to face that tonight. Rafe, oh, Rafe, she thought despairingly, why did I ever have to fall in love with you?

The ringing of the doorbell behind her was a startling intrusion into her abstraction. For a moment she didn't know what it was, but then comprehension dawned on her, and with a clearing shake of her head, she went to answer it.

The man waiting on the steps outside stifled the breath in her throat. It was as if her desperate need of him had been miraculously made manifest. She stared at him disbelievingly for several palpitating seconds, and then she went towards him urgently, hands outstretched, hungry for the security of his arms.

'Rafe . . .' she breathed, lifting her face to him, and then halted abruptly at the sight of the boy just coming up the steps behind his father. 'I—why—Thomas!'

'I brought him with me. I hope you don't mind.' Not letting her draw back, Rafe bent his head and bestowed a light kiss on her parted lips. 'I hoped I wouldn't be too late. The traffic coming into the city was murderous.'

'But—I——'

Catherine got out no more than that before Thomas had reached them, and Rafe let go of her fingers to place a reassuring hand on the boy's shoulder.

'Hello, Miss Tempest.' Thomas grinned up at her cheerfully. 'I bet you're surprised to see us.'

Catherine gave a helpless shake of her head, and as she did so, Mrs Hartley came bustling through from the hall. 'Catherine! Who are you keeping waiting on the step? Is it a friend of Graham's? Oh—I'm awfully sorry . . .' She had seen Rafe and Thomas. 'Do I know you, Mr—er——'

'This is Mr Glyndower, Mother,' Catherine explained, with some reluctance, and Mrs Hartley gazed at her incredulously.

'*Mr Glyndower?*' she echoed, turning to look at Rafe again. 'I—don't think I understand.'

'I've come to drive your daughter home, Mrs—er—Hartley,' Rafe declared politely, only the tightening of his fingers on Thomas's shoulder giving any indication of his feelings. 'I—had business in town, and I thought I would save her the trouble. I've brought my gardener's son with me to drive her car back.'

'Oh, but you're mistaken, Mr Glyndower,' Mrs Hartley put in quickly. 'My daugher is not driving back to Wales tonight. We—er—I've persuaded her to stay over for a couple of days——'

'One day, Mother!' Catherine turned desperate eyes in Rafe's direction. 'I—I was going to drive back tomorrow.'

'Oh, I see.' His disappointment was almost tangible, and suddenly she knew she could not let him go. She loved her mother, of course she did. But her mother was not alone, she had Graham, while she might never have more than this small part of Rafe's life. How could she give it up?

'I—I think,' she said carefully, 'in the circumstances, as Mr Glyndower had gone to the trouble of—of coming here——'

Her eyes met Rafe's across his son's head, and her pulses raced at the passionate darkening of emotion she saw there. It was as if there was only their two selves, isolated in the awareness of their feelings for one another, sharing an intimacy as penetrating in essence as if he had touched her.

'You're not leaving, Catherine!'

Her mother's cry of protest was superseded by her step-father appearing behind her, adding his voice to the proceedings. 'What is going on, Emily?' he grumbled, but Catherine was no longer perturbed by their combined weight of disapproval.

'Er—this is Mr Glyndower, Graham,' she explained coolly, guessing he would recognise the name. 'Rafe, this is my stepfather. My mother, I think, you've already met.'

'Must we carry out these introductions on the door-step?' Graham Hartley was disconcerted by the other man's presence, and at his invitation they all moved into the hall, Thomas looking about him inquisitively as the nuances of the conversation went over his head.

'Do I hear correctly? You've come to take Catherine back to Pendower?' Graham raised his brows interrogatively, striving for superiority, and Rafe inclined his head. 'But she's come in her own car.'

'He's brought someone with him to drive Catherine's car,' inserted Mrs Hartley stiffly. 'Isn't that right, Mr Glyndower?'

'What are those things?'

Thomas chose that moment to intervene, and Catherine bent to him eagerly, glad of the momentary interruption. 'What?' she asked, and then discovering in which direction his attention was drawn, she laughed: 'They're knob-kerries,' she told him. 'African clubs. They're a kind of weapon, and very heavy.'

'Really, Catherine, I think you might pay attention to the conversation,' her stepfather exclaimed, but Thomas was asking where they had come from, and it was Rafe who spoke for her.

'I'm sure you'll agree that the journey to Pendower is a long one to make alone, Mr Hartley,' he said politely. 'I assume part of the reason for persuading Catherine to stay was to avoid her driving all that way in the dark. That was my own intention also.'

Catherine straightened after answering Thomas's questions. 'I'll get my things,' she said, patting her mother's arm appealingly in passing. 'Why don't you give Rafe a drink, while I get ready?'

Their departure was decidedly chilly, but Catherine knew her mother well enough to realise that some small part of her appreciated Rafe's concern, even if she did deplore their relationship. She had never approved of her daughter driving long-distances alone, and she unwillingly agreed to hand over the keys of the Renault to Philip Laurence, when he returned from visiting his sister in Fulham.

Thomas had given up his seat in the Volvo, at his father's request, and scrambled goodnaturedly into the back, but Catherine, loath to spoil the boy's pleasure, said she could easily sit in the back herself.

'No, you can't,' Rafe stated shortly, and the pressure of his hand at her elbow deterred any further argument in the matter. He saw her seated before closing the door, and then strode round the vehicle to climb in beside her.

After the small Renault, the Volvo felt big and luxurious, and almost unconsciously Catherine relaxed against the soft upholstery. She was going home, she thought with satisfaction, and she could think of nothing else she would rather do—except perhaps go home with Rafe.

'Are you glad we came for you?' That was Thomas, jumping about in the back, resting his elbows on the backs of their seats, and arousing his father's impatience when he completely blocked the rear-view mirror with his head. 'This is a better car than yours, isn't it? Much bigger. Do you wish you had a car like this?'

'Shut up, Tom, will you?' After listening to Catherine's patient assurance that it was indeed a nicer car, Rafe silenced his son with a quelling glance. Then, glancing at his other passenger, he said: 'Did you really want to come back tonight?'

'Oh, yes.' Catherine looked sideways at him, her eager expression still visible in the light from the shop windows they were passing. 'But it was so late when I arrived last night——'

'I know. Your aunt told me how late it was when you left Penwyn.'

'My aunt?' Catherine gazed at him, and he moved his shoulders in an offhand gesture.

'How else do you think I found out your mother's

address?' he asked practically, and her lids lowered abruptly.

'Was that—wise?' she murmured, concentrating on pleating the folds of her camelhair skirt, and his fingers came to change the gear with a certain amount of suppressed violence.

'Probably not,' he agreed, turning his head to ascertain that the road was clear before joining the dual carriageway that would eventually take them out of the city. 'It was necessary, that's all.'

Catherine's tongue circled her lips. 'Why—why did you have to come to London?' She glanced over her shoulder at Thomas, now engaged in counting the cars they were passing. 'Or was that invented for my mother's benefit?'

Rafe's sideways glance was eloquent. 'No,' he said, at last, adjusting the heat control. 'I brought Sir George Marland back to town.'

'Oh!' Catherine felt suitably chastened by this news, but before she could say anything more, he added dryly:

'You may be interested to know that the mine project has been abandoned. The consensus of opinion is that there's not enough ore there to warrant the expense that would be involved.'

'Oh, Rafe!' She couldn't keep the warmth out of her voice, but her fingers which had automatically reached for his arm were hastily withdrawn. 'I mean——' she was restricted by the awareness of his son behind them, 'I'm so *relieved*!

'I thought you might be.' Rafe's lips twisted wryly. 'It solves your uncle's problems, at least. I gave him an undertaking that if the mine project was abandoned, he could buy Penwyn.'

Catherine looked at him helplessly, wanting to touch him, yet unable to do so. 'Have—have you told Uncle Mervyn yet?' she asked, trying to keep the emotionalism out of her voice, and Rafe nodded.

'I used that as an excuse to call at the farm,' he replied. 'I think I've redeemed myself, as far as your family is concerned.'

'Mummy was furious!' put in another voice, from the back seat, dispelling once and for all Catherine's hopes that perhaps Thomas was not listening to them. 'She said she was fed up with being as poor as a church mouse, and if Daddy didn't find some money soon she'd divorce him!'

'Tom!'

His father's harsh use of his name silenced the boy, but Catherine's attention had been caught by the boy's words. Turning sideways, she met Rafe's look of entreaty, and for once in their relationship, she could not condone it. Instead, she looked down at her hands in her lap, wondering why the phrase 'Out of the mouth of babes and sucklings . . .' should suddenly have such bitter connotations.

The pregnant silence stretched, and Catherine sought desperately for something to say. Anything to divert attention from her own shaken disposition. It was necessary to behave as if Thomas's words had never been uttered, as if she had never learned that Lucy might consider a divorce.

'*Catherine!*' When her spirits were at their lowest ebb, Rafe spoke again, his voice harsh and desperate. 'Catherine, don't prejudge me, please! You don't know the half of it!'

'No.' Catherine made an offhand movement of her shoulders. 'Probably not.' She forced a note of indifference into her voice. 'And you don't have to explain yourself to me. I mean, it's nothing to do with me, is it?'

'*Damn you!*' His knuckles stood out sharply as his hands closed tightly against the wheel, squeezing it between his fingers, as if it was some kind of symbolic instrument of torture. He looked sideways at her, exhorting her response, and then dragged his eyes back to the road, blinking in the glare of undipped headlights. 'Catherine, won't you at least give me the benefit of the doubt? I've never lied to you. Why should you assume I've done so now?'

Thomas was looking from one to the other of them with interested eyes and casting an eloquent glance in the boy's direction, she said: 'Isn't it late for Thomas to be up? Doesn't he have to go to school tomorrow?'

'School's still closed,' the boy declared cheerfully. 'They haven't fixed the roof yet. You know—after the storm.'

'Oh, yes.'

Catherine nodded, and Thomas went on: 'Do you know, Daddy had to drive to Pendower that night, and when he came back the road was flooded.'

'Tom!'

That was his father again, sounding rather weary now, and Thomas took advantage of the change of tone. 'It's true!' he declared, as Catherine cast a frowning look in Rafe's direction. 'He had to spend the night in the car, and that was how he caught 'flu.'

'Was it?'

Catherine addressed her question to Rafe, but he only shook his head. 'Tom is exaggerating, as usual. The road was flooded for a time, but I got home before morning.'

'He helped Mr Lloyd move some of his sheep to higher ground,' declared Thomas proudly. 'I wish I'd been with him. I'd have liked swishing around in all that mud!'

Catherine felt disturbed. 'You—you didn't tell me you—got marooned,' she said, and Rafe made a sound of resignation.

'It wasn't important.'

Catherine hesitated. 'You—you should have come back.'

His self-mockery was denigrating. 'Oh, yes? Oh, yes, I should have done that.'

Catherine looked distractedly at him, then, once again, she was aware of Thomas's inquisitive attention, and changed what she had been about to say into: 'Are you fully recovered now? I—wondered.'

'Physically,' he agreed, allowing the car to accelerate past a stream of slower-moving vehicles. 'Shall we stop somewhere for a meal? Tom's had nothing since lunch time.'

Catherine had no objections, and they entered the next service area and ordered dinner in the grill room. Thomas was excited at the prospect of eating out so late, and his chatter throughout the meal healed the gaping chasms in the conversation. He waded through soup and salad, beefburgers and chips, and a strawberry-flavoured ice-cream before sinking back happily in his chair.

'Hmm, that was super!' he declared, grinning at his father. 'Have I made a pig of myself?'

'You have rather,' observed Rafe dryly, but his tone was not unsympathetic, and his son took advantage of his amiability and asked if he could have another Coke.

In the car again, the miles were soon eaten away. Oxford, Cheltenham, Hereford; Catherine watched the signposts with a deepening sense of despair, wondering if ever she would drive with Rafe again.

Glancing over her shoulder, she found that Thomas had fallen asleep at last, worn out by the journey, and comfortably full after his enormous meal. She had noticed that Rafe, like herself, had eaten next to nothing, and been glad of his son's diversionary tactics. But now the boy was asleep, and for the first time she could speak freely.

'I've been thinking,' she said quietly, drawing Rafe's attention to herself, 'I might—close the Pendower shop.' There was complete silence and, not at all reassured, she went on: 'I thought—I thought I didn't care what people might say about me, but I do.'

'It's your decision, of course. I can't stop you,' he conceded bitterly, when she had begun to think he was not going to answer her. He shrugged his shoulders heavily. 'I presume this has to do with what Tom said earlier, hasn't it?'

Catherine pressed her lips together, trying not to succumb to the defeated appeal of his low voice. 'Not—altogether,' she admitted at last, choosing her words with care. 'I've thought about—about our relationship, and—and I can see no future in it.'

'I told you that,' Rafe reminded her harshly. 'Just two nights ago. But you ignored it. Just as you're ignoring the real facts now.'

Catherine lifted her head. 'What real facts?'

Rafe made a sound of impatience. 'We have laws in this country of ours,' he stated grimly. 'Laws about marriage, and laws about divorce. Like—if Lucy divorces me, she gets half of everything I possess, including Penwyth. And I don't mean the estate, although there's that too. I mean the house—the manor. The place where my father was born, and God help him, the place where he wants to die!'

Catherine gasped. 'But—surely she wouldn't——'

'Oh, yes, she would.'

Catherine shook her head. 'Then aren't you taking a—a terrible risk? Seeing me at all? I mean, does Lucy know about me?'

Rafe's sigh seemed to have been dragged up from the depths of his being. 'She suspects,' he concurred wearily. 'But you have to understand our relationship to understand how Lucy's mind works.' He hesitated. 'Lucy and I, to use an old cliché, are not compatible. Oh, she appreciates this as well as I do, and she's not—unreasonable.' His lips twisted. 'She allows me my little—how shall I put it?—foibles?'

Catherine stared at him. 'You mean—other women?' She felt sick. 'Like me?'

'No, not like you,' he snarled angrily. 'But I am male, Catherine. And sometimes——' He broke off abruptly. 'Well, that's the kind of relationship we have.'

'Oh, Rafe . . .' Catherine felt helpless, but his expression had hardened.

'Don't feel sorry for me,' he snapped. 'I was quite content, until you came along.'

'And—and Lucy?'

'She doesn't care what I do, so long as there isn't any gossip.'

'But there's gossip now!' Catherine protested, and he nodded.

'I know. And that was the main reason for that row Thomas partially overheard.'

'Oh, Rafe!' It was a futile cry, but she couldn't help it. Half turning towards him, she put her hand on his leg, allowing her fingers to close about the taut muscle, and then whispered despairingly: 'What are we going to do?'

'You're planning to leave,' he told her stiffly, steeling himself not to respond in any way. 'It's probably just as well. I was getting to the point where I was beginning to question my own integrity. The needs of the estate, my father's needs—my son's needs—were becoming blurred by emotion. There've been times during the past two days when I've actually asked myself whether what I was doing was right, whether I didn't deserve to snatch my happiness, whatever the expense to others.' He shook his head. 'It's as well you didn't put me to the test. At least this way, I can maintain a semblance of my self-respect.'

Catherine slowly withdrew her hand. Until that moment she had not really considered what their relationship might be doing to Rafe. She had been so wrapped up with her own feelings, with avoiding discovery, she had forgotten that the two people most closely involved must carry the heaviest burden, unless they were completely without conscience, and she knew that was not true. But what did his words mean to her? How could she go back on her word now?

'I—I'm sorry I've been the cause of so much—soul-searching,' she got out jerkily. 'I'm glad we've had this talk. Without—without being blinded by—by——'

'—emotion,' Rafe finished flatly. 'I know. When I'm near you, I don't always think coherently.'

'Oh, Rafe . . .' But the words were silent, choking the breath in her throat and making further conversation between them impossible.

She wondered what had happened to the lighthearted girl who had got into the car. She seemed to have made such a mess of everything. She loved Rafe, so why was she letting this happen? Why was she giving in when she had so much to fight for? She didn't want to close the Pendower shop. She had spoken recklessly, in the heat of the moment; she hadn't really intended to let it go so far. What would she do? Where could she go? Not back to London. Her spirit rebelled at such a thought. But where, *where*?

Yet, if she stayed, what could she do? Wait for an old man to die? *No*! Not because she didn't love Rafe enough, because she loved him too much to put that kind of pressure on him. It would be better for everyone if she left. Uncle Mervyn had his farm again. Gillian could have her baby with confidence, and Owen would no longer accuse her of fraternising with the enemy.

Thomas was still asleep when the Volvo stopped before her cottage gate. Gathering her things together, Catherine made a concerted effort to act naturally.

'I—I want to thank you,' she began, fumbling for the door handle, when his mouth silenced her good intentions.

'Don't say it,' he muttered, his breath warming the contours of her ear. 'Don't say anything. Just let me know where you are. I'll come and find you.'

Catherine pushed open the door and got out. That kind of talk was intoxicating, and she needed a clear head to face the future.

'Look—look after yourself,' she managed, chokily, and then almost ran up the path to her door.

Lucy came to the boutique the following morning.

Catherine was serving a customer when the green Volvo stopped in the High Street, and for a heart-shaking moment she thought Rafe had changed his mind and come back. But even as the colour came and went in her pale cheeks, and the customer she was serving regarded her with some curiosity, she heard the click of Lucy's heels on the pavement, and the duller tread as they encountered the rubber-backed carpeting of the boutique.

Mary went to attend to the newcomer and Catherine endeavoured to concentrate on what she was doing. But her mind buzzed with questions as to why Lucy was here, and she couldn't prevent her ears from straining to hear what Mary was saying.

Presently, however, Mary approached her. 'Mrs Glyndower wants you to serve her,' she whispered confidentially. 'Shall I take over here?'

'Oh—if you wouldn't mind . . .' Catherine cast a smile of apology in her customer's direction, before excusing herself and crossing the floor to where Lucy was waiting. 'Good morning, Mrs Glyndower. Can I help you?'

'Indeed you can.' Lucy's eyes snapped as she surveyed the serving area with critical appraisal. 'Do you have an office? Where we can speak privately?'

Catherine trembled, but she stood her ground. 'I think

anything we have to say to one another can be said here, Mrs Glyndower,' she insisted. 'Is it the gown you bought? Has something happened to it?'

'You dare to stand there and ask me about some cheap gown I bought weeks ago!' Lucy hissed. 'You know perfectly well why I'm here. And if you're prepared to have your affairs bandied about the streets of Pendower, I most certainly am not!'

Catherine followed Lucy's pointed stare to where Mary and the woman she was serving were watching their encounter with interest. Pressing her lips together, she realised they could not continue their conversation out here, but equally, she was loath to take Lucy into her office. It was so small, and the perfume Lucy wore was unmistakable. She didn't want that small room permeated by its fragrance.

'You'd better come into the stockroom,' she declared reluctantly, leading the way down the steps, and after a moment's hesitation Lucy followed her.

The stockroom was filled with racks of suits and dresses, some still in their plastic containers, like shrouds. Looking about her, Catherine quailed at the task that confronted her, of transporting all these garments to some other stockroom in some other store, and after the sleepless night she had spent, every task seemed overpowering.

'Now . . .' With the door closed behind them, Lucy came straight to the point and Catherine was forced to put her own needs aside. 'I have only two things to say to you—one, stay away from my husband, and two—get out of this valley!'

Catherine gasped. She couldn't help it. It was so much like a scene from some melodrama. Did Lucy really think she could come here and say such outrageous things to her? Who did she think she was? She had no right to order her about, no authority over her actions whatsoever.

But even as the words of protest sprang to her lips, she stifled them. What was the point of arguing with Lucy? What could she hope to gain from proving the other woman did not intimidate her? Maybe this was what she wanted. Maybe she hoped Catherine would defy her. Who could honestly tell what Rafe's wife was thinking?

Still, it was not easy to say quietly: 'Thank you for your advice, Mrs Glyndower,' even if Lucy was taken aback by her composure.

'I mean it, you know,' she persisted. 'I know what's going on. Rafe tells me everything about his little—affairs.'

Catherine's cheek muscles stiffened. 'Thank you, Mrs Glyndower. If that's all——'

'Damn you, it is not all!' Lucy was very much on her dignity now, her narrow nose shrunken to a sharp point. 'You'll listen to everything I have to say before you show me the door!' She snorted. 'Don't think I don't know what your game is. I do. You're thinking—don't get involved with her, don't let her upset you, don't listen to what must be the most painful truth of your life!'

'Mrs Glyndower——'

'*Mrs* Glyndower! Yes, Mrs Glyndower, *Miss* Tempest. And don't imagine Rafe will ever change that situation, because he won't.'

'Please——'

A distinct pain was making itself felt behind Catherine's eyes now, and she wished she had been better prepared to face this. For her part, Lucy could see how her continued assault was affecting the other girl, and as Catherine's confidence dwindled, hers swelled.

'Yes. You don't like to hear that, do you, Miss Tempest? But it's true, nevertheless, and I think you know it.'

'Mrs Glyndower . . .' Somehow Catherine had to stop this tirade. 'You're making a terrible mistake. You—you have no need to ask me to leave Pendower. I'd already decided to go.'

'What?' Again, Catherine had succeeded in disconcerting Lucy. 'Why, I—I don't believe you! Thomas—Thomas told me how—how Rafe came to your mother's house yesterday evening——'

'Thomas?' Catherine raised her eyebrows, a feeling of faint understanding bringing a tingling warmth to the inner coldness that gripped her.

'Yes, Thomas!' Now she had said it, Lucy didn't try to change her words. 'But Rafe would have told me, sooner or later. He always does.'

'Mrs Glyndower, I think you'd better leave . . .'

'Don't you tell me what to do!' Lucy clenched her small fists. 'And remember this—if you do change your mind about leaving, I'll do everything in my power to make things as difficult for you as I can. And you know what I mean. How long would Rafe care about you, I wonder, if every time he looked at you he remembered that because of you he had to sacrifice Penwyth. That house means something to him, even if it is only that old man upstairs. *Lord* Penwyth!' she sneered. 'He doesn't even know his own name!'

The opening of the door behind them saved Catherine from answering her. In all honesty, she didn't know if she could have done so anyway. Her head was throbbing, and the tight feeling in her throat wasn't just emotion.

'Did you call, Miss Tempest?'

Mary's inquisitive little face had never been more welcome, and Catherine put out a detaining hand.

'I—will—will you show Mrs Glyndower out, Mary?' she asked unevenly. 'She—she was just leaving.'

There was a moment when she thought Lucy was going to defy her and say something more, but discretion won. Tucking her handbag under her arm, she strode abruptly up the steps, and without waiting for Mary's escort, left the boutique.

Mary looked after her departing figure with curious eyes, and then turned back to Catherine, her expression changing to one of concern as she saw her employer clinging weakly to a rack of dresses.

'Hey, miss, are you all right?' she exclaimed, hurrying towards her. 'Good heavens, you're like a fire, you are! Got a cold coming on, I shouldn't wonder. Or was it that spiteful old bitch who's upset you?'

'Mary . . .' Catherine had hardly the strength to remonstrate with her. 'Oh, but yes, I do feel slightly woozy. I think I'll sit down for a while . . .'

Mary shook her head. 'Strikes me you'd be better off at home,' she declared. 'After all, I didn't expect you in today, did I? I can manage—I told you so.'

Catherine brushed back a few tendrils of hair that had strayed on to her forehead. It was a great temptation to give in and go home, even if she could not escape from her thoughts as easily as from her duties.

'Oh, Mary . . .' she began, but she was weakening, and Mary knew it.

'You're getting 'flu, by the looks of things,' she said disapprovingly. 'I don't know where you've got it, but I don't want it.'

Catherine bent her head, so that Mary should not see the revealing weakness of her tears. 'No,' she murmured quietly, 'you're probably right. People who have 'flu should stay at home'

CHAPTER TWELVE

DURING the next couple of days, Catherine did not have the energy to seriously consider what her next move should be. Committed now to leaving Pendower, she knew she must make some arrangements soon, but the idea of telling Mary, and the part-time assistant, that they were out of a job filled her with regret. What would Mary do if the boutique closed? There were few enough jobs in the small town, and the chances of her finding alternative employment were slim. Yet she was not old enough or experienced enough to run the boutique herself, and even if she was, that would leave Catherine with no alternative but to return to London and the Hammersmith branch. Sarah wouldn't like that. She had become accustomed to being her own boss. Unless she could be persuaded to take over the Pendower boutique . . .

But there Catherine baulked. She didn't want Sarah coming to Pendower, taking over where she left off, living in this cottage. This was her home. She had been happy here. And the truth was, she didn't want to leave.

The weather continued to be unpredictable, with days of rain, when the temperature was almost mild, alternating with days of icy brilliance. Catherine's cold kept her confined to the cottage, and secretly she welcomed these days of respite, when she had an excuse for not making any irrevocable decisions. Curled on the couch before a cosy fire, she tried to shut out the world and its problems, deliberately numbing her mind to the inevitable step she would have to take.

The first days of December slipped by. Then one morning Catherine was awakened by a distinct tapping at her door. She was feeling a lot better, well enough to go to work, in actual fact, and as she pulled on her dressing gown with some reluctance and went drearily down the stairs, she reflected that she could no longer put off the evil day. Maybe this was a sign. The postman, or the milkman, or whoever it was knocking at her door, had awakened her, and now she was up, she might just as well resign herself to the fact that she could not go on avoiding her problems.

Releasing the chain, she opened the door a crack, peering round it wearily. At first she thought there was nobody there, and then her eyes were drawn to the boy standing shivering on the step.

'*Thomas!*' she exclaimed disbelievingly, blinking as she registered that he was alone. 'Thomas, for heaven's sake! What are you doing here?'

'Can I come in?'

His teeth chattered as he spoke, and automatically she opened the door wider to allow him into the hall. Then she closed the door again, staring at him with anxious eyes.

'You've run away, haven't you?' she said, trying not to sound as disturbed as she felt. 'Oh, Thomas! You shouldn't have come here!'

'There was nowhere else,' he replied simply, and her heart went out to him.

'No—I don't mean—how that sounded,' she fretted, expelling her breath on a sigh. 'What I meant was—you shouldn't have run away.'

'I had to,' he declared tremulously. '*She—she* was going to send me back to school—to—to St Matthew's—and I couldn't go back there. I couldn't—I couldn't——' And without waiting for any invitation, he threw himself at her, burying his face in the soft folds of her dressing gown.

He was shaking, shuddering with sobs, and shivering with cold. She didn't honestly know where one ended and the other began, but what was painfully obvious was that Thomas was dreadfully distressed, and in no fit state to be chastised. Yet, as her arms closed almost instinctively about him, and she felt the dampness of his clothes, the thought uppermost in her mind was how on earth had he got here? Surely he hadn't been out all night? Surely he hadn't *walked* from Penwyth?

Smoothing her fingers over his dark hair, so like his

father's, she soothed his desperate sobbing with gentle words. 'Don't,' she breathed. 'Honey, you mustn't upset yourself so. Come along. We must get you something to drink, something to warm you up, and then you must tell me how you got here.'

He allowed himself to be helped out of the duffel coat which was obviously his school attire, but underneath, Catherine was appalled to find he was only wearing his vest and underpants. Her questioning gaze brought his lids drooping over his eyes, and realising how delicate the situation was, she merely gathered up a woollen jacket of her own, and draped it quickly over his shoulders. He was cold, chilled to the bone, and she felt a sense of bewilderment that his parents could have allowed this to happen. There were so many questions that needed answers, and while her initial instincts were to ring Rafe and tell him where his son was, she was loath to risk destroying the boy's confidence in her. Perhaps, after he had had a warm drink, he would tell her what had happened, allow her to contact his father . . .

The kitchen was chilly, which wasn't surprising considering the hour, thought Catherine bleakly. Six-thirty! she registered, looking at the clock on the cooker. Dear God, Thomas had to have been out all night!

Trying not to show her alarm, she said: 'I'll put some milk on to boil, and then we'll go and stir up the fire in the living room. You'd like some Horlicks, wouldn't you?'

She was trying to think of things that might warm him up. One couldn't give a boy of his age brandy, and besides, he probably wouldn't like it.

Thomas didn't say anything. He gave a sort of half-hearted nod, and then stood shivering while she poured milk into a saucepan. But she was reluctant to let him out of her sight, and after plugging in the kettle she hurried him into the living room.

The fire spluttered into life. A few small sticks of wood soon had it crackling away, and she noticed how Thomas huddled near it, trying not too obviously to warm his frozen fingers. Discretion gave way to determination, and taking him by the shoulders, she set him down on a chair in front of the fire. Then she knelt down beside him, tugging off his shoes and socks, and taking his icy little feet between her hands.

The brisk massage she gave them brought the blood tingling beneath her fingers, and his tears gave way to smothered giggles as he tried to pull away. 'You—you're tickling me,' he gulped, though his mirth was brief and quickly controlled, but when Catherine left him to make his drink, she had the satisfaction of knowing that he was beginning to lose that pinched look of exposure.

With a mug of Horlicks between his palms, he eventually stopped shivering altogether, although he still continued to sniff from time to time, little indrawings of his breath that ended on a sob. Catherine made herself a cup of coffee, cast a doubtful look at the telephone, and then closed the living room door before joining Thomas by the fire.

'Now,' she said, 'don't you think I deserve an explanation?'

Thomas licked a moustache of milk from his upper lip. 'I—I s'pose so.' He cast her an anxious look, then muttered: 'You won't send me back there, will you? I—I—can't go back.'

It was worse than Catherine had imagined. What could she say to him? How could she make promises she had no way of keeping? How could she explain now that there was no possibility she could care for him? That only his parents had that right?

Sighing, she said quietly: 'Tell me why you ran away. Does anyone know where you are? Does anyone know you're missing? Because if they do, Thomas, they must be out of their minds with worry.'

'No one knows,' he said, sniffing again. 'They—they think I'm in bed. *She* always puts me to bed if she wants me out of the way.'

Catherine stared at him unhappily. 'Honey! Don't judge your mother so harshly.' She paused, trying to be objective. 'I mean, it isn't always—easy to know what's best for a child. Your mother obviously feels——'

'—that I'm a nuisance!' declared Thomas tearfully. 'She doesn't want me around. She never has. She never wanted me, you know. She hates me——'

'Oh, Thomas!'

'She does, she does. She said so.'

Catherine endeavoured to school her features. 'Darling, you know people can say things in anger that they don't mean.'

'She does.' Thomas gulped into his Horlicks, and Catherine removed it from his hands while she gave him a tissue to blow his nose. Then, when he had taken hold of it again, he added: 'She said—she said I couldn't stay at Penwyth because it was going to be sold——'

'Sold?'

'Yes, sold.' Thomas nodded. 'She said Grandpa would have to go into a home, because she wasn't going to put up with either of us any longer.'

Catherine was aghast. Penwyth—sold? Surely Rafe would never allow that.

Thomas rubbed his nose with an unsteady finger, and then went on: 'There—there was the most awful row after—after I was sent upstairs.'

'Then how do you know all this?' Catherine knew she was taking advantage of him, but she had to know.

'I—I listened. On the stairs.' Catherine remembered he had listened there once before. 'I—I wouldn't have, if—if Grandpa hadn't gone downstairs.'

'Grandpa?'

'My grandfather,' said Thomas simply, and Catherine nodded.

'I know. But doesn't he usually go downstairs?'

'No. Not for years and years. He—he and my mother don't get on, you see.'

'They don't?' Catherine's voice was faint.

'No. She's always grumbling about him. He's old, you see, and he drops ash on the carpets, and sometimes he spills things.'

'I see.'

'He smokes in bed, too, and that really makes her mad.'

Catherine shook her head. 'It can be dangerous.'

'Oh, yes, I know, but everything Grandpa does makes her mad. I think—I think she expected him to die much sooner.'

'Thomas!'

'Well, anyway, when Grandpa went downstairs, I *had*

to listen. He had heard her arguing with Daddy, you see—about me. The Pendower school hasn't opened again. It's not expected to open until after the Christmas holidays, and she said that she wasn't going to put—put up with me any longer.'

'But it's only three weeks to Christmas,' Catherine protested.

'I know. But—but she wants Daddy to take her away at Christmas. She—she said he—he *owed* it to her. Because—because of you!'

'Me?' Catherine was horrified. 'What did she say about me?'

'Not a lot. It was mostly about me. Until Grandpa called her an—an unnatural woman, and she said he was a stupid old man!'

Catherine pushed back her hair with unsteady fingers. 'And—your father? What did your father say?'

'He—he said he'd go to prison before—before he'd sell Penwyth.' His eyes widened in terror. 'He won't go to prison, will he, Miss Tempest? If—if he does, I'll never be allowed to come home . . .'

'Oh, love . . .' Unable to withstand the agony in his face, Catherine put down her cup and went to him, lifting his thin little body up from the chair and sitting down herself with him in her lap. 'Going to prison . . . that's just a figure of speech. Your father won't allow that to happen. And—and your mother—well, she'll get over her anger —'

,'She won't.' Thomas's jaw wobbled. 'She told Daddy she was going to drive me back to—to St Matthew's today! This morning. That—that's why I ran away.'

He buried his face in her shoulders, shuddering as more tears came to claim him. Catherine shuddered, too, at the realisation that the boy had walked the ten miles from Penwyth. No wonder it had taken him all night! Thank goodness, he had had the sense to put on his duffel coat. He'd have died of exposure without it. As it was, she was sure he ought to be examined by a doctor, but that could come later. After she had contacted Rafe, as she would surely have to do . . .

'Tell me about St Matthew's,' she said quietly now.

'Tell me why you don't want to go back there. Why do you hate it so?'

Thomas burrowed closer. 'I just don't like sleeping there,' he insisted, 'that's all.'

'But why don't you like sleeping there?' persisted Catherine. 'Why won't you tell me what it is that's frightening you?'

'I'm not frightened.' Thomas lifted his head at this, rubbing his eyes with the back of his hands, leaving grubby smudges across his cheeks. 'I just don't want to go to boarding school.'

Catherine sighed. 'But don't you see? That's illogical. If you can't give any reason why you don't like boarding school, how can you expect anyone to understand?'

Thomas's lips pursed. 'I've told you. I don't like sleeping there.'

'But why? You're not a baby, are you? You don't need someone to tuck you up, do you?'

'No!' Thomas was indignant. 'I can put myself to bed.'

'There you are, then.'

Thomas hung his head. 'You don't know what it's like. At—at home, I can get up if I want to.'

'Get up?' Catherine frowned. 'Why would you want to get up, after you've gone to bed?'

Thomas's cheeks went red. 'You know,' he muttered.

Catherine hesitated. 'You mean—to use the bathroom?'

Thomas nodded.

'But can't you do that at school?'

Thomas shook his head.

'Oh, Thomas! That's not true.'

'It is true. It is.' Thomas stared at her, his long lashes damp and silky. 'After—after lights out, no one's allowed to leave their beds until the morning.'

Catherine's frown deepened. 'But—that's ridiculous!'

'I know.' Thomas looked down at his hands.

A dawning comprehension made Catherine suddenly stiffen. 'You mean——' she bit her lip in disbelief, 'even in an emergency——'

Thomas sniffed. 'Mr Walton said that boys have to learn to control themselves. That—that it's just a—a matter of self—self-discipline.'

Catherine's shoulders sagged. 'And didn't Mr Walton explain the situation to your father?'

Thomas shook his head.

'I gather—there were times . . .'

'Yes, yes!' Thomas was distraught. 'The other boys used to laugh. It was awful, awful!' His sobs broke out anew. 'You see—you see why I can't go back there. I can't, I can't!'

Catherine let him cry, realising tears were not just a self-indulgence, but a release of tension. And she could sympathise with him. She could imagine exactly how it was. A boy like Thomas, a sensitive boy, forced to endure nights of torment, without anyone to whom he could turn. It was a mother he needed at times like this. He wouldn't want to admit the situation to his father. But his own mother never had any time for him . . .

'Look,' she said now, making him dry his tears, 'shall I speak to your father? Shall I tell him?' And as Thomas started to shake his head, she added: 'I promise he won't be angry—honestly. And—and he just might be able to do something about it.'

Thomas blew his nose vigorously, then looked sideways at her. 'You like Daddy, don't you? I know you do. I wish—I wish you and Daddy——'

But Catherine stopped him there, getting up from the chair and depositing him on it. And as she did so, the telephone started to ring.

Immediately Thomas shrank back into the chair, his face mirroring the agony he was feeling. 'Don't—don't tell them I'm here,' he begged, and they both knew who they guessed was calling.

'I—I have to, Tom. Can't you see that?' Catherine protested gently. 'Darling, you can't hide for ever!'

Thomas said nothing, drawing up his knees and wrapping his arms around them, as if to occupy the smallest space possible. Catherine was reluctant to leave him, but the telephone was insistent and she had to answer it.

It was not Rafe, however, but her Aunt Margaret at the other end of the line, and her first words dispelled any doubts Catherine might have been feeling.

'It's Penwyth,' she said, without preamble. 'I thought

you ought to know. There's been a fire, and—and the old man and the boy are—are dead!'

'Dead?'

Catherine couldn't take it in at first. It was so unreal, so unexpected, and with the awareness of Thomas behind her in the living room, ears pricked to every word she uttered, she could hardly comprehend what her aunt was saying.

'Yes, dead,' went on Aunt Margaret flatly. 'It was terrible! *Terrible*! Rafe—Rafe tried to go back into the flames, but they wouldn't let him.'

'*Rafe!*' Catherine tried desperately to understand what her aunt was relating, and as she did so, she heard the storm of weeping break out behind her.

'Daddy?' Thomas was screaming. 'Daddy's dead? Daddy's dead!'

'No . . .' Somehow, Catherine managed to grasp the boy's arm, pulling him close to her and saying urgently: 'Your father's all right. Believe me, he is!'

Thomas's sobs were starkly audible, and her aunt could be heard to catch her breath. 'You've got the boy there?' she cried in disbelief. 'Dear God, Catherine, what is going on?'

'He's here, he's here,' Catherine exclaimed, her voice eloquent with feeling. 'Aunt Margaret—please! What happened?'

'No one knows. But the old place went up like tinderwood.'

'And—and Lord Penwyth——'

'The fire caught that wing first. He must have been asleep, overcome by the fumes. They couldn't get to him. And—and they couldn't find the boy . . .' Aunt Margaret's voice broke. 'Catherine, is Thomas really there with you? Oh, God! Wait till Rafe hears!'

'Yes.' Catherine's breathing was constricted, and aware of Thomas still gazing up at her through tear-soaked eyes, she said: 'I—I'd better telephone—oh, oh, no! I can't do that, can I?' She squeezed Thomas's shoulder in an effort to reassure him. 'Oh, lord, what am I going to do?'

'Owen can go up and tell them,' said Aunt Margaret firmly, controlling her own emotions. 'Rafe's still up at the house—what's left of it. You—you keep the boy with you.'

'Where else would he go?' demanded Catherine huskily,

and Aunt Margaret made a sound of acceptance.

'I won't ask what he's doing there now,' she said. 'But thank God he is. Thank God!'

With the receiver replaced, Catherine went down on her haunches beside Thomas, taking his small face between her hands and saying gently: 'You've got to be very brave——'

'You—you said Daddy——'

'Daddy's fine. Daddy's well. But—but Penwyth—the manor—your home——' She sighed, realising there was no way of breaking it to him gently. 'There was a fire. The house has burned down.'

Thomas absorbed this with a curious lack of emotion. 'And what—what about Grandpa?' he asked, with poignant dignity, making Catherine's task that much more painful.

'He—he died,' she said, realising she could not lie to him. He had heard his grandfather's name mentioned, and he knew someone was dead. 'I'm sorry.'

Thomas nodded, but it was as if he was cried out. No tears welled from his eyes then, just a strangely adult acceptance pulled down the corners of his mouth, as if now there was no hope of reprieve.

Catherine didn't know what to do, what to say to him. Pulling away from her, he trudged back into the living room, and when she looked through the open door she saw he had resumed his curled-up position on the chair. She wanted to comfort him, to hold him close and reassure him that nothing was ever as hopeless as it appeared, but she knew he would not believe her. He had not even asked about his mother. Only his father could assuage his grief. His father . . .

Licking her lips, Catherine turned doubtfully towards the stairs. She ought to dress, to make herself respectable for when Rafe and Lucy arrived, for she had no doubts that they would come, once they knew their son was safe. But she didn't like to leave Thomas, and with a feeling of despair she admitted that Rafe would not look at her while his wife was with him. And in any case, she had no secrets from him. So instead she resumed her seat opposite the boy, staring into the dying flames with a curious sense of unreality. She had not known old Lord Penwyth, but she pitied anyone who died in such tragic circumstances. She could imagine Rafe's feelings. He had loved his father so much. How awful that he should have his prophecy of his father wanting to die at Penwyth fulfilled in such a terrible way.

And Lucy; how would Lucy feel now that the old man who had stood in the way of her ambition was dead? She was Lady Penwyth now, Catherine had to remember that. And Rafe was *Lord* Penwyth. How hollow the title sounded. Not at all like the strong, virile man she knew he was.

And Thomas . . . Her eyes shifted to the boy facing her. How would he face up to the future, a future that had never seemed more uncertain in his eyes?

It seemed hours before they heard the sound of a car in the square, and then they both stiffened, as if arming themselves against the confrontation that was bound to come.

'Wait here,' Catherine told Thomas, as she went to answer the imperative ring of the doorbell. 'And don't worry. Your father loves you. Remember that!'

As she crossed the hall, it was less easy to give herself advice. She dreaded the look of triumph she would see on Lucy's face, and she wished with all her heart that she could hide her own emotions more successfully. Think of Thomas, she kept telling herself. Think of him, and don't let Lucy see what depths of misery she had plumbed.

But when she opened the door, only Rafe stood on the threshold, tall and dark and familiar, streaks of soot making the weariness in his face that much more marked. His parka was torn and soot-stained, his hair unkempt, as if he had constantly raked his fingers through its overlong thickness, and his eyes were dark and red-rimmed from the smoke—yet filled now with the light of relief.

'Tom's here?' he demanded huskily, and when she nodded, he came towards her into the hall, slamming the door behind him with his foot, jerking her into his arms. 'Oh, God! Catherine,' he groaned, burying his face in the scented hollow of her throat, 'I've been through hell tonight, but it's over now . . . over now . . .' and his mouth sought and found hers.

Catherine didn't understand, but he had always been able to rob her of any resistance against him, and his arms about her were so wonderful after the awful hours they had spent waiting for him to come. Her lips parted automatically, submitting to the exploratory caress of his, and she clung to him weakly for a moment, desperately trying to keep her head.

Then, as if aware they were no longer alone, Rafe lifted his head to regard his son, who had come to stand at the living room door. With a wry smile for Catherine he put her gently aside and went towards the boy. Thomas seemed to hesitate, as if uncertain of his reception, and then, when his father held out his arms, he ran into them, pressing close to him and letting the tears he had swallowed earlier come through again.

'Easy, son, easy . . .' Rafe squatted down beside him, holding him between his hands gently, waiting for the storm of tears to subside. 'I gather you've heard that Grandpa's dead, hmm? I know how you must feel. I love him, too, you know. But he wanted to die at Penwyth, you know that. And he did.'

Thomas's lips quivered. 'The house is gone?'

'Just about,' Rafe nodded. 'I'm sorry, son.'

'I'm not. Now I don't have to go back there.'

Rafe ran long fingers over the boy's hair. 'Was it so bad?' he mused softly. 'I'm sorry. We'll try and make it better from now on.' He shook his head. 'It—it's just so—good, having you back again. You'll never know the night I've just spent.'

'What do you mean?'

Thomas frowned and now Rafe looked again at Catherine, rekindling the feelings of emotive confusion he had ignited earlier. 'You didn't tell him?' She shook her head, and he nodded in understanding, getting up and stretching his long legs. 'Oh, well, that's something else we have to straighten out, Tom.'

'I—I'll go and get dressed.' Catherine needed something to do, and after a moment's hesitation Rafe nodded.

'Very well.' He glanced towards the kitchen. 'Can I make myself a cup of coffee while you're gone? I could surely use some.'

'Oh—of course.' Catherine chewed on her lower lip.

'Do you—that is—shall I make it?'

'No, I can manage.' Rafe glanced significantly at Thomas. 'We—er—we have things to say to one another. You understand?'

She didn't really. She wanted to ask about Lucy, where she was, how she could allow her husband to come alone to collect the son they had both thought dead. But instead she nodded, and went towards the stairs, realising that it was really no business of hers, and she should not read more into that kiss he had given her than he wanted her to read.

The wash she had was skimpy to say the least, but she gave her teeth a thorough brushing, gaining a certain release from the exaggerated effort. Then she pulled off her nightgown, and quickly donned a button-through shirt and navy cords. She was brushing her hair, trying to put it into some semblance of order, when her bedroom door opened to admit Rafe. He was alone, and her hands trembled uncontrollably as he closed the door behind him and leaned back against it, successfully cutting off her only means of escape.

'Hi,' he said softly, and she had to grip the dressing table behind her with both hands to support her uncertain knees.

'I—I was so sorry to—to hear about your father,' she murmured. 'It must have been a—a terrible shock . . .'

Rafe straightened and came towards her, halting only a foot or so from her. 'Yes,' he said. 'I've had some shocks in the last twelve hours, I don't deny it. The worst was imagining Tom was dead.' He shook his head reminiscently. 'That was without doubt the worst moment of my life to date.'

Catherine bent her head. 'And—and Lucy's,' she said chokily, but Rafe's smothered expletive brought her eyes up to his.

'No,' he said, shaking his head. 'Not Lucy's. That came when she heard that he was still alive!'

'You can't—you can't be serious!'

'Oh, but I am.' Rafe was bitter. 'It was hard for her to hide her feelings when we thought Tom was dead. It was impossible when we discovered that he wasn't.'

'Oh, Rafe!'

'I wasn't the only one to see it. Your aunt was there, and your cousin. They would tell you. All Lucy ever cared about was her possessions. And no court in the land will grant her custody of a boy she obviously cares nothing about   I'll see to that.'

Catherine moved her shoulders helplessly. 'Sometimes   sometimes people say things—when they're distressed   '

'You're not defending her to me, are you, Catherine?' he demanded, putting strong fingers beneath her chin and lifting her face to his. 'Oh, no, love, Lucy needs no advocate. But I know what this means to me—to *us*. I shall be free soon. Free!'

Catherine quivered. 'But—you're Lord Penwyth. Lucy wanted the title.'

'I shall rescind it. I don't want it, and after tonight, nor will she. But you may not want *me* when you hear all I have to say.'

'Want you?' Catherine faltered weakly. 'Oh, Rafe, I love you. You know that. I—I'll always want you.'

His eyes darkened passionately at her words, and with a sound of satisfaction he pulled her against his hard body, seeking her mouth with his. When she protested that Thomas was downstairs and might come looking for them, Rafe told her that Thomas was making an effort to eat his breakfast, and would be satisfactorily employed for at least ten minutes.

'I hope you don't object,' he murmured wryly, 'but I boiled two eggs. That is, apparently, what you allowed him the last time he breakfasted here.'

Catherine shook her head. 'I—I can't believe any of this . . .'

'You'd better believe it.' Rafe drew her down on to the bed beside him. 'But first, there's something I have to tell you.'

'Yes—'

'Yes.' He took her hand between both of his, smoothing the soft skin almost absently. 'I may not get any insurance money from the fire. In fact, I'm pretty sure I won't.'

'No?' Catherine was puzzled. 'Why not?'

Rafe sighed. 'It's a long story . . .'

'Thomas told me there was a row last night.'

'Did he?' Rafe raised his dark eyebrows. 'Yes, of course he would. That, I hear, was why he ran away.' He shuddered. 'Thank God he did!'

'You'd have got him out,' exclaimed Catherine eagerly. 'You know you would. My aunt said you couldn't find him.'

'No.' Rafe nodded reminiscently, his face twisting with remembered agony. 'God, I nearly went out of my mind! I was sure he must be in there. And the flames were so fierce. I imagined them on his skin . . .'

'Don't!' Catherine touched his cheek with her free hand. 'It never happened. It never would. He would have been unconscious long before the flames touched him. As—as your father would be . . .'

'My father? Oh, yes,' Rafe nodded, 'I was coming to him. Did Tom tell you? He came downstairs.'

'Yes.'

Rafe sighed. 'Lucy threatened him, do you know that? She actually threatened him with a nursing home!'

'But you wouldn't allow that.'

'No.' Rafe closed his eyes for a moment. 'Although we both knew how ruthless Lucy could be.' He sighed. 'That's what I wanted to tell you. I think—my father may have started the fire deliberately.'

'Oh, no, Rafe, he wouldn't do that!'

'He may have done.'

'With his grandson, as he thought, asleep in bed? No.' Catherine shook her head. 'Thomas told me—sometimes he smoked in bed.'

'An accident, you mean?' Rafe frowned. 'It could have been, I suppose. But—oh, God! Who could tell what was in his mind? I only know that the fire started in or around the area of his apartments. I tried to get to him but I couldn't.' His eyes darkened with remembered horror. 'The bed—the bed was ablaze from end to end.'

'Rafe, Rafe . . .' Now it was she who comforted him. 'Forget it! Forget it! Oh, not your father—I know you'll never do that. But there was nothing you could do, remember that. Do you think he would want you to blame yourself? You must know he wouldn't.'

Rafe's faint smile was a reassurance. 'I guess I'm just—confused. Whatever—Penwyth's gone, and with it, everything it stood for. All I'm left with is the land, acres of it, but hardly the estate my father offered my mother. Nevertheless, it—and myself—are yours, if you want us. And Tom, of course, but that goes without saying.'

'Rafe . . .' Catherine turned to him fully, resting her arms on his shoulders, linking her fingers behind his head. 'How—how can you say this? Lucy——'

'Lucy and I are through,' declared Rafe huskily. 'You know that. I'd never have let her send Tom back to St Matthew's, whatever she did. I don't know why he hates it so much, but he does, and so far as I'm concerned, that's enough.'

Catherine gazed at him with her heart in her eyes. Later, some time, they would talk about Thomas, and she would tell him what the boy had told her. But for the present, it was enough that they were together, more than enough . . .

With a groan of satisfaction, Rafe slid his hands round her waist, arching her against him, his lips teasing hers until the urgent demands of his own overcame his restraint.

'Will—will Lucy give you a divorce?' Catherine breathed, when his mouth moved to caress her ear, and he propped on one elbow beside her, stroking her lips with his forefinger.

'I think so,' he conceded. 'After the last twenty-four hours, I don't think we have anything more to say to one another, and without Penwyth, I'm of little use to her. With the money I get from the sale of Penwyn, I intend to build a modest house in the grounds, and we should just about manage to break even.' He grinned. 'I always wanted to take up farming seriously. Do you think your uncle would give me some advice?'

Catherine smiled. 'I think he might.'

'Good.' Rafe's fingers slid possessively over her breast, and then were abruptly withdrawn. 'Come on,' he said huskily, getting up. 'If we stay here any longer, Tom *will* begin to wonder what's going on.'

Catherine sat up, buttoning her shirt. 'Do you think—that is—will he mind? About me, I mean?'

Rafe pulled her to her feet. 'Stop fishing for compliments! You know how Tom feels about you.'

'But Lucy . . . how *could* she not want to see him?' Catherine couldn't forget that.

'She *never* wanted to see him,' replied Rafe simply, bestowing a final kiss on her parted lips. 'Can you wonder that he ran away? Or where he ran to . . .'

It was the most wonderful Christmas that Catherine had ever spent. There was just Rafe, Thomas and herself at the cottage, a real family for the first time in Thomas's young life, with a Christmas tree and a Christmas stocking, and the awesome beauty of the carol service at the chapel. It no longer mattered what anyone said about them. Lucy had agreed to give Rafe a divorce, and in a few short months they would be married. The plans for the new house Rafe was building had already been drawn up, but it would be months before it was ready, and until then the cottage was their home.

Catherine had kept her job, and she delivered Thomas at school on her way to the boutique in the mornings, while Rafe conducted the business of the estate from her uncle's study at Penwyn. Despite his misgivings, the insurance for Penwyn had been paid, although what with death duties and Lucy claiming most of the remainder as her share of the estate there was little left. But there was enough left over to pay for the honeymoon. Of which, Rafe said, his father would have approved.

It was like a dream come true for Catherine, and when she awakened each morning to find Rafe beside her, she sometimes had to pinch herself to convince herself that it was real. Of course, her mother didn't approve of their temporary arrangements, but as soon as Rafe's decree was made absolute, they were married in the chapel at Penwyn, to Thomas's unbounded delight. He was to stay at Penwyn while they were away, sleeping in the bedroom where his stepmother had slept as a child. He was quite excited about it. He had never known what it was to have aunts and uncles and cousins who actually welcomed him into their homes, and Gillian's baby was a great attraction.

For Catherine, waking on their first morning at the hotel in Paris, there was a curious satisfaction in knowing she was actually *Mrs* Glyndower at last. Rafe never used his title, and the simple designation suited her. She was his wife, and that was enough.

Becoming aware of his eyes upon her, she flushed becomingly, arousing a chuckle of amusement from her husband. 'The blushing bride,' he mocked tenderly. 'After everything, you can still be embarrassed. I like that. It's very feminine.'

Catherine burrowed close to him. 'Oh, Rafe, you've made me so happy!

Rafe's fingers slid through her hair. 'It's good being alone together at last,' he mused lazily. 'Shall we spend the whole day in bed, or shall we stir ourselves later and have dinner downstairs?'

Catherine giggled, pressing her balled fist into his midriff. 'You know I want to go sightseeing. I must see the Louvre, and Notre-Dame, and I must do some shopping in the Faubourg St-Honoré.'

'Oh, lord!' Rafe closed his eyes in mock despair. 'This is our honeymoon, you know. We can go shopping at any time.'

Catherine wrinkled her nose at him. 'And you know we're leaving for Provence the day after tomorrow. We'll have plenty of time there to laze and—and other things.'

Rafe rolled over, imprisoning her beneath him. 'We'll never have enough time,' he said huskily, but there was satisfaction in the words. 'My wife!' He held her face between his two hands and bent his mouth to hers. 'I love you. How can I have lived so long without you?' He stroked the silky hair back from her forehead. 'Do you think you can handle two adoring males?'

'Easily,' whispered Catherine eagerly, and did her best to prove it.

Take romance with you on your holiday

Holiday time is almost here again. So look out for the special Mills & Boon Holiday Reading Pack.* Four new romances by four favourite authors. Attractive, smart, easy to pack and only £3.40.

*Available from 11th June.

Summer in France Lorna Cameron	**Escape to Love** Claudia Jameson
The Emerald Coast Margaret Mayo	**Ripening Vine** Ellen Clare

 Mills & Boon

The rose of romance

How to join in a whole new world of romance

It's very easy to subscribe to the Mills & Boon Reader Service. As a regular reader, you can enjoy a whole range of special benefits. Bargain offers. Big cash savings. Your own free Reader Service newsletter, packed with knitting patterns, recipes, competitions, and exclusive book offers.

We send you the very latest titles each month, postage and packing free – no hidden extra charges. There's absolutely no commitment – you receive books for only as long as you want.

We'll send you details. Simply send the coupon – or drop us a line for details about the Mills & Boon Reader Service Subscription Scheme.

Post to: Mills & Boon Reader Service, P.O. Box 236, Thornton Road, Croydon, Surrey CR9 3RU, England.
*Please note: READERS IN SOUTH AFRICA please write to: Mills & Boon Reader Service of Southern Africa, Private Bag X3010, Randburg 2125, S. Africa.

Please send me details of the Mills & Boon Subscription Scheme.

NAME (Mrs/Miss) _____ EP3

ADDRESS _____

_____

COUNTY/COUNTRY_____ POST/ZIP CODE_____

BLOCK LETTERS, PLEASE

Mills & Boon
the rose of romance